Blood Lines

Blood Lines

KATHRYN CASEY

Minotaur Books ♏ New York

This is a work of fiction. All of the characters, organizations, and events portrayed in this novel are either products of the author's imagination or are used fictitiously.

BLOOD LINES. Copyright © 2009 by Kathryn Casey. All rights reserved. Printed in the United States of America. For information address St. Martin's Press, 175 Fifth Avenue, New York, N.Y. 10010.

www.minotaurbooks.com

Library of Congress Cataloging-in-Publication Data

Casey, Kathryn.
    Blood lines / Kathryn Casey. — 1st ed.
        p.   cm.
    ISBN-13: 978-0-312-37951-3
    ISBN-10: 0-312-37951-X
    1. Texas Rangers—Fiction.   2. Criminal profilers—Fiction.   I. Title.
    PS3603.A8635B56 2009
    813'.6—dc22

                                                                2009007914

First Edition: July 2009

10 9 8 7 6 5 4 3 2 1

For Nick, Zack, and Emmie

Blood Lines

One

H idden in a below-stage passageway, Cassidy Collins felt the rumble of the SRO audience. A week earlier, Tina Turner rocked Las Vegas's opulent Colosseum at Caesars Palace, but tonight the fans stomped and whistled for Cassidy, the newest teen sensation.

"Cassie! Cassie! Cassie!" they chanted.

How long would it be? When would the star of the evening appear?

The warm-up act sauntered off, and Cassidy's team took over. The stage manager triggered a pulley system that positioned the platform bearing the twelve-piece band's instruments, as the soundman turned on the mixer, lighting up the long panel of switches and levers plugged into the theater's sophisticated audio system. At the same time, chain-hoisted spots clicked into place, and crew members slid out scenery, constructing a make-believe jungle, replete with trees bearing glittering leaves. As the work finished, the lights flashed, and the audience hurried to take their seats.

"We're ready," the stage manager shouted into his walkie-talkie.

Two performances a week, twenty weeks a year, Cassidy had experienced it many times, but she always felt the excitement of the big shows, the spectacles of light and sound. Over the past two years, traveling from city to city, she'd memorized every detail, learned to listen for anything out of place. She had to. It was, after all, her show, her life.

Yet on this particular night, Cassidy feared that the cries of the crowd masked danger.

The percussion section kicked in, rumbling drums in sync with a recorded track of rainforest sounds: growling cats, pounding rain, croaking frogs, screeching birds, and buzzing insects.

The audience hushed as a single beam of light appeared center stage, shining down from the rafters directly into the shaft where Cassidy waited. It was time, and the teenage superstar slipped into the nylon cocoon coated with 14-karat gold that lay at her feet, pulled it up to cover her from head to toes. That accomplished, Germaine Dunn, Cassidy's stylist, climbed a ladder and sprinkled flakes of gold foil, covering Cassie's long blond hair, her costume, even the outside of the gossamer cocoon. Onstage, the gold would splinter the spotlights into rainbows, radiating into the crowd. With Cassie's entrance, the theater would shine as if doused in light cast from thousands of clear white diamonds.

"Ready?" Germaine asked.

"I hate this stuff," Cassie said, referring to the precious specks that drifted about her. "Always bothers my eyes."

"Keep them closed until the cocoon drops," Germaine advised, as she did every night, all for no good. Even though Cassie followed instructions, a spec of the gold invariably worked its way out of her hair and costume and irritated her wide green eyes, so much so that she couldn't wear her contacts onstage. Yet, the effect was worth it. From the audience, Cassie's appearance would be spellbinding, breathtaking. Every teen magazine from *Tiger Beat* to *BOP* had gushed over the show's hundred-grand, opening-act costume.

"Sure," Cassie said, not really meaning it. "Let's go."

A crack of thunder echoed via the soundtrack, and the keyboard guy hit the opening notes, leading to a renewed wave of squeals from the audience, as the transparent fly harness strapped about Cassidy's chest lurched, and she slowly rose. At stage level, she felt a slight breeze as she entered the open theater. The platform she stood on stopped level with the floor, but the harness pulled her higher, until Cassie dangled above the stage, exposed and vulnerable.

It's just another night, Cassie thought. *No big deal.*

Her stomach didn't believe her. It cramped tight, and she fought a building anxiety. *Breathe*, she thought. *Breathe.*

As hard as she tried, Cassie's admonitions didn't quiet her fears. *He's out there*, she thought. *He's watching.*

A renewed surge of screams, whistles, and catcalls from the audience as the wires pulled Cassie higher. The band played the intro to her latest hit, "Young Girls," and Cassie released the golden cocoon from her right hand, bringing it out of the top, as if stretching, giving the audience a first glimpse. They responded with a sharp gasp. At the second chord, Cassie let go of the costume, allowing it to fall. The precious wrap slipped past her head, her shoulders, and breasts, dropping onto the stage below. The shrieks of the audience swallowed the thud of the costume hitting the stage, as a black-clothed stagehand emerged from the shadows to scoop it up and whisk it away.

Suspended high over the stage, Cassie opened her eyes. Clad in a shimmering leotard, she contracted her arms and legs into a fetal position, and then slowly, deliberately unfolded her body. Off stage someone triggered a computerized command and iridescent wings, the orange and black of a monarch butterfly, unrolled from her back. Cassidy shook out her long blond hair, and bits of the gold foil scattered in the spotlight like glowing rain, prodding young voices to a painful cry.

From the audience, Cassie appeared encased in a sparkling pyramid of pure gold light.

"Hello, Las Vegas," she shouted, her voice amplified by the microphone in the thin, flesh-colored tube near her lips.

"Cassie! Cassie! Cassie! Cassie!" the audience responded.

He's out there, she thought. *He's out there, somewhere in that crowd.*

The theater throbbed with anticipation, yet Cassidy Collins hesitated. She blinked, a fleck of gold sending tears down her cheeks. The music grew louder, but she felt scattered, and before she realized it her prompt had passed. The band covered for her. Another opener, a second cue, and Cassie remained silent. She knew the song. She'd written it. She opened her mouth, but only silence.

The audience screamed again, their young voices impatient. Determined to take control, Cassie nervously laughed. She knew what they wanted. Her building sense of panic bounced off their exhilaration. She, like the audience, rode a jagged edge.

"Were you expecting something?" she taunted.

The young voices in the audience boiled over, as Cassie's mechanized wings beat at the excitement-charged air. Her arms and legs extended, she peered down apprehensively at the faceless crowd. Again the music poured around her, again her signal to join in, but she still wasn't singing. She flew above the audience, as below her the tweens reached upward, hoping to claim her as their own. Abruptly, Cassie turned in midair and flew back over the stage. Her Peter Pan–like flight ending, the guide wires lowered her. Her dancers rushed forward. They reached out to cushion her descent, yet Cassie's eyes searched the audience, watching for danger. She missed her mark and came down hard, stumbling.

One of the dancers grabbed her. "It's okay," he said. "I've got you."

Another night, Cassie would have been grateful. She might have even enjoyed it. The young man was handsome and devoted to her. Tonight was different. She was not in the mood for hollow reassurance. She had to pull herself together. It was time.

As the band circled the music around yet again, Cassie stood her ground, staring out into the crowd, tears cascading down her cheeks, willing herself not to be afraid. "*Young girls,*" she sang to the opening chord. "*It's time to live, to break free and fly.*"

The music pounding, Cassidy Collins tried to lose herself in the song, yet without success. She danced and the troupe of young men shadowed her well-rehearsed moves. But the superstar faltered. As familiar as it all was, she couldn't keep focused. All she could think of was the stranger whose eyes watched her from the audience. He was there, that she knew. She fought back flashes of what he'd said he'd do to her.

She had to control her fear. Cassidy reminded herself that any girl in the audience would have gladly traded places with her. Any girl would walk away from her mundane life for a shot at what Cassidy Collins had: power, money, and fame. Yet, the teen whose face graced magazine covers around the world still couldn't put *him* out of her mind, the stalker, the man who watched her, terrified her.

He's going to kill me, she thought. And she knew it like she knew the streets of the trailer park where she grew up. She knew it like she knew the lines alcohol traced in her mother's face before forty. Cassie knew it like she knew every detail of her mother's agonizing death from liver disease.

No one else understands. But I do, she thought. *That man's going to kill me.*

As she danced across the stage, fighting to retain control,

Cassidy considered the weeks ahead, especially two upcoming concerts in Texas.

That's where it will happen, she realized. *That's what he's waiting for. And when he comes for me, no one will be able to stop him.*

Two

What's wrong here? I wondered. *What's wrong?*

I'd stared at the woman's body for a full fifteen minutes. Elizabeth Cox was thirty-six, a slender woman dressed in an expensive St. John knit suit, the jacket a bold black-and-white hound's-tooth over a narrow black skirt. Her soft Italian leather heels had severely pointed toes. The responding detective theorized that Cox had arrived home from work that Friday, sat on her bed atop a thickly tufted tapestry bedspread, rested her back against her ornately carved eighteenth-century headboard, and aimed a 9 mm pistol at her right temple, inches from where her coiffed dark brown hair pulled tight into a perfectly executed French twist, just behind her almond-shaped eyes rimmed in thick mascara-lined lashes. This woman, who had money, beauty, position, and power, apparently found her life so untenable that she then pulled the trigger.

The bullet entered in front of and slightly above her right ear, traveled nearly straight through her skull, and blew out the left side of her head, leaving a trail of destruction and a cavernous wound that spewed brain matter and high-velocity blood spatter all over the headboard and faux-painted wall. A bloody mist covered the body, ruining her pricey suit and the exquisite bedspread. The gun lay beside Cox's extended right arm, near her hand. A typewritten suicide note lamenting a failed love life rested on her lap.

> *I thought I'd find More in life than business and financial Success, but that didn't happen. I needed More to inspire me to go on. I am Sorry. To those I leave behind, PLEASE FORGIVE ME. I Never meant to hurt anyone. I needed someone to love. I needed to be loved. Please Forgive me.*

Success was an understatement. Elizabeth, a.k.a. "Billie," Cox ran Century Oil, one of the most lucrative medium-size oil companies in Houston. Oil had been on a roller-coaster ride for two years, the past six months headed straight up. With the price of a barrel skyrocketing and money spurting through the oil industry faster than crude from a gusher, Century had reported profits of $100 million in the previous quarter alone. Cox was the youngest and highest-profile woman in the inner circle of the Houston energy business. Her bedroom was on the second floor of her six-thousand-square-foot River Oaks mansion, which sat on an acre of Space City's priciest real estate.

How bad could your life have been? I wondered. *Come on, Billie. What's really going on here?*

"You planning to tell me something about this case or just stare at that photo," my boss, Captain Don Williams, barked.

The captain glowered down at me from his vantage point, three feet above, as I sat at my home-office desk, digesting the police file on the Cox case. Even when I stood, the captain had a formidable advantage. I'm not a small woman, five-foot-six, 130 pounds or so, a bit wide in the hips, but he's a former University of Texas basketball player, a broad-shouldered man, with dark brown skin and a thick-boned jaw that locks into place when he's unhappy, as he was now. He'd been patient with me, bringing the photos out to the ranch, not asking me to go to the office or the scene. But then, he'd been handling me with kid gloves ever since the previous spring when the most grueling investigation of my career, the Lucas case, went south and nearly destroyed my entire world. For months after, I didn't know if I'd ever wear a badge again. Coming back had been slow, a six-month leave followed by half-pay with the understanding that I review case files at home. How long would his patience last?

The truth is that I have something of an ace in the hole. I'm one of only two women Texas Rangers, but that's not particularly important. What makes me unique is that I'm the only one in the department FBI trained in criminal profiling. When a law enforcement agency anywhere in the Lone Star State needs an assessment of a scene or help narrowing a list of suspects, I'm the one they call. Plus, the captain and I have history and a healthy respect for each other. I'd counted on that for nearly a year, to cut me enough slack to work through my situation at home.

"Why are we involved in this case?" I asked, giving him a wary glance. His eyes narrowed and the captain frowned.

"Sarah, let's not worry about that. Just look it over," he said, motioning at the thin file on Billie Cox's death, the one I held in my hand. "This is simple. Just give me your thoughts."

Something didn't smell right—the captain's answers, I mean. It wasn't that we didn't have the authority to look at the case. The Texas Rangers are a branch of the Department of Public Safety, DPS—we report to the governor—and our jurisdiction is the entire state. It's tradition. Back in the days of Stephen F. Austin, my predecessors got their name by patrolling the vast Texas range.

That said, since the commotion the year before, I hadn't strayed much outside my own fence line. Half an hour from Houston, the

Rocking Horse Stables lies on the outskirts of Tomball, a small town that's being swallowed up by the city. I live with my mom, Nora Potts, who makes her living baking fancy cheesecakes for caterers and boarding horses for folks without the land to stable them. My jailers are Mom and my twelve-year-old, Maggie. It hasn't been a particularly hard time. The Rocking Horse is a pretty pleasant place to watch the world go by.

What bothered me about the Cox case file was that we rangers rarely step into a case uninvited. "Well, this file says Houston P.D. and the medical examiner have both already ruled Cox's death a suicide. They didn't ask for my opinion," I said, glancing up at the captain. "Is there some theory that they aren't shooting straight with the investigation? Some reason to be suspicious of the local uniforms?"

"No, nothing like that," the captain said, waving off my concerns.

"Why then?" I pushed.

The captain sighed. "Damn, Sarah. Nothing's easy with you. The truth is that Billie Cox has a sister, Faith Cox Roberts. She's been calling the governor's office and her state senator, saying Billie wouldn't have killed herself, demanding a full investigation," he said, irritated. "But that's not important. All the director asked for was a look-see. You tell me this is a suicide. I tell the director, who conveys your take on the case to the governor. That done, we're clear, before we rile up anybody on Travis. We're out of this, clean and quick."

Travis was 1200 Travis Street, the address of Houston P.D.'s skyscraper headquarters, the building where the chief of police offices are, in the center of downtown. What the captain implied was that, unless we had to, he saw no reason to irritate a department we work closely with, one where we count on good relationships to get things done.

"You do think this is a suicide, *don't you?*" he prodded.

"Well, I guess," I said, squinting up at him.

"Hell, Sarah, there's a note, the gun's right where it should be, they got her prints off it, the damn thing is hers, and her hand tested positive for gunshot residue," he said. "Show me a single piece of evidence that suggests this isn't just some rich woman who decided she'd had enough and wanted out."

There he had me.

"I can't. I'm not sure it is any more than a suicide," I admitted. "But the scene looks too perfect. All that's missing is the bow."

"That's it? It looks too much like a suicide to be one?" the captain fumed. "Sarah, if we're going to bash heads with the locals, give me something I can use to justify our take to the governor, some reason to step on toes."

I'd hoped the questions would get easier. They weren't.

"You know, I'm just not sure," I said. "Maybe this is a suicide. But . . ."

"That's not like you," he said. "You're usually pretty quick on the draw when it comes to zeroing in on a case. Why in that Lucas mess—"

"Yeah," I said, cutting him off. I had no desire to ever again rehash the worst case of my career, one that sent me across Texas hunting a twisted killer who ultimately set his sights on me. "Captain, give me overnight to study the file. Maybe I'm just a little rusty."

As soon as I heard myself say it, I regretted the choice of words.

"Rusty is right," the captain said, storming through the barn door I'd unwisely swung open. "You know, Lieutenant Armstrong, that Lucas case happened in spring, and now it's nearly spring again. I'm as sympathetic as anyone, but we need you back. You can't do cases justice sitting out here on the ranch." With that, he pushed the paperwork back into the Cox file folder and closed it. "If you'd been in the office, we would have called you to the scene on this one, given this woman's position in the business community. You wouldn't be looking at photos three days later trying to figure out what happened."

"I know," I agreed. Then, mistake number two, I pushed that door open even wider. I couldn't seem to help myself. "I can't say that I'm not having the same thoughts."

"Why not then, Sarah?" he asked, softer. "Why not report in tomorrow morning? It's time."

My slips weren't unintentional. The truth? I wanted my life back. As much as I loved the ranch, being tied to the place grated on me. I've got to admit that I'm headstrong, maybe even downright stubborn. A lot of us rangers are. Back in the bad old days, when rangers fought warring Mexicans, Ranger Captain Jack Ford pretty much said it all about how a ranger sees a situation, when he ordered, "Whip them, and then talk of treaties."

So I was eager to work full-time again, but I wondered if Mom and Maggie, especially Maggie, were as prepared to put the past behind us. They'd faced the devil with me, and I couldn't force them to move on until they were ready. Still, the kid did seem stronger. And how long could I stay in lockup? Oh, it wasn't really a hardship. I left whenever I wanted, went wherever I wanted, as long as it didn't have anything to do with a crime scene and a murder.

"Tell you what, Captain. I do want to come back," I confessed. "I didn't know if I would, but I miss my work. Leave this file with me overnight, and I'll talk to Maggie and Mom and have answers for you on both matters in the morning. Fair enough?"

The captain, looking more pleased than I'd seen him in a long time, reclaimed his sharply creased, silver-belly Stetson off my worktable, flicked off a bit of flesh-colored clay stuck on the rim, and nodded. "Fair enough. We need to get all this behind you, Sarah. I'll drop in early tomorrow morning, on my way to the office, for the file and your answers," he said. "We need you back where you belong."

My combined home office and workshop is on the second floor of the garage. The captain left, and I proceeded to tidy up. When he'd arrived, I'd been working on a skull. I'm a bit of a contradiction. My college degree is a double major: psychology and art. Instead of my original career plans, using art to counsel traumatized kids, I utilize my psychology training in my profiling, diagnosing crime scenes and suspect lists. And in my spare time, I sculpt clay faces on unidentified skulls, hoping someone will recognize the dead and claim them, and that it'll help put away a killer.

Lately, I've had a lot of spare time.

We rangers are a close-knit bunch, and we take care of our own. In my case, that's meant a lot. My husband, Bill, was a ranger, too, actually the reason I got into law enforcement. When he died two years ago, the captain and the whole department closed in around Maggie and me, offering help. Then, last spring, crisis number two, a case we were lucky to survive, and again Captain Williams and the good souls in the office were patient and understanding. Even the folks in ranger headquarters, in Austin, didn't push. But the captain was right. It was time for Maggie, Mom, and me to stand on our own feet again. It was time for us to pick up our lives.

My hands were rough from tending stock on the ranch, and I had to soap up twice to remove the last of the clay. My forehead felt tight, and I took the rubber band out of my dark blond hair, letting it bunch out around my shoulders. A long-standing tradition of neglect left it verging on wild. One of these days, I'd have to splurge on a good haircut. Maybe even a new shampoo and conditioner. Of course, there didn't seem to be any urgency, no one to impress. A year ago, I had a new man in my life, an FBI profiler named David Garrity. We met in the thick of the Lucas debacle, partnered up for the investigation, and got tight fast. To my disappointment, he hung around briefly afterward but suddenly stopped calling.

Since David Garrity's departure, worrying about my looks wasn't high on my list.

Outside, the fresh air hit me with the heavy scent of pine after a rain, and Maggie and Strings were on the porch putting up her telescope. These last days of February already felt like spring. Winter on Texas's Gulf Coast doesn't have the punch it does up north, and the thermostat hovered around sixty. But at just after six, dusk was crawling in. It appeared that Maggie and her best friend, Strings, more formally known as Frederick Allen Jacobs Jr., planned to take advantage of the situation with a little stargazing.

"Hey, Mrs. A," Strings shouted when he saw me. His dark eyes were playful behind wire-rimmed glasses, dangling low, and his skin was the rich hue of coffee with cream. He scrunched up his broad nose and pushed his glasses back with one finger. "Are you going to watch tonight?"

"Watch what?" I responded. Strings shrugged at me. Obviously, I was supposed to know. Maggie, who was on her knees positioning the telescope's spindly legs, peeked around the porch railing at me and frowned.

"I've been talking about this for a week, Mom," she said. "The Alpha Centaurids are at their peak, and the weather's good to see them tonight."

"Oh, I forgot," I said, stating the obvious. Then, to prove I'd retained a tidbit from her lectures, I added, "Meteors, right?"

"Yeah," Maggie said, rewarding me with a generous grin. Her front teeth were crooked, and I thought about scheduling an appointment with an orthodontist. I'd heard braces could cost as much as a year's college tuition. "They're named after the constellation Centaurus, and they're near its brightest star, Hadar."

"Well, we'll have to have a look," I said. "I wouldn't miss it."

At that moment, the timer kicked in and the corral lit. The elm in the center shone with thousands of tiny white lights along with a new addition, icicle lights lining the fence. It appeared that Maggie had been busy that afternoon.

"More lights?" I asked.

"Strings helped me. Gram found them in the bargain bin at the hardware store," Maggie said, her dark hair falling over her hazel eyes. She looked an inch or two taller. I thought about the lights and considered protesting, but I knew how much they meant to Maggie, the comfort they gave her, as if their glow kept her father near.

Just then my mother, Nora Potts, walked down the hill from the stable, followed by the ranch hand she'd hired a month or so earlier, Frieda Cavazos, a woman in her forties with coarse black hair tied back in a single braid. Frieda's jeans and plaid shirts hung on her narrow frame, and her haggard brown leather cowboy boots looked gray under a coat of dust. In her hands, she dangled a worn leather halter.

"Hello, Mrs. Sarah," Frieda said, nodding slightly.

"*Buenas tardes*, Frieda," I said, nodding back.

Mom and the ranch hand stopped next to us, and I noticed that Frieda looked troubled, her sun-worn face pinched in thought. I didn't have to ask why.

"Mrs. Potts, I think maybe I stay with Emma Lou. Watch over her longer," she said, handing Mom the halter. "I like to spend more time with her, just to see."

"That's a good idea, Frieda. I'll bring you dinner," Mom said, absentmindedly winding the halter into a thick loop. "Thank you."

"What's wrong with my horse?" Maggie asked, immediately

concerned as Frieda ambled back up the hill to the stable. Emma Lou was heavy with her first foal, due in a little more than a month.

"Probably nothing, dear," Mom said. "Frieda just thought the horse looked a little peaked, so she's sitting with her for a while."

"Now about those lights?" I asked, bringing the conversation around a full one-eighty.

"They were on sale, a real deal," Mom said, using the sleeve of her old red shirt to wipe sweat from her forehead. "Maggie and I talked about expanding the light show, so I snapped them up. I even bought a batch for the front gate. Good idea?"

I considered giving her a little nudge, but decided against it. "I've got to admit, they look good," I said. "But someone is going to have to pay for all the electricity."

Mom lifted her eyebrows and gave Maggie a look, the kind that signals, *I told you so.* I shot Maggie one of my best *okay, what's up?* expressions, and she giggled. Strings broke the silence.

"Guess you'll just have to work full-time to pay the bill then, huh, Mrs. A?" he said, grinning.

"Am I that transparent?" I asked. "No secrets from all of you?"

"Gram, Strings, and me talked about it awhile, back," Maggie said. "How the captain would want you back soon."

"And that's good or bad?" I asked. Maggie frowned, then looked at Mom.

"You should do it, Mom. Gram and I decided you should. It's why Gram hired Frieda, so you didn't have to worry so much about the ranch."

"So you two were preparing for this? And I should go back to work?" I said, giving Mom a glance.

"It's time, Sarah," she said. "It's been long enough."

"Well, I'll be," I said, amazed. "You're sure?"

"We're sure," Maggie said. "Aren't we, Gram?"

"As sure as anyone can be in this crazy world," Mom said, taking off one of her work gloves and ruffling her hand through Maggie's mop of hair. "We're sure there's a big world out there, and we can't stay locked up here."

"Well, this is a pretty picture," Bobby Barker said as he rounded the curve from the front yard, appearing from behind the side of the house. A solidly built man, his white hair fringed over muddy green-gray eyes, and instead of a business suit he wore a pair of jeans and an open-neck shirt. I wasn't surprised to see him. The one good thing that came out of the Lucas case was that Bobby was no longer the father of a suspect but my mother's gentleman caller, even if she insisted they were only friends. Just to prove my point, Mom flushed and tried to rearrange her short white curls. It was hopeless. After working with the horses, she really needed a shower and a change of clothes.

"If you gave a woman more notice, Bobby, she'd be more presentable," Mom said, taking a playful swipe at him with the halter. "How's a person supposed to look her best without time to fuss?"

"You look beautiful, Nora," Barker assured her, brushing his hand gently across Mom's cheek. "You always look beautiful. And you invited me for dinner. Remember?"

"Of course," Mom said, looking flustered. "I've been so busy with the horses, I guess I forgot."

Just then, Frieda called down from the hill: "Mrs. Potts, I think maybe you should call Doc Larson. I think maybe something is wrong with Emma Lou."

"What I'm worried about, Nora, is that the foal isn't due for more than a month, and its lungs aren't quite there," said Doc Larson, drawing blood from the black and white pinto's right jugular vein. The mare looked weary, and her awkward girth bulged, wide and heavy. "But if it's what I think it is, Emma Lou may deliver sooner. We've got to hope not too early."

"What do you suspect?" Mom asked. "What's wrong?"

"Well, I hate to speculate," Doc said. At five-foot-five and maybe 150 pounds, Doc was a small, fidgety man. His dad's family was Norwegian and his mom Irish, and his hair used to be red before it grayed like the stubble that covered his chin. The best horse vet in the county, Doc wasn't fond of delivering bad news and when faced with the prospect always appeared to have one foot headed toward the door.

"We won't hold it against you if you're wrong, Doc," I said. "But we need an idea of what's wrong with the mare."

Chewing on the inside of his mouth like he used to on plugs of tobacco before his missus made him quit, Doc said, "Well, I figure this mare of yours has most likely come in contact with some pesky bacteria."

"Emma Lou has an infection?" Maggie asked, her voice a couple of octaves higher than usual. Doc turned to her and frowned.

"It's not as bad as it sounds, Maggie," he said, trying to be reassuring. "Thanks to Frieda, we caught it early."

On her return trip to the barn, Frieda noticed that Emma Lou's eyes were irritated, the lids red. We now knew that the horse was also running a low-grade fever.

"How sick is she?" Maggie asked. "Is my horse going to die?"

Doc frowned again, looking at her straight on. "I'm not going to lie to you, Maggie. If it's what I think it is, it could cause the foal to abort, leave one or both horses blind, and, in the worst cases, it can be fatal," he said, his brow furrowed in worry. "But it's treatable. When we get Emma Lou's blood work back, we'll know more, but in the meantime, I'm going to put your girl on an antibiotic, to get a head start."

"I'll take care of her," Maggie said, her voice small and frightened.

"Of course, you will," Doc said.

After he gave the horse an antibiotic shot, Doc left, and we carried out his orders, cleaning out the shed behind the house for Emma Lou's temporary home, to prevent her from infecting the rest of the horses. Instead of one of Mom's home-cooked suppers, we ate pizzas from the freezer, and Maggie and I munched ours in chairs outside the shed. Every time Emma Lou made a sound, Maggie jumped up to check on her.

The celestial events occurred that night without notice, at least at the Rocking Horse Stables. Maggie's telescope remained on the porch, unused. At ten, I coaxed my exhausted daughter into the house. In her room, Maggie climbed into bed and I flicked on the strings of Christmas lights that hung across her ceiling. As I prepared to leave, I turned the lights off.

"No," Maggie said. "Please, Mom. Leave them on."

I flipped the switch back on, and the ceiling glowed softly with the small, white lights. Before I left, I bent down and kissed her again.

"Don't worry, Maggie," I said. "I'll watch over Emma Lou."

Maggie nodded and quickly fell fast asleep.

Three

The captain stared down at me with an amused grin when I opened my eyes early the following morning. In the two years since Bill's death, I'd noticed that the men I work with often have that kind of reaction. I guess they see me less as cop tough and more single-mom scattered. I could consider that a bad thing, but most of the time it works to my advantage, so I don't fight it. I'd slept on an old cot outside the shed, to the dismay of my back and neck. Cold, I pulled the sleeping bag up around me. Even Texas can be chilly on a winter morning.

"I knew you were excited about talking with me, but I didn't expect that you'd sleep outside to greet me," he said with a chuckle. The sunlight bounced off his captain's badge, like mine, a lone star inside a wagon wheel. My silver lieutenant's badge was stamped out of a Mexican *cinco peso*, but the captain's, anchored onto his brown leather vest, was gold. When I put up my hand to block the glare, I noticed he carried a thick file folder.

"Late night," I said, reluctantly unzipping the sleeping bag and pulling my legs out, still wearing my jeans and sweater from the night before. I wrapped the open sleeping bag around my shoulders, attempting to keep warm. "We moved Maggie's pinto into the shed. She's sick. Some kind of infection, it looks like."

"Isn't she carrying a foal?"

"Yeah," I said. "She is."

"I'm sorry about the horse, Sarah. I hope she and the foal pull through," he said. "But I need a couple of answers. First, any more thoughts on the Cox file?"

The truth was that I'd been unsettled half the night, thinking and rethinking the case. "It's not easy to fall asleep out here in the cold," I said. "I had lots of time to consider it."

"And?" he prodded.

"I see no reason to irritate our friends at H.P.D., at least not about this case," I said. "There's nothing in those photos to indicate this is anything other than a suicide."

"Good," he said. "I would have stood by you if you thought it was more, but I'd hate to have a showdown over a hunch."

"I agree," I said. The case still nagged at me, but I had no evidence, nothing to hang my suspicions on. Bending down to retrieve the Cox file from under the cot, I said, "I've got it right here."

"Great. And regarding that other matter?" he said, taking the folder in his meaty hands.

I'd almost forgotten about the question of my return to the rangers. Maggie and Mom said it was all right, but now with Emma Lou . . . ? "How about I work half-days at the office and half-days at home, just for the first couple of weeks, until Emma Lou and the foal are out of the woods?" I proposed. "Then you've got me back in the office full-time."

"Well, it's about time!" the captain crowed. "Sarah, you're going to make a lot of folks happy. You've been missed."

"Thanks, Captain," I said. "It'll make me happy, too. I'll see you at the office in a little over an hour. I'll work this morning, so

I can be here when Doc Larson swings by this afternoon, if that's okay?"

"Couldn't be better," he said. "It's more than okay."

"It's settled then," I said, shaking his hand, cementing our deal.

The captain turned to leave but then swung back. "I almost forgot," he said, handing me the folder he'd brought with him. "This is a new case. Some young girl, a singer, has a lowlife obsessed with her. Her security people think it's a guy from Houston, although we're not positive they're looking at the right man. Anyway, this girl is pretty scared. She lives in Los Angeles, but she's scheduled to give a concert in Dallas this weekend, Saturday night, and then open the Houston rodeo with a concert next Monday evening."

"And you'd like me to . . . ?"

"Figure out if this stalker is really dangerous or just some crackpot fan," he said. "Also, maybe you can tell if the man they're looking at is the right guy."

I scanned the folder and noticed the girl's name. "That's the singer? Cassidy Collins?" I asked.

"Yeah," he said. "You know who she is?"

"Maggie has every one of this kid's CDs," I said. "And that's something that hasn't made me happy. Collins is a teenager but she acts like she's twenty-four. Some of her songs are, well, let's just say not what I want Maggie listening to."

At that moment, Emma Lou neighed softly in the shed behind us, reminding me that I had a sick expectant mom to care for.

"I better go, Captain," I said. "I'll look at this later."

"Yup, duty calls," the captain said. "Sarah, I'll see you at the office."

Another neigh, this one coupled with an impatient snort, and I waved at him as I turned toward the barn. I had an appetizing bucket of oats and hay to fetch for the pinto's breakfast. When I walked into the shed, feed bucket in hand, Emma Lou shook her white mane, and I ran my hand over her muscular back, giving her a solid tap on her right hip. She's one beautiful animal, the foal of Mom's favorite brood mare and a neighbor's prime sire. We'd picked her parents and raised her, then had her bred to extend her bloodline. But the truth is that folks who love horses understand you never really own one. You don't buy the horse, just the right to care for one of God's noblest creatures.

"I'm here, girl," I whispered. I ran my hand down to her round belly and felt the foal move. Emma Lou nudged my shoulder, pushing my arm away. "Tender down there?" I asked. I remembered my own pregnancy, the rush of watching my infant daughter's feet pushing against my abdomen, as if eager to enter the world. "Don't be in such a hurry little one," I whispered. "It's a big world out here. A crazy world. You stay inside your momma as long as you can, where you're safe."

Four

Getting Maggie on the school bus that morning wasn't easy. She doted over Emma Lou, talking to the horse, rubbing her neck, helping Frieda put drops in the pinto's eyes and arguing that a few days off school wouldn't matter.

"Mom, my grades are good. My teachers won't care," she pleaded. "Just today, so I can talk to Doc when he comes this afternoon. Please?"

I assured her that Mom and I would memorize every word Doc had to say, but it wasn't until Bobby showed up and cajoled her with promises of his and Mom's uninterrupted care for the horse that she climbed onto the bus. I guess sometimes a new voice helps. Maggie's probably pretty used to Mom's and mine.

That settled, I left the ranch in my burgundy Tahoe right after rush hour, when the freeways in Houston no longer resemble slow-moving parking lots. The entire staff swarmed me when I walked in, clapping and hugging. The captain's secretary, Sheila, a plump woman wearing a beige dress covered with red orchids, brought donuts, remembering that I like chocolate frosting and jimmies.

Munching on my second disc of fried cake, except for worrying about Emma Lou, I felt like all was pretty right with the world.

My office was as I'd left it, papers piled in neat stacks on the desk, photos of Bill, Maggie, and Mom on the shelves, along with my most recent *Criminal Laws of Texas* volume and manuals on skull reconstruction, crime-scene investigation, and forensic techniques. I soaked in the place for a minute, glad to be back. Then I stowed my brown leather purse and my rig, the black, tooled-leather double belt with silver buckles that holsters my Colt .45, in the bottom right drawer. Settled in, I opened the file on teenage idol Cassidy Collins.

It started with a photo of Collins, a head shot I think they call them, the kind performers use for publicity. Collins was a pretty girl, long blond hair, a turned-up nose, and green eyes set wide apart. Second was a report from a guy named Rick Barron, the head of the kid's private security force. It was odd to think a sixteen-year-old needed bodyguards, but one look at Barron's report and there was no doubt that Collins did. Celebs, it seemed, attracted a lot of attention, not all good.

Barron started out by recounting instances with stalkers in Collins's past, men and women who fixated on the teenager. Two years earlier a Des Moines pharmacist sent a then-fourteen-year-old Collins love letters and Ecstasy pills along with directions to his house. At one point, a thirty-six-year-old woman harassed Collins for nearly a year, wanting to adopt her, insisting Collins was a love child she'd put up for adoption at birth. Then there were the young girls who swarmed her at concerts, wanting to be her BFF, best friend forever, and the men, some well into their fifties, who claimed to be in love with her.

"In all these cases and others, suspects ceased their behavior when afforded a personal visit by local law enforcement officers. With some, we went a step further, serving restraining orders. In the end, all gave up, or at least appeared to," the report read. "In no case was it necessary to further involve law enforcement."

While reluctant to broaden the scope of the current investigation, Barron said he had no choice since he didn't have the authority for subpoenas he needed to obtain the records necessary to confirm the identity of the stalker. "This person has been highly resourceful," Barron wrote. "At each juncture, he's known what actions we're taking to block him. We've been unable to trace his e-mails and text messages. All attempts to positively identify the stalker have failed."

Barron's prime suspect was a student at Rice University's prestigious Shepherd School of Music, a young pianist named Justin Peterson. A brilliant musician and composer, Peterson started college at sixteen and, although he'd just turned twenty-one, was finishing up his doctorate. According to Barron's report, Peterson, who had a genius-level intellect, wrote Collins letters. They started out pedestrian enough, but quickly turned threatening. The letters ended after Peterson was briefly hospitalized and visited by a campus police officer. But Barron was convinced that the kid had simply switched to an anonymous, electronic route, threatening texts and e-mails sent under an alias, Argus.

"Mr. Peterson has an extensive background in computers, using them to compose his music. So he has the technical knowledge to electronically stalk Miss Collins," Barron wrote. "We have no concrete evidence, but Peterson is the only suspect we've found who makes sense."

Finished with Barron's report, I read Peterson's first letter to Collins. It was short, to the point, and, to say the least, cordial:

"Dear Miss Collins," he began. "I have watched you on television, and I've become something of a fan. While I am five years older, we have much in common. I, too, am devoted to my music, and I am an aficionado of dance, something at which you are quite talented. It has occurred to me that perhaps I could help a young woman like yourself become more knowledgeable about her chosen field, to share my comprehension of music with you. While as a pianist my venues are classical, not rock or pop as your compositions are, I share your love of melody and tone, your obsession with getting the song right. I would very much like to meet with you at your earliest convenience to discuss how I might help you in your musical career."

Weeks later when Collins hadn't personally replied, her publicity agency sending only a stock photo and a canned thank you letter, Peterson's correspondence became more insistent, going on for nearly a dozen pages: "I explained in my previous letter how valuable my counsel is for you, how I can help you become a better composer. Cassidy, I know that our paths are destined to cross. I see in you what no one else does. I know that I am the only one who truly understands you. I'm the only one who knows who you are and what you need. We have a common bond that transcends our mutual love of music. But how am I to explain all of this to you, to introduce myself and tell you what I can do for you, unless you meet with me?"

There were a few more letters, before Peterson's final one. That correspondence was a full twenty-six pages. The first fifteen, as with his earlier letters, were typed, but the remainder was hand-written, single-spaced, with additions scratched into the margins. In the last half-dozen or so pages, Peterson held his pen so tight, pushed so hard, that he dug into the paper. It was obvious that his initial interest in Ms. Collins had digressed into an angry obsession.

"Listen you little bitch," it began. "I've written and written, but you've ignored every letter. What am I supposed to think? What do I have to say before you understand that I must meet you? If you think your refusal to answer my letters will keep me away, you are wrong. I know we are meant to be together. A young girl like you needs someone to guide her. Think of me as your teacher. I know what you need. I know what you want, and it's what only I can give you. I am the only one who understands you."

By the end of that final letter, Peterson's handwriting was nearly unintelligible, little more than a scrawl. His words were a string of expletives, attacking Collins, threatening her. "I am not responsible for what I will do to you if you ignore my letters. I am not accountable. The blame is all yours," he ended. "You will meet with me. You will see me, or the repercussions will be tragic."

The day that last letter hit Barron's desk, he contacted Jim Herald, a Rice University police officer. Sergeant Herald pulled up Peterson's school records and discovered that he'd been seen frequently in the university clinic, but the available records, due to privacy constraints, didn't indicate why. Herald then learned that Peterson's supervising professor had repeatedly contacted authorities, alarmed by her student's odd behavior, including angry outbursts. When Herald tried to contact Peterson, he found out that the grad student had checked himself into a private psychiatric facility.

Three weeks later, Herald heard Peterson was discharged and on campus.

When Herald went to the Shepherd School and knocked on a practice room door, the student amiably invited the officer in. Throughout their conversation, Peterson appeared forthcoming, explaining that a hospital psychiatrist had diagnosed his condition and prescribed meds. "Mr. Peterson was rational and cooperative. He was well-groomed and calm," Herald wrote. "He assured me that his obsession with Cassidy Collins has ended now that he is properly medicated, and that she would have no further correspondence from him. He asked me to explain the situation to Mr. Barron and Ms. Collins and to apologize for the concern his actions caused."

When Herald contacted Peterson's professor, she reported that her gifted student had returned to his prior commitment to his studies and his music. At the end of his report, Officer Herald pre-dicted Ms. Collins no longer had anything to fear from Justin Pe-terson.

Then, one week later, in mid-November, the stalker made his initial approach to Collins in the form of a text message she re-ceived while in a restaurant with a friend: "I look @ U & I C blood. Enjoying lunch? Argus."

"That must have ruined her appetite," I whispered, although there was no one to hear.

Curious about the stalker's name, I keyed "Argus" into the Inter-net on my office computer and came up with Wikipedia: "From Greek mythology . . . a giant with a hundred eyes" that never slept. According to legend, Hera, jealous of the relationship between Zeus and a young princess named Io, sent Argus to watch the girl. Later, the goddess placed the slain giant's eyes into the tail feathers of the peacock.

What part of this ancient lore convinced the stalker to take Ar-gus as his name was unknown, but another term popped up on the screen: Argus-eyed, defined as hawk-eyed, always vigilant. Certainly that fit Collins's stalker, who seemed to know her every move.

"I C U w/o ?, now & always," Argus text messaged a few days later. Then, that night, "Do U C me? No? U will."

As Cassidy Collins became more anxious about the text mes-sages, e-mails arrived from *Argus-eyed@* . . . , *WatchingU@* . . . , and *NeverEscape@*. . . . All were short and to the point. "You belong to me. I will claim what is mine," read one.

Some implied that the stalker was near, in the shadows, watch-ing, like the one that read: "The drapes in your bedroom were open last night. I could have reached out and grabbed you."

"Who is that U had lunch w/?" Argus text messaged, after Collins left a posh L.A. restaurant where she'd hobnobbed with her agent. "Y R U w/him?"

Then, that night, the stalker e-mailed: "Y R U sleeping w/ your drapes shut? Scared? Of me?"

"When she saw that message, Ms. Collins was terrified. She did have her drapes shut the night that text message came in, which is unusual for her," Barron noted. "She is convinced that the man was indeed watching her. The grounds to her estate are surrounded by a high brick wall and gated, patrolled by guards who saw no one, and we thoroughly searched, but we found nothing unusual."

Finally the e-mail that haunted Collins, the one that came back to her when she woke up panicking in the middle of the night, showed up on a brand new e-mail account Barron had set up for her only hours earlier: "You are dead. Argus."

"Two nights later, Ms. Collins performed at the Colosseum at Caesars Palace in Las Vegas. Right before she went onstage, she received another text message, this one saying that Argus would be in the audience, waiting for her," Barron wrote. "Luckily, we'd hired extra men to patrol the theater. Nothing happened, but Argus must have been there. The next day he e-mailed Ms. Collins again, and he knew that during the prior evening's concert she'd missed her cue for her opening number.

"Ms. Collins has appearances in Texas approaching, and we request that the rangers do a risk assessment on this Argus, to give their opinion on the level of danger, and an evaluation of Peterson, to determine if he is a suspect," Barron concluded on the last page of the file. "We also need subpoenas for records from all the Internet providers this stalker has used. We want this man or woman identified, charged, and arrested."

Straightforward request, I thought. Too bad it's not that simple.

Flipping again to the front, I found Rick Barron's phone number on his letterhead. "Mr. Barron, I'm Lieutenant Sarah Armstrong, with the Texas Rangers," I said when he answered his cell phone. In the background, I heard what sounded like young girls screaming, a car door slam, and then the roar of an engine. "I've been asked to review the file you've pulled together on Mr. Peterson and the stalker Argus."

"It's about time," Barron said, irritated. "I've been waiting for some action from you rangers for days. Cassidy's Dallas gig is this weekend and she's scheduled to open the Houston rodeo two nights later. We need to handle this situation quick, stop this jerk, before she gets on the plane for Texas."

I'd forgotten that the captain said Collins would be opening the rodeo in a week. There isn't a bigger event in the city. It literally takes over Houston in early March, weeks of Stetsons, spurs, steer wrestling, and barrel racing. Reliant Stadium, the city's massive football arena, transforms into the world's biggest rodeo stage and, at the end of each competition a country and western, pop, rock, or Tejano star puts on a show. Most of the year, Houston looks about as Western as L.A. But come rodeo time, folks polish their boots, get their cowboy hats steamed, and the whole city gets rodeo fever.

Considering his version of the events, however, I wasn't sure how Barron figured Texas was the issue. "I understand Ms. Cassidy's concern," I said. "Yet, obviously this man, whoever he is, he's mobile."

"Mobile?"

"The text messages indicate that Argus knew what Cassidy did in L.A. and what happened at the Colosseum in Las Vegas," I said. "Maybe in L.A. the texts were lucky guesses, based on the time of day? Early afternoon means lunchtime. But in Las Vegas, I gather you believe Argus *had* to have been in the audience?"

"You bet he was. That SOB *must* have been there. No other way he would have known she missed her cue," Barron said. "We're not saying he can't travel, but, assuming it is Peterson, we'll be coming to his home turf. Isn't that more risky?"

"Well, it depends," I said.

"Are you thinking this guy isn't dangerous? He was in the audience in Las Vegas and didn't try anything. I've been telling Cassie that he's probably just a big talker trying to scare a young girl. Why if that son of a—"

"No, that's not what I'm saying," I interrupted. "If Argus left his home territory, wherever that is, and traveled to be in the same city as Ms. Collins, bought a ticket to her concert, that means that he has to be taken very seriously. Most stalkers, especially those who use the Internet, don't do that. They don't travel and physically shadow their victims."

"Is there another possibility?"

"Yes," I said. "It's possible that this Argus lives in Vegas, and that's why he was in the audience that night."

"So, what do we do? How do we find out who this sicko is?"

"You need to keep an open mind, not restrict the investigation to Texas," I suggested. "And you need solid evidence."

"I'm all for that. What do you suggest?"

"Unfortunately, we start by going down what will most likely lead to a dead end," I said. "As you requested, I will subpoena the Internet records. But I predict it'll be of little or no use, because anyone savvy enough to find unlisted phone numbers to text message and private e-mail addresses knows how to cover his tracks."

"So, what do we do?" he asked. "Lieutenant, we have to stop this guy. Cassidy's a wreck. She's hardly sleeping. You've gotta have more than that for us."

"I'll talk to Los Angeles P.D., since that's your home city, and we'll put traces on all her phones, all incoming text messages, to see if we can track one."

"They're coming through on the kid's cell as all kinds of numbers," Barron said. "Sometimes the caller I.D. shows 'number withheld' or 'private'."

"Your guy's scrambling the numbers," I explained. "But if we can trace the text messages in transit, maybe we can determine where they're originating. While L.A.P.D. helps us out with that, I'll investigate this Justin Peterson. Just to see if he could be your guy."

"Okay. Sounds like a plan. But if this Argus isn't stopped, what do you think he's capable of?"

"Like I said earlier, Mr. Barron," I warned. "From the tone of the text messages and e-mails, and assuming this stalker is really physically trailing Miss Collins, he needs to be taken very seriously."

Now that we had a plan, I needed to get busy. I hung up the telephone and called the captain's secretary. "Sheila, get me a number for special crimes at L.A.P.D.," I said. "And send in Janet. I need to have some subpoenas drawn up." Janet was Janet Kirk, our civilian employee, a whiz at writing subpoenas.

"Sure," Sheila said. "But there's someone here to see you."

"I don't have any appointments. Who even knows I'm back?"

"There's a lady in the lobby. She says her name is Faith Cox Roberts, and she wants to talk to you about her sister, Billie."

Five

"My sister did not commit suicide," the woman who'd taken over my office insisted, pacing in front of my desk like a nervous prosecutor addressing a jury in opening arguments. "I know it like I know my own name, like I know that the clock on your wall reads one o'clock. My sister would not, did not commit suicide. She was murdered."

"How can you be so sure?" I prodded.

"I saw her that afternoon. We had lunch at the Four Seasons. We talked and laughed," she said, strain pinching her voice tight. "Billie wasn't depressed. She was successful, growing rich, and loving it. She invited me to fly to Manhattan with her to shop. Does that sound like a woman so miserable she fired a bullet into her head?"

"Mrs. Roberts," I said, trying to calm her. "I'm really not the one you should talk to about the case. The detectives at H.P.D. are in charge."

"I've tried to reason with that detective," she said, her lips anchored into a lopsided frown. Older than her sister, Faith Roberts didn't appear to have her sister's funds. She wore an ill-fitting pin-striped skirt and a long-sleeved white sweater. Cut short, her dark brown hair tapered awkwardly into a bob around her ears. Yet she had on an impressive pair of canary yellow diamond stud earrings, marquis cut, and carried a black purse with the Fendi symbol zig-zagged across the fabric. Gifts from her dead sister?

"The Houston detectives have decided that this is a solved case, period, and they're not about to open it back up. The governor's of-fice tells me you agree," she said, becoming even more agitated. "I know why H.P.D. won't listen to me. That detective thinks I'm some kind of a loon. But I'm not. You have to listen to me. You just have to."

"This is understandably a highly emotional time for you," I said, looking down at my watch. Doc Larson was supposed to be at the ranch at two. I had to leave and head home soon or risk miss-ing him. "It's difficult to accept that a family member could commit suicide, and it's not unusual for families to disbelieve it, even when it's obvious."

"Too obvious," the woman stormed. "I saw the photos. It looked like a made-for-TV suicide. The whole thing was unbeliev-able. She even had the note right there on her body."

Had someone told her that I questioned the scene in the bed-room, troubled that it appeared too perfect? That wasn't possible. I hadn't told anyone except the captain. Even if she had heard some-how, it didn't matter. I'd found no evidence of homicide and already passed on the case. Faith Cox Roberts was H.P.D.'s headache, not mine. I'd learned my lessons. I'd taken on more than I should have a year earlier on the Lucas case and regretted it. I'd gotten in too deep.

"I'm sorry they showed you the photos," I said, meaning it. "You shouldn't have had to see that. I'm sure it was disturbing."

"I demanded to see them," she said, standing across from me at the desk, her hands locked in tight fists at her sides. "I had to see what they said my sister did. I had to know for myself."

"Mrs. Roberts, you need to limit your inquiries to the detectives in charge of the case," I said again. Sorry I'd agreed to talk to her, all I wanted was for the woman to leave. "This is inappropriate. It's H.P.D.'s case, not mine."

"I'm telling you that detective already made up his mind. He doesn't believe me. He doesn't care," she said, tears spilling down her cheeks. "You're my last chance to get justice for my sister, to find out who murdered her."

Damn, I thought. *I promised Maggie. If I'm not out of here in ten minutes . . .*

Faith Roberts dropped into the chair opposite my desk. Her shoulders sagged, and she appeared to wear the weight of her sister's death like the heaviest of shawls. Finally, she spoke again, confessing, "I think I said some things to the Houston detective, things that made him conclude I wasn't thinking clearly. Things that led him to believe that I'm some kind of a nut. But I'm not. I promise you, I'm not."

"What kind of things?" I asked.

Roberts hesitated and shook her head. "I'd rather not say," she said, nervously drumming her fingers on the wooden chair's arm in a swift *rat-a-tat-tat*. "Obviously, I made a mistake confiding in the detective. I'd rather that you don't get the same impression, that I'm some sort of maniac."

"Your reactions, under the circumstances, are entirely understandable. You've suffered a terrible loss," I said in my most reassuring voice. Still, I needed to know. "But if you don't tell me what you said to the detective, I'll simply call and ask him. Wouldn't you prefer to explain the situation?"

"Shit," she said, spitting out the word with all the force of a more substantial curse. She covered her mouth with one hand, her tomato-red polish chipped and splintered, as if she'd been absent-mindedly peeling it away. When she spoke again, she pleaded, "I don't know why I even said that, about what I told that other officer. It has nothing to do with why I'm here. Can't we talk about my sister's death? What does it matter what I said?"

"If you don't tell me, I'll call H.P.D. and ask the detective," I said again. "He *will* tell me."

The woman frowned, looking regretful and tired. She gathered her mouth into a tight bow. "Hell," she said, and then she paused. She waited for me to interrupt and let her off the hook. I didn't. "Well. I didn't really say anything all that shocking," she said, finally. She squared her shoulders, bracing, I gathered, for my reaction. "I just told him that my sister's communicating with me, letting me know she wasn't the one who pulled the trigger."

"Communicating with you?" I asked, glancing at my watch. I really needed to leave.

"Yes. Communicating with me," she said again. "Can we just leave it at that?"

"Not a chance," I said. "You've got me for four more minutes, so I suggest you take a deep breath and go for it. Tell me how your dead sister's sending you messages, and why you're convinced she was murdered."

My intentions were good. I meant to leave for home in plenty of time to talk with Doc Larson, to be ready to answer all Maggie's concerns about Emma Lou. Instead, forty-five minutes later, I weaved through traffic, rushing home, hoping to beat Maggie's school bus. I tried the ranch phone and Mom's cell but she didn't answer either. I figured she was out in the shed with Bobby and Doc, getting the rundown I should have been there to hear.

Still, how could I have left? I couldn't take my eyes off Faith Roberts, much less tell her to go away.

"It happens every evening, right about six o'clock," she said. "Six, you know, is about the time the coroner estimates my sister died."

"What happens?" I asked.

"It's always different," she said. "The day Billie died, before I got the bad news, I was home, picking up a pile of newspapers my husband left on the den floor, when the television clicked on. I hadn't turned it on, and no one else was there."

"Some kind of a fluke," I said, dismissively. "Mrs. Roberts, you can't place emphasis on a chance occurrence."

"When the television clicked on, it was on one of those crime channels, you know, the ones who have the real stories about real murders," she said. I nodded, and she started again. "I never watch those channels. I've never had any interest in them. Neither does my husband, so why our television would be set there, that puzzled me. The topic of the program was a New York case, a forensic show featuring a coroner."

"Well, there are a lot of crime shows on television. It's not surprising that the TV was on one."

"That day's episode was about a murder covered up by making it look like a suicide."

That was odd, I had to admit, but I said, "Coincidences do happen."

"I stopped and watched it. I'm not sure why. Like I told you, I never watch those kinds of shows," she said. "I guess it was about two hours later, when the detective called to tell me that my sister's body had been found. He read the suicide note to me over the telephone."

"You think your sister was talking to you through that television program?" I asked. No sense in dancing around the implication. I'm almost always in favor of getting everyone's hand laid out, cards right side up on the table. "Mrs. Roberts, certainly you don't truly believe that?"

"Not at that point. As you say, I assumed it had to be some kind of bizarre coincidence. But then, late the following afternoon, I was at the funeral home with my husband, picking out my sister's casket," she said. "I was crying. I had been ever since I'd heard the news. I was struggling with why Billie would have done this, when she'd been so happy at lunch. I hadn't thought much about the TV show the day before. Really very little."

"Well, then, why are you now thinking it was anything more than chance?"

"Because of what happened next. I had a hard time choosing, so we were there a long time. Just before six o'clock, my husband excused himself to return a business call and walked into another room. While I stood there surrounded by open caskets, wondering how something so terrible could happen and where I would get the strength to bury my sister, my cell phone rang," she said. Faith Roberts brushed a tear off her right cheek, and paused. "My cell phone rang, and I answered it. I said hello, but there wasn't anyone there."

"A wrong number," I speculated.

"My sister's name and cell phone number were on the caller I.D.," she said.

That, of course, was rather interesting. "Where was Billie's cell phone?" I asked.

"She'd forgotten it on the table at the restaurant the day before. I left after she did and took it with me," she said. "Since I hadn't seen her to return it, I still had Billie's phone in my purse."

Sure it was odd, but not unexplainable. "Phones sometimes dial by mistake. It's happened to me," I said with a shrug. "I was the last one somebody called, and his redial button was accidentally pushed, and my phone rang. My mom has my number programmed into her cell phone. Something triggered the button once without her know-ing, and my phone rang. I could hear her talking to someone, but she didn't know I was listening. It's most likely that something in your purse hit the button and made the call, that's all. You can't assume anything more than that."

Faith Roberts bit her trembling lower lip, and stared down at her hands. I wondered if she'd be able to go on. To move the con-versation along I asked, "I gather something happened again Sun-day, at about six P.M.?"

Roberts nodded.

"Yes. I was in the sunroom at our house when the breeze picked up from an open window," she said. "It flipped the pages on an al-bum I'd been looking through, collecting photos for the funeral. The page it opened to was a photo of Billie and me as children. We were holding hands. It was taken shortly after our mother died. The last thing my mother asked me to do was to always look out for my sister."

Faith was crying openly now, wiping away tears. It was getting harder to leave, but I really had to.

"This is very interesting, even quite sweet," I said. "But we're talking about easily explained events, and I need to be on my way."

"Late yesterday, Monday, I was in my sister's office at Century Oil, cleaning out her personal items," she said. "Her company com-puter was turned off, not on standby, *turned off*. At precisely six, it clicked on, all by itself. No one else was in the room, and I was standing at least five feet away, boxing up family photos, so I didn't do it by accident."

It all sounded too farfetched, ringing cell phones and computers and televisions that flick on by themselves, so I renewed my deci-sion to pass the buck to H.P.D., and I ventured, "As I said, this is in-teresting, but it really doesn't mean anything. You have nothing solid to investigate. Nothing to base a case on."

"Please, just listen. I never touched the keyboard, but somehow this popped up on the screen," she insisted, pulling a sheet of computer printer paper out of her purse. "As soon as I saw it, I knew my sister's death wasn't a suicide. Billie didn't pull that trigger, Lieutenant Armstrong. Someone murdered my sister."

Six

I'm on my way," I told Mom when she finally answered her cell phone. "Is Maggie home yet?"

"She'll be here any minute," Mom said, sounding worried. "It's okay that you weren't here to see Doc, Sarah, but I hoped we'd have a chance to talk before Maggie gets home."

I knew from the tone of her voice that Doc's news wasn't that Emma Lou had made a full recovery. "Maybe you should tell me now, on the phone," I said. "So I'm prepared."

It was a bright, warm winter day with a cloudless blue sky, and I drove down one of my favorite stretches of road, not far from the ranch. I crossed a small bridge over a creek and drove under a canopy formed by the strong, gnarled branches of black-trunked live oaks. I maneuvered through an S-curve and passed Liber- tyville, the post–Civil War settlement where Strings's dad pastors a white-clapboard church. On the other side of the road sat the Jacobses' brown brick one-story house and a fenced pasture, where Bruce, Strings's 4-H project, chomped on high grass growing along a barbed-wire fence. As I passed, the gray Brahman reared its head back, ruffling the thick flap of skin draped from its chin to its chest and scattering the white egrets at its feet. The birds unfurled their long, elegant wings, and flew off, their slender bodies soaring gracefully overhead.

"Doc was right," Mom said. "The blood tests show Emma Lou has that bacterial infection he worried about."

"Damn," I said.

There was no mistaking the worry in her voice. "Based on when we had her bred, Emma Lou is two-hundred and ninety-eight days into the pregnancy, Sarah. There's a good chance that the infection will cause the foal to birth early," she said. After a long, quiet pause, she explained, "If it's born in the next few days, Doc says the foal won't survive."

"Now Maggie, you have to trust that Emma Lou and her foal will be all right," I said. Mom and Bobby were seated on one bench at the kitchen table, and Strings was beside my daughter on another across from them. The only one standing, I couldn't see their hands, but I suspected Strings held Maggie's under the table.

"But Emma Lou could be blind, and what happens if Doc is right and the foal comes early?" Maggie asked, her voice urgent with fear. "The foal could die, Mom. Doc said the foal could die."

"We can't guarantee anything, Magpie. I wish we could, but we can't," I said, using the nickname Bill and I gave her at birth. "None of us has the power to control what will happen. But we will do everything we can for Emma Lou and her foal."

"Maggie, honey, your mom, Bobby, and I, we're all going to take care of Emma Lou," Mom said. "She'll have everything she needs. With just a little bit of luck, both the horses will be all right."

I walked over and slipped my arms over my daughter's shoulders. She shivered just slightly, I guessed from fear. "Yeah, they'll be okay, Mom," she said, sounding not quite convinced. "We've been through a lot, all of us, and we're going to make sure Emma Lou is okay."

"That's what I like to hear," Bobby Barker said, slapping a thick hand on the hard, bare wood of the table. "Why this family, this group of women, you three could lick anything, couldn't they, Strings?"

"I think they could even lick us in a fight," Strings agreed. "Maybe not one-on-one but . . ."

"Oh, we could so," Maggie said, the prospect edging away her frown. "Couldn't we, Mom? We could wrestle both of them and win."

Glad my daughter was up for the fight ahead, I didn't disagree. "I bet we could, Magpie," I said. "I bet we could."

The discussion ended, and Mom and Maggie drew up a schedule listing everyone's responsibilities, from giving the mare her medicine to cleaning her shed. I suggested we put the baby monitor, the one Bill and I used for Maggie, in the shed. As the lightest sleeper, I volunteered to cover the nights, listening for Emma Lou from my bedroom.

It seemed we were thinking of everything. Maggie and Strings even decided to download music from the Internet, to play in Emma Lou's shed to relax her and the foal. To my chagrin, what I heard the kids playing were Cassidy Collins songs.

While Mom made ham and macaroni and cheese for dinner, and Maggie coddled her horse, I disappeared into my workroom to make phone calls. Listening to Collins sing had reminded me that I'd run out so quickly after Faith Roberts left, I didn't have time to follow through on any of the things I'd wanted to do for either of the cases dumped on my lap that first day back at work. Number one on my list, I called an L.A.P.D. special crimes officer who Sheila had already alerted. The sergeant who answered listened to my assessment of the stalking situation and agreed to get an L.A. prosecutor to set up traces on landline phone numbers Barron would supply him with later that evening. If the calls were being rerouted, caller I.D. wouldn't work. Barron had already contacted the cell phone company and asked them to do tower checks on all incoming text messages and calls, to narrow down where the signals were coming from. Meanwhile, Janet, the clerk at my office, was busy writing subpoenas for any information associated with Argus's e-mail addresses.

Confident that the Collins case was being worked, I dialed the Houston morgue, and asked for Dr. Joe, a.k.a. Joseph Fernandez, M.D., one of the assistant medical examiners. "Dr. Joe, will you check and see if you still have a body there? It's an apparent suicide from last Friday," I said.

"What's the name?" he growled back. A thick-necked, round man, Dr. Joe had been in a foul mood for the past month, ever since he'd crashed his motorcycle into a pickup truck and cracked a few ribs. In his sixties, he was probably too old for speeding through the countryside on his Harley, but I would have paid to see anyone tell him that. This was not a man who pampered those who saw things differently.

"Elizabeth Cox," I said. "Her sister tells me that the body is ready for transport, but she hasn't sent a funeral director to do a pickup yet."

"Just a minute, Lieutenant," he said. Only silence until he clicked the telephone back on and said, "Yeah, she's still here, but she shouldn't be. Anyone planning to claim this body anytime soon?"

"I need to check a few things out," I said. "I'll be there in forty-five minutes. After that, I think we can get the sister to call the hearse and transport Ms. Cox."

"Hallelujah," Fernandez said. "I've got bodies waiting in the wings for a vault. I'll be glad for the extra room."

One last thing to do before I left for the morgue, I called an old friend, a retired FBI profiler named Mike Davis. Back in the day, as Mom likes to say, Davis headed the document analysis branch at the FBI Academy in Quantico, Virginia. We'd met what seemed like a lifetime ago, when I studied profiling. What had popped up on Billie Cox's computer screen the day Faith was claiming her sister's personal possessions was the suicide note. From the form of the note, including the random capitalization, Faith claimed there was no way her sister would have written it.

"My sister was a meticulous woman," Faith had told me. "She had a masters degree in geophysics, but right out of college, when jobs in the oil industry were scarce, Billie worked briefly as an executive assistant. Her language skills were impeccable, and years later, even as company president, she wrote her own correspondence. She wouldn't have left something so poorly written as her final communication with her family and friends."

It was Billie Cox's suicide note that I wanted Mike to evaluate.

A brief hello and the required niceties out of the way, I suggested we catch up another time, and told Mike what I needed. "I have six documents I want you to examine," I explained. "The first is a suicide note left by a woman named Elizabeth Cox, the head of an oil company. The other five are documents we know Cox wrote. No question. They're all personal notes and letters written to her sister."

"You want me to compare all six and let you know if I think the dead woman authored the suicide note?" Mike asked. "You're figuring that maybe this wasn't a suicide?"

"Not necessarily. Maybe there's nothing out of whack here. Could be this is just what it looks like, a tragic suicide," I said. "I'm figuring maybe you can clear up the mystery. You're the best documents-guru I know, Mike."

"E-mail the paperwork," he said, not arguing the point. "I'll get back to you in a couple of days."

"You've got it. It'll be on its way in a flash," I said. "And Mike, by the way—"

"Let me guess," he cut in. "Don't tell anyone I'm doing this for you?"

"Mike, you are the best. Hell, you can even read minds," I said with a laugh. "The truth is that this is H.P.D.'s case, and I want to find out if there's even a crime before I get called on the carpet for poaching."

Seven

"What're you looking for?" Dr. Joe asked.

Hands tucked in his lab coat pockets, he watched with interest as I circled the cold, lifeless body of Elizabeth Cox on a steel exam table. Dr. Joe hadn't been happy when I asked his assistant to remove Cox's remains from the refrigerated vault and black body bag. I needed to see her laid out as she was now, under a bright exam light, so I could get a good look. Not that I particularly wanted to. Despite my chosen profession, I've never been at ease around dead bodies, at least not those who meet their ends through violent means. The way I see it, these are folks who die unfinished. I'm sure there are those who'd argue it with me, but I've never believed deaths like Billie's are God's will. Someone else makes the decision, fires the fatal bullet. Was the killer in this case also the deceased? That was what I was there to figure out.

"Lieutenant Armstrong," Dr. Joe said again. "You want to tell me what you're looking for?"

"Sure," I said. The truth was that I didn't have a clue. That said, I figured I'd know it when I saw it, so I suggested, "Give me a couple of minutes."

We were in an autopsy suite on the first floor of the county forensic center, a redbrick building just outside the skyscraper hospitals that make up the Texas Medical Center. In this part of the state, the M.E.'s office is a stop on the way to eternity for not only crime victims but any questionable death. Texas law stipulates that anyone who dies by homicide, suicide, in an accident, or from undetermined causes, anyone who's not in a doctor's care, and folks in hospitals for less than twenty-four hours before their deaths must be examined by a medical examiner. About a quarter of the time, an autopsy is unnecessary, because it's apparent that a terminal disease, like cancer, has reached its logical conclusion. That means that 75 percent of the time, the docs ready their scalpels and fulfill their role as combination physicians and investigators. In this building, pathologists and technicians not only dissect human bodies but conduct DNA and toxicology tests, study recovered bones, collect and process evidence, and in the cold, lonely vaults, the remains of the dead silently wait to be claimed.

For the most part, forensic pathologists are curious individuals, intent on piecing together the clues death leaves behind. What they learn can help the living, hence the Latin motto over the door in nearly every morgue I've encountered: "*Hic locus est ubi mors gaudet succurrere vitae.*" In a more familiar language: "This is the place where death delights to help the living."

Two days earlier, Dr. Joe began with a visual examination of Billie Cox's body, and then cut through her chest in a "Y," from clavicle to pelvis, opening her up to inspect her insides. He examined and weighed all her internal organs including her kidneys, heart, and liver, dictating his notes as he progressed. Like many who die violently, Billie Cox was a fine specimen, in good health. The physician found nothing organic to portend an early death. After he documented the outer appearance of her GSW, the gunshot wound, he cut through her skull with a small electric saw and carefully removed her brain, to trace the path of the bullet. There would be no surprises. Billie Cox died of the GSW to the brain. The damage was catastrophic, and death was instantaneous. Finished, Dr. Joe turned her body over to an assistant, who repaired the pathologist's incisions with V-shaped stitches, the same type used to bind baseballs.

As I patrolled the exam table, I also noticed a few stitches closing a small incision on Cox's side, the point at which a probe had been inserted on the scene to record liver temperature. At 7 P.M. on the night of her death, in a seventy-degree bedroom, her body didn't yet show signs of rigor mortis and her liver temp was a nearly normal 98.4, leading to the conclusion that she'd been dead for less than two hours. The M.E. couldn't be more precise than that.

"You did the GSR testing here at the morgue?" I asked.

Dr. Joe frowned, looking impatient. "Of course," he said. "The woman's hands came in bagged from the scene. We did the testing for gunshot residue here, as we always do. What's up, Lieutenant? Why are you here? Isn't this H.P.D.'s body?"

Not looking up, I said, "I was asked to consult." It wasn't a lie. I had been asked to look over the file, even if this trip to the morgue could be considered extracurricular. "I thought perhaps seeing Miss Cox's remains might settle some questions."

"What questions?" Dr. Joe asked.

"Well," I said. "The death scene looked a little too perfect, almost staged to me. It's probably nothing, but did you see anything at all that contradicted the conclusion that this was a suicide?"

Dr. Joe thought about that for a little while. His final report hadn't been typed up yet, but he flipped through his notes on Billie Cox, all the while standing on one foot and rubbing his calf with the opposite heel. There's very little humidity in the morgue, not the best environment for living flesh. "Just what I already told the detective, about the bruising," he said, closing the report folder. "That's already been discussed, and I can't find anything else of interest."

"Refresh my memory," I said. "What bruising?"

"Didn't Detective Walker fill you in?" he asked. He stretched out his left arm, and rubbed the elbow, scratching. As he did, I noticed a tattoo just above his wristwatch, a new one. From the occasional glimpse and death-house rumors, I knew the pathologist had an impressive collection covering his body from his wrists up, extending over his chest, to just below the neck of his blue surgical scrubs. In fact, along with motorcycles, tattoos were a pet interest of the good doctor, which explained why his new one depicted wings emanating from a motorcycle wheel. Somewhere in the lab, legend had it that he kept a three-ring binder filled with tattoos he traced off dead bodies. He referred to it as his "research project."

"Detective Brad Walker?" I asked.

"Yeah," Dr. Joe said. "This is his case. Didn't you know that?"

I hadn't noticed Walker's name in the file. That was why Faith Roberts received such a cold reception at H.P.D. Like all officers, Walker had a jacket, a reputation. I'd never met him, but I'd heard he was a black-and-white kind of guy. He didn't leave much room for the possibility that things weren't as they seemed. When Faith Roberts mentioned communication from the dead, Walker must have flipped. If I'd realized he was on the case, I would have asked more questions from the start.

"Just slipped my mind," I fibbed. "Guess the detective forgot to clue me in. Why don't you, Dr. Joe? What bruising?"

Everyone who dealt with the medical examiner's office knew Dr. Joe hated explaining anything more than once. As was usual when his patience was taxed, he stared at the one who strained his goodwill as if inspecting bacteria. At such times, he had this look about him, kind of a dead, cold stare. Frowning at me, he took a ballpoint pen from the collection in his breast pocket plastic protector. He bent over and used the tip to point at the skin just below the entrance wound in the right side of Billie Cox's head.

"Take a look here," he said. "It's faint but definitely there. You'll have to stand close to see it."

I did as instructed, getting within inches of the raw, angry hole in Cox's temple, and I saw just a slight yellow hue, faint but there, on the lower lip of the entrance wound. "That shouldn't be there," I said, stating the obvious.

Suffering from my apparent stupidity, Dr. Joe shook his head. "Lieutenant, when people shoot themselves through the head, depending on the position of the body, standing, sitting, or lying down, there are variations on where the arm holding the weapon ends up and where the gun lands. When the victim is seated, as Ms. Cox was, the most likely scenario is what we see in the scene photos. The pistol's recoil pushes the hand and gun away from the head, and the body is found with the gun lying near the extended hand."

"I understand that, but a suicide entrance wound isn't usually bruised like this," I asked. "Why is she bruised?"

Again the good doctor sighed, staring at me as if it required all his patience to proceed. "As I explained to the detective, sometimes things don't happen precisely as we expect," he said. "There are multiple possibilities, but my guess is that this woman held the gun so tight against her skull, with so much force, that the recoil bounced it, causing the peri-mortem bruising."

"I've never seen that before," I said. "Not in a suicide."

"Nor have I," he answered. "But that doesn't mean it isn't possible."

"I have seen this type of bruising in homicides," I said. Offering nothing more, I waited for the physician to jump in. He didn't at first, as if considering how to take my observation. When he spoke, it was again to dismiss my concerns.

"Of course. And I discussed that option with Detective Walker," he said, with an air of finality.

"Just to make sure I get the right version, how about one more time with me?" I asked.

Scowling at me, Dr. Joe cinched his face into a taut frown.

"You're absolutely right," he said, eyeing me as if my very presence irritated him more than his aching ribs. "The usual scenario with this type of bruising is homicide. Someone holds a gun tight against a victim's skull. A living, breathing shooter has the strength to fight recoil, and that increases the odds that a jerking reaction brings the pistol back toward the head, hitting near the entrance wound. The result? A peri-mortem bruise, just like this one."

"In this case, there's some reason you don't believe that's what happened? The file I reviewed had a notation that your conclusion on the autopsy report will agree with a finding of suicide," I said. "You didn't find that bruise a convincing reason to consider murder?"

"No," he said.

"Why not?" I asked.

"Everything else fits a suicide, so my opinion is that this bruise is simply an aberration. Detective Walker agreed with me that when the rest of the scene screams suicide, something so minor isn't enough to question manner of death."

I thought about that for a few minutes, and then asked one more question. "When you did the GSR test on the shooting hand you only tested the back of the hand?"

"Of course. Why?" he asked.

"Humor me and test her right palm."

"We're not going to find anything, Lieutenant. She was grasping the gun, so the grip blocked residue from her palm," he said. I said nothing, just waited, until the good doctor shrugged. "But if you'd like, sure. We can do that."

"Thanks," I said, with a smile. "It's appreciated."

"Now, since I've been such a good sport, you will, of course, return the favor by getting this woman's sister to claim her corpse, won't you?" he said. "As I mentioned on the telephone earlier, I need the room. These days the morgue has a permanent NO VACANCY sign."

I knew he wouldn't be happy, but what the heck. "I'd like you to keep Ms. Cox's body a bit longer, while I look into the case," I suggested. "Until we're sure we've got it right."

Predictably peeved by my request, Dr. Joe glared at me but said, "Okay, Lieutenant, but let's make every attempt to hurry this woman along to her final resting place."

On the way home from the M.E.'s office, I called the captain and filled him in on what I'd learned about the autopsy and the bruising. "I'd like to poke around a bit," I said. "I want to make sure we're not closing the book too soon."

"That's fine," he said. "Now that you've got something to back up your suspicions, I'll notify H.P.D. in the morning, tell them you'll be investigating further. Keep me posted."

"By the way, Captain," I added. "You didn't mention that this is Brad Walker's case, and I don't remember seeing his name on the file."

Even on the telephone I could hear the captain's sigh. "Sarah, I didn't want it to color the way you saw it, make you second-guess if there wasn't anything there," he said. "Maybe I was wrong, since now you do have suspicions, but I took out H.P.D.'s assignment sheet because I didn't want it to complicate matters."

"Okay," I said. "That makes sense. I've got an appointment in the morning on that Collins stalking case. I'll see you at the office, not sure when."

"See you then," he said.

It was well after dark when I arrived at the ranch and found Mom and Bobby winding white Christmas-style lights over the wrought-iron gate at the entrance. They'd crisscrossed the circular emblem at the top with the white cord so many times that the Rocking Horse insignia was hidden under what looked like the web of a Chippewa dream catcher. I hoped it would capture all our bad dreams and spirit them away.

I stopped and lowered my window.

"I didn't know you two were doing that tonight," I said.

"It's a surprise for Maggie," Mom said, looking proud. "It was Bobby's suggestion, something to lift her spirits."

"Good idea," I said, thinking Mom looked cute when she's smitten.

"I've got a full day at the office tomorrow," Bobby said, explaining that his family business, Barker Oil, was getting into a bidding war over an oil company that had just recently gone up for sale. "The company president died suddenly. I figured if your mom and I were going to do this for Maggie, we needed to do it tonight."

"Well, it looks great. See you two at the house." That said, I drove up the driveway, parked the Tahoe, and got out. Then I decided to walk back to the gate for a little talk.

"Which oil company?" I asked Bobby, who was bending over, picking up the remains of the packing materials from the lights.

"What?" he said, looking at me over his shoulder.

"Which company are you bidding on?" I asked. "Is it Century Oil?"

"How did you know that?" he asked, standing beside me. He looked uneasy, as if called on something he found distasteful. "I hated to pick it up like this, but with the whole place in chaos after

Billie Cox went and shot herself, the two old guys who own it are selling, and companies are lining up to put in a bid. Oil as high as it is right now, it's a no-brainer. But how did you know?"

Ignoring his question, I asked, "Did you know Cox?"

"Sure," he said. "Great gal. Lots of fun, and a great business-woman. I thought the world of Billie. Can't understand why she'd do anything so blatantly stupid. Just not like her. That gal, why she was smart as a whip."

"When's the last time you saw her?"

"A couple of weeks ago," he said. "We were getting ready to do a deal together, buy up an old field in East Texas and co-develop it. Combining our assets made it easier. Now, I'm looking at buying the field alone, for Barker Oil. It's a good investment. They're widow wells, abandoned decades ago because it was too expensive to get to the oil. But we figured with prices so high and new tech-nology, we could cash in, big time."

"That's interesting, and I'd love to hear about it sometime, maybe the same day we discuss the loan I need to take out to fill up my gas tank?" I interrupted.

"You know, finding more oil isn't a bad thing, Sarah," Bobby said, patiently. "More supply brings down prices, not raises them."

He, of course, had a point.

"We can argue about oil prices later," I offered. "But for now just tell me what you're hearing from folks in the oil patch. What're folks in the business saying about Cox's death?"

Mom moved forward, as interested as I was in hearing what Bobby had to say. He looked at both of us and a small smile inched across his face. "You know," he said, with a chuckle, "I've been hop-ing to find a way to get this kind of attention from you two women. Didn't know all I had to do was spread a little gossip."

"Don't think of it as gossip. I have reasons for wanting to know," I told him. "What are you hearing?"

"Most folks don't think she did it, Sarah—killed herself, I mean," he said. "She was a gung-ho kind of gal, Billie was, but not the kind to do anything rash. Billie was young and aggressive. Under her, Century pulled together one hell of a portfolio, one of the best in the industry for a medium-size company. With its share of this field we were buying, the company would have been the envy of nearly every privately owned oil company in Texas."

"Folks who aren't questioning why she did it," I said. "What are they saying?"

Bobby sucked in a breath. It was obvious he'd prefer not to talk about those rumors. My mom's suitor was more the strong, quiet kind of man, one who offered a steady hand without a lot of fanfare. I'd grown to believe that was what Mom saw in him, the same quality I'd always recognized in her, someone there for the long haul, no matter what.

"Well, there are folks who say someone broke Billie's heart," he said. "And there are others, a few, who, the way I hear it, are spreading rumors that she'd been seeing a therapist, maybe because she was having a hard time splitting off from the guy. The way folks tell it, Billie had an affair of the heart that went wrong, because the man she was after was married."

Mom scowled, and I figured talk of an adulterous relationship had crossed the line for her. She'd never been one to approve of what she called "such shenanigans." Of course, she didn't know the reason for my questions, and, at least at this juncture, I preferred that no one, not even Bobby and Mom, know that I was looking into Billie Cox's suicide as a possible murder. If the news broke, it would only add fodder to the swirl of gossip around her death.

Appearing intent on changing the subject, Mom said, "Let's light this gate up and see how she looks."

Figuring I had enough information for the time being, I didn't object. "Good idea, Mom," I said. "It looks like I got here just in time for the grand unveiling."

With that, Mom bent down and plugged the cord into an out-let under the coach light on the post next to the gate. The lights flared, covering the arch over the gate like a bright, white rainbow, and we stood there for just a moment enjoying the view. "Beauti-ful," I said. "Just beautiful."

"It is pretty," Bobby agreed. "Maybe it'll help give Maggie some peace about Emma Lou."

"You don't think the horse will make it, do you Bobby?" Mom said.

"I think the pinto will pull through, but that foal is in for one hell of a fight," he admitted. "I'd be willing to bring in a specialist, someone to treat the horses, if you'd like, Nora?"

Mom thought about that a bit, but shook her head. "I trust Doc Larson," she said. "He's been watching over our livestock for years. And I don't want to give Maggie false hope. If the foal comes too early, no vet's going to be able to keep it alive. Seeing some expert will only give the wrong impression. At least for the next few days, until the mare's pregnancy hits three hundred days, that foal is in God's hands, not ours."

"You're right, of course," he said, and I saw him slip his arm around Mom's waist.

"We'll be up at the house in a few minutes, Sarah," Mom said, and I took that as my dismissal. As I headed toward the back door, I turned for another glimpse of the gate glowing in the night. Maggie would love it. Like the corral, the lights were another bit of heaven brought closer to earth. Mom looked happy, too. Bobby had her in his arms and they were locked into a long, slow kiss. I thought about how I missed those, and how I missed Bill, but I couldn't help but think that even with so much pain in the world, life had so much to cherish.

Inside the house, I found Maggie at the living room window, barefoot and in her nightgown, holding the blinds apart so she could see the gate. She must have expected me, because she didn't seem startled when I walked up behind her.

"It's wonderful, Mom. Don't you think so?" Maggie asked, staring out at the lights in the darkness.

"It is, Magpie," I agreed. "It truly is."

In the kitchen, I made myself a cup of Mom's chamomile tea, and then decided on one last phone call before I turned in for the night.

"Was your sister having an affair?" I asked Faith Roberts.

"No, at least not lately," she said. "I thought awhile back there was someone, but I was never sure. For a time she seemed busier than usual, and I didn't hear from her like I typically do. She never told me about any particular man, although we usually shared everything in our lives. That stopped before her death, maybe a couple of weeks. I saw more of her, and things got back to normal. But even if Billie had an affair, she didn't kill herself over it."

"How do you know that?" I asked.

"Like I told you, those last weeks, I'd never seen Billie look happier," she said.

"One last question," I said. "Was your sister seeing a therapist?"

The phone went quiet. "Well, I guess I should have told you about that," Faith said, finally. "But it's not what you think. She's not the usual kind of therapist. It wasn't because Billie was depressed."

"What kind was she seeing?"

Again, silence.

"Faith, I can't help if you're not honest with me."

She must have considered that and decided I was right. "My

sister and I shared a belief in the supernatural. Perhaps that's why I'm so certain she's communicating with me," Faith said. "The therapist she saw deals primarily in hypnosis and past lives."

"You want to say that again?" I asked.

"Past lives, like reincarnation," Faith said. I could tell from the tone of her voice that she realized how bizarre I thought this sounded. "I know it's pretty unusual, but you really need to talk to Dr. Dorin. She'll explain it. It's not really that eccentric, I promise."

As I wrote down the doctor's name and phone number, I thought that this just might be the oddest case of my career. If it weren't for that bruise Dr. Joe showed me, by now I would have agreed with H.P.D.'s conclusion and written the whole thing off. It didn't help my mood any when Faith said she had something else she wanted to tell me.

"This is the first evening since Billie's death that six o'clock came and went and nothing unusual happened," she said. "I think it's because she knows you're going to help us."

"I'll do my best, Faith," I said. "But please remember, in the end it may turn out that H.P.D. is right, and your sister's death is a suicide."

Thinking about how much I would have liked it if Bill had dropped in to leave messages after his death, then shrugging off even the thought that that was possible, I hung up the telephone, and went into the living room to check on Maggie. She wasn't there, but I knew where to find her. I walked out to the shed, and there she was, in her soft flannel nightgown, slumped down in one of the old metal chairs, in a light sleep. I peeked in on Emma Lou, who slept peacefully in her temporary home. Confident that, at least for now, all was well, I nudged Maggie a bit, whispered her name, and she woke up. We were past the point where I could carry her. She opened her eyes, and I walked her down the hill. As we approached the house, she caught another glimpse of the Christmas light dream catcher over the gate, with Mom and Bobby still stand-ing beneath it.

"It really is beautiful, Mom. Just like the stars," Maggie said. She smiled, and then cuddled against me for the rest of the walk into the house.

Eight

Cassidy Collins's heart pounded so hard as she walked onto the stage, she worried it might rivet its way through her chest. She used to look forward to performances, but now they filled her with an acute dread, an overriding foreboding. *I've got to pull it together,* she thought. *I can't let this perv get to me.*

Oblivious to her plight, all around her the San Diego audience cheered, called out to her, a sea of strangers that intensified her fears. Were they, as they appeared, simply a throng of parents, daughters, and sons? Were they *all* there just to have a good time? Or had something else brought one spectator to the concert?

He could be out there, she thought. *He could be watching.*

The tempo built, hard and solid, the music pulsing around her, and Cassidy concentrated on the beat, trying to ease her disquiet. The stage was her territory, where she felt the most alive. *I'm not going to let some dude with an overblown ego ruin this for me,* she thought. *He won't try anything, not here, not now, not with all these people watching. That creep wouldn't dare.*

Behind her the band kicked into a hard-rocking number, and

Cassidy relied on instinct for the dance moves that maneuvered her across the stage. In the audience, a girl in the front row reached up toward her, holding a red rose. Cassidy bent down to take it. As her hand closed around the stem, a searing pain pierced her palm. Four more dance steps and as she began the song's second verse, she threw the rose back into the audience, where a heaving patchwork of bodies rushed forward to catch it. Still singing, she glanced at her hand and saw red, a bloody smudge. She needed to be more careful. *Leave the roses and take the daisies*, she thought. *Remember the thorns.*

Per the routine, the dancers shadowed the superstar stage right, and she spun and fell back into a web of their bodies. They held her up by her extended arms, an ear-to-ear smile resolutely anchored on her face. Her hand throbbed and tears formed in her eyes, but from the audience, Cassidy appeared to be exhilarated by the excitement of being on stage.

In truth, she couldn't get him out of her mind.

Five rows back, she thought she saw a glint in the audience, something bright. She wondered if it could be a knife, and if the hand holding it belonged to Argus. It passed quickly. *Silly*, she decided. *Probably just one of those battery-operated fans, the ones with the whirly bird tips that light.*

She shook it off.

Calm down, she thought. *I have to relax before I drive myself crazy.*

As the evening wore on, she sang, danced, and fought back waves of anxiety. Until, nearly an hour into the concert, after the fourth costume change, Cassidy realized she had only fifteen minutes left on stage. The concert was nearly over. For the first time that day, she began to loosen up. One more concert and nothing had happened. *I'm freaking myself out for no reason*, she thought. *This creep just gets off scaring people.* If so, she assured herself, Argus had picked on the wrong girl. Life had fed Collins more than her share of pain, and she'd always survived. She needed to take it one day at a time, and before long the stalker would be nothing more than a bad memory.

Suddenly, her in-ear monitor went dead, quiet.

Cassidy turned and looked at Jake, the audio guy, off in the wings, and saw him frantically search the sound mixer, flipping switches. The lights had all gone out, and nothing was working. He looked up at her and shook his head. *Not a clue*, he seemed to be saying.

Then, as unexpectedly as it clicked off, the equipment flicked back on. Dancing and singing her way across the stage, Cassidy trembled with relief. *It was nothing*, she chastised herself, *a computer glitch*.

Shaking it off, she sang as the dancers formed a circle around her for the song's finale. Cassidy moved into place, and the muscular young men dropped to their knees. Four grabbed her by her calves and thighs, lifting her up, until two moved beneath her and slipped her onto their shoulders. Cassidy thrust her arms up into a triumphant "V" and belted out the final refrain, just as again, without warning, her in-ear monitor went stone silent.

As the dancers walked the stage, displaying her in front of more than twenty thousand screaming fans, Cassidy's monitor snapped back on. Rather than music, she heard a voice, an unfamiliar voice.

"I'm here," he taunted, mocking her. He let lose a thick-throated laugh, and then whispered, "I'm here, and I've come for you."

Nine

There's no doubt about it: it's easier to work one case at a time than balance multiple investigations. If I ever meet a cop who routinely has the luxury of focusing entirely on a single case, I'm going to leave the rangers and sign on with her department, whether it's Detroit, Miami, or Sacramento. So far, I sure haven't been that lucky. That is, unless I'm in crisis mode, like last year on the Lucas case. That's different. But on your average day I work two, often three cases. Then there are the files sent in from across the state, the ones that pile up on my desk, waiting to be reviewed. Not to mention the cold cases, those I've never been able to solve. Some nights, one or another wakes me up in a sweat, reminding me that I haven't given the victims justice. It's a juggling act, trying not to let any case fall, afraid the one I drop is the one that takes me down. I love my work, but I'd only been back on the job a day, and it was already getting wild.

That's what I was thinking sitting in the Rice University Police office waiting for Sergeant Jim Herald. Emma Lou and I had both slept peacefully the prior night, not a blip on the baby-now-turned-horse monitor. Doc figured this was day number 299 of her pregnancy. Anything over three hundred and the foal had a chance. Aware that I had a full day ahead, I got up early, checked on the pinto, and then called Sergeant Herald to tell him I'd be dropping by. If Faith was right and her dead sister was keeping tabs on me, for the time being Billie Cox was just going to have to trust that I'd get back to her. Right now, Cassidy Collins and her stalker had my undivided attention.

I'd asked Herald to get an update on our prime suspect, Justin Peterson, from his professor, and to find out where the piano protégé was on the night Argus was in the audience in Las Vegas. Afterward, I planned a knock and talk. I'd knock on Peterson's door and talk my way in. The truth is that I didn't have nearly enough probable cause to get a search warrant, but I wanted a look inside his apartment. You can tell a lot about folks from the way they live.

At least that was the plan.

Fifteen minutes later than we'd agreed, Sergeant Herald, a tall, angular man with hollow cheeks and a precisely cut brown flattop, walked in the door and guided me to his cubicle. We'd barely begun talking when my cell phone rang. I noticed the 213 area code, Los Angeles, and realized it was near dawn on the West Coast. This wasn't going to be good news.

"Argus was at Cassidy's concert last night," Barron said. "You have to do something, Lieutenant Armstrong."

"Let me talk to her," a young female voice shouted in the background. "They're not taking this seriously. I want this perv stopped, now!"

"I'm working on it, Cassie," Barron said. "I'll get it done!"

"Get real, Rick. You've been handling this, okay, and what have you done to stop this creep?" the voice demanded. "Give me that stupid phone. From now on, I talk to the cops."

Barron must have handed over the telephone, for the next thing the girl said was directly to me, "I want you to take care of this Peterson jerk for real. Get him the hell out of my face. You got that, cop?"

"Who are you?" I asked.

"Cassidy Collins, Lady Cop," she said. "And like I said, it's like . . . this is it, you know? No more excuses. You need to arrest this jerk now."

"My name is Lieutenant Sarah Armstrong, and I'm a Texas Ranger," I said. "If you'll just explain to me what happened last night, perhaps I can help you."

"Rick told you. That Peterson guy showed up again, this time while I was onstage in front of twenty-thousand kids. All of a sudden the dude talks into my ear monitor. He was laughing and stuff, threatening me," she said. "You need to stop him, now. No excuses. I want this guy gone."

This case wasn't going to be easy, and it sure wasn't turning out to be fun. "Did Mr. Barron call San Diego P.D.?" I asked. "Did you file a report?"

"We've filed enough paper to supply the johns in Caesars Palace. Ask me if it helped. It didn't," she said. "I've had it with this dude. I can't go to bed without figuring he's outside my window. I just bought the hottest red Porsche, but I can't drive it without a bodyguard because this Argus dude could follow me. You getting this, cop? You understand?"

"Yes. I understand. And one more time, my name is Lieutenant Armstrong," I said. It shouldn't have mattered, but this was one irritating sixteen-year-old.

"Whatever. I don't care what your name is, Lady Cop. All I care about is that you catch this dude. Give him one of those lethal injections you Texans are so good at, and get the hell rid of him."

There were things this kid was going to have to understand.

"Despite stalking not being a death sentence offense, I recognize your need to find and stop this man," I said. "So tell me everything that happened last night, and maybe instead of attempting to bully me, you can help me figure out how to stop him."

The kid balked some, but got over my "dissing" her. By the time I hung up, I was not only convinced that when I returned to the ranch that night I would burn every one of Maggie's Cassidy Collins CDs, but also that the ill-mannered pop star had more than enough justification to be frightened. It had to be unsettling to be up on a stage in front of thousands of strangers and hear someone whisper threats in your ear. His final words were enough to haunt anyone: "You will die."

While San Diego police attempted to determine how Argus intruded on the facility's closed-circuit sound system, what I wanted to know was where Justin Peterson spent the evening. If he wasn't in Houston, was he in San Diego?

Sergeant Herald had listened to the entire exchange, and when I hung up, he gave me a sympathetic nod. "I've dealt with those Hollywood people," he said with a sideways grimace. "They aren't easy to get along with."

"Bet that kid doesn't get many votes for Miss Congeniality," I agreed. "But I can't blame her for being upset."

"Maybe, but it sure sounds to me like they're going after the wrong guy," Herald said. He handed me his report with the information I'd asked for, documenting Herald's whereabouts on the evening Cassidy performed at Caesars Palace. "On that particular day, Mr. Peterson worked most of the afternoon with his supervising professor on a musical composition, in the piano lab," Herald said, while I paged through the file. "Mr. Peterson didn't leave until eight that evening. He was seen later that same night taking out the garbage, at about ten-thirty, by the couple who lives in the apartment next to his in grad-student housing. Mr. Peterson wasn't anywhere near Las Vegas."

"Okay," I said. "What about last night?"

"I'll check," he said. With that Herald picked up his telephone and dialed, talked to someone briefly, then hung up. "That was Peterson's professor," he said. "She had dinner with Peterson last evening in the student center and then they worked on his composition together until nearly nine. Mr. Peterson was in the piano lab again early this morning."

"Sounds like you're right. The Collins folks are targeting the wrong guy."

"Unless the guy can teleport," Herald said, with a rueful grin. "For what it's worth, his prof says Peterson hasn't missed a work session since his hospitalization and appears to be doing well on his medication. Maybe it's a California stalker Mr. Barron ought to be looking for instead of a Texas one."

"Could be," I agreed. "I'd like to visit with Mr. Peterson anyway, just to be sure."

"Is that really necessary?" Herald objected. "Obviously, he's not your guy, and he is one of our students. His professor says Peterson is pretty sensitive and stress hurts his work. Attracting the kid to Rice was a big deal, I'm told. We competed against dozens of other universities to get him."

You don't need much interaction with campus police to know that most want everything that happens kept hush-hush. When possible, I've accommodated them. This wouldn't be one of those times. "It's necessary," I said. "I want him to know he's under suspicion, just in case he's playing some kind of game."

"If you say so, Lieutenant," Herald reluctantly agreed. "I guess Mr. Peterson is probably in the piano lab. If he's not there, we'll try his apartment."

We drove in Herald's squad through the campus, as close to an Ivy League school as Texas has to offer. The same architect who'd designed Notre Dame and West Point drew up the plans for the campus's original gothic-style buildings, so Rice certainly looked the part. The live oaks that lined the road were lush, and spring green flecked the pale winter grass. I followed Herald through the Shepherd School of Music's vast foyer, past an overflowing flower arrangement on a pedestal, and down an all-white hallway lined by lockers, toward a windowless, first-floor practice area students call "the dungeon." There, in a square rehearsal room with sound buffers on the walls, we found a young man seated all alone at a black lacquer piano.

Solidly built, Peterson didn't fit my image of a classical pianist. Looking older than his twenty-one years, he had a coarse, not a delicate look. His hands and fingers, although long, were strong and solid. Stubble covered his chin, and he had a scar on his right cheek, about two inches long, vertical, just above his upper lip. His disheveled almond brown hair gave him an untamed look. Head bent over the piano keys, his eyes remained closed, as if he were intent on finding inspiration. We stood next to the piano, two feet from him, but Peterson didn't react.

"Mr. Peterson," I said. "Forgive us for interrupting, but I'd like to introduce myself. I'm Lieutenant Sarah Armstrong, with the Texas Rangers."

Justin Peterson took little or no notice, failing to respond to my words. Instead, he lightly touched the piano and hit a series of three keys, holding the last note until it gently faded. As the sound dissipated around us, Peterson's eyes blinked open and he reached for an eraser he used to wipe away the last line of handwritten music on the paper before him. He then penciled in three new notes, perhaps those he'd just played. Apparently finished, Peterson looked straight at Sergeant Herald and me, smiling broadly.

"Lieutenant Armstrong," he said. "This is an honor. And Sergeant Herald, how good of you to drop in again. As you can see, I'm hard at work. It's wonderful to be able to concentrate on my work."

"Have we met before, Mr. Peterson?" I asked, shaking his strong hand.

"No, I didn't mean to suggest that," he said, rising. "I recognize you from last year's headlines. I followed the Lucas investigation in the newspapers."

"I thought you composed your music on a computer," I said, motioning at the piano.

"At times," he said. "But for the most part I prefer the feel of the keys."

As he talked, I sized up the young man. Herald's file explained that Peterson grew up in Chicago, in a small house in the suburbs, the only child of a factory worker and a nurse. He began playing the piano at six, and quickly displayed a remarkable ability. By thirteen, the word "genius" was bandied about, and he gained the attention of a renowned teacher, who took him on as his protégé and transported him to national and later international competitions, where Peterson amassed a collection of first-place trophies. As Herald had said, college music programs across the country put on dog-and-pony shows to attract Peterson. To win, Rice offered him a full scholarship.

"I see," I said. "Do you know why I'm here today, to see you?"

"I'd like to think it's to hear my music, but since Sergeant Herald is with you, my guess is that this has something to do with that ridiculous fascination I once had with Cassidy Collins," he said, matter-of-factly. "I'd hoped that I'd eased everyone's concerns in that regard last time we talked, Sergeant Herald."

"You convinced me, Mr. Peterson," Herald said, obviously uncomfortable at being questioned. "But the ranger wants to ask a few questions. I hope you won't mind?"

"No problem," Peterson said. Rather than bothered with our inquiry, he appeared pleased, which I found rather confusing. Folks aren't usually all that delighted when I knock on their doors in an official capacity. "Ask whatever you'd like, Lieutenant. If I can help, I'm happy to."

"Where were you last night, Mr. Peterson, around ten o'clock?"

"That's easy," he said. "I worked here, had an early dinner with my professor in the student center, we worked a bit more, I guess until about eight or nine. I stopped and bought a latte at Starbucks, and then went home to do a little reading until sometime around eleven. Then to bed. It was, actually, a rather typical night for me. I gather it wasn't for Ms. Collins?"

"Why would you gather that?" I asked.

"Why else would you be here inquiring about my whereabouts?" he asked, his voice restrained but with just a hint of pleasure. No doubt about it, this guy was enjoying the heck out of our visit.

"When was your last attempt to communicate with Ms. Collins?" I asked.

"That unfortunate letter that brought Sergeant Herald here," Peterson said, with a slight laugh. "Right after that, I was hospitalized and prescribed my new medications. I haven't had the urge to write her since. I trust you're not here because she misses my letters?"

"Nothing since then? No letters? No e-mails? No text messages?"

"Nothing," he said.

Something about the man I didn't trust. Still, I had no reason to believe Peterson was Argus. In fact, unless he had not only musical but magical talents, Peterson couldn't have been the man we were looking for. The kid wasn't in Las Vegas a week earlier, and he wasn't in San Diego the previous night. That didn't prevent me, of course, from wanting to know more about him.

"Mr. Peterson," I said. "Rather than talk here, where anyone can see us and wonder why you're being questioned by two police officers, I'd like to continue this conversation in your apartment, where it's more private. Sergeant Herald's car is right outside. Why don't we drive there together?"

Peterson smiled that same unnervingly friendly grin.

"That's nice of you to be concerned, but it's not necessary," he said, softly. "There's no one here but us. And if someone stumbles upon us talking, it's not a problem. My doctoral advisor understands that I had a breakdown and that I'm better now. There's no one to hide from."

"I would prefer going to your apartment to talk," I said again, more forcefully. "I would consider it a sign of your cooperation on this matter if you'd accommodate me."

To my disappointment, Herald spoke up. "I don't think we need to do that, Lieutenant," he objected. "Mr. Peterson's working, and we have enough, don't we? We know he wasn't in Las Vegas or San Diego."

I assessed the sergeant out of the corner of my eye, annoyed. "There are some things I'd like to discuss further," I said. Turning my gaze back on the kid, I said, again, "Mr. Peterson, I would appreciate your cooperation. It would go a long way toward convincing me that you're working with us on this matter."

Briefly quiet, as if considering my request, before long Peterson shook his head. "No. As the sergeant said, I'm working," Peterson said, holding out his hand to shake mine. "But I thank you for stopping by to meet me. It's always interesting to meet someone who has made front-page headlines. That's quite a feat, don't you think? So few people ever accomplish it."

"I can think of loftier goals," I said, sizing him up and still feeling uneasy. "Perhaps writing a musical composition that brings joy to others?"

"Of course," he said. "But then, there is something to be said for fame."

Peterson never stopped smiling, never raised his voice. He'd remained composed and friendly throughout, even when he turned his back to return to his piano. As Sergeant Herald and I walked from the piano lab, I heard those same three notes the young pianist played when we first arrived, and then one more, a fourth, lower and richer than those preceding it. His alibis were airtight, yet as my visit with Justin Peterson ended, I felt more wary of him than when I arrived.

Once Herald took off for his office, I called Rick Barron in Los Angeles from the Tahoe. "Justin Peterson wasn't in Las Vegas or San Diego on the nights of the concerts. We have witnesses placing him in Houston both nights," I told him. "Are you positive he had to be on location to break into the sound systems?"

"Yes. That's what all the experts tell me," Barron said.

"If that's true, he's not Argus. But just to be sure, where is Ms. Collins playing next?"

"Why?"

"I'm going to have Mr. Peterson under surveillance," I said. "Just in case he has a Lear jet parked somewhere we don't know about."

"Like we talked about, this coming Saturday night in Dallas, then the following Monday evening at the Houston rodeo," Barron said. "But both concerts may have to be cancelled. I know what you're saying about Peterson, but coming anywhere near Texas has Cassidy freaked."

Ten ·

The waiting room at Dr. Senka Dorin's office was small and cramped, and the door resolutely shut with a yellow IN SESSION: DO NOT DISTURB sign hanging from the knob. I thumbed through a two-year-old *Ladies' Home Journal* looking at recipes for low-cal pasta salads while I considered stopping for a barbecue sandwich for lunch, when the door finally opened, and two women walked out.

"That was amazing," said the first woman, tall, with big blond hair. Wearing a burgundy suit with a brightly colored scarf around the neck, she appeared flushed and happy, relaxed.

"Getting in touch with your past lives relieves stress," the other woman, the one I took to be Dorin, said, as if it were something she repeated often. "You'll find this type of therapy opens you up to enjoy your life, raising awareness that we are all visitors here, and that what we do wrong in this life we have the opportunity to rectify in the next."

"Yes," the patient said. "I can see that now."

"You should sleep well tonight," the doctor said, patting the woman on the arm. "I'll see you for your appointment next Wednesday."

The blonde grabbed Dr. Dorin's hand and eagerly pumped it. "I can't tell you how wonderful it is to finally find someone who can help," she said. "I've suffered for so long. Now, I understand."

"Understanding our past lives allows us to drop our burdens," the doctor said, again sounding as if she said those same words to patient after patient. "As we progress, you'll experience how past life therapy can improve this life, allowing you to forgive yourself for past transgressions and move on."

Clearly enthused about whatever happened during her session, the blonde nodded in agreement. I had to stop myself from guffawing. This promised to be one interesting interview. *What was a bright, successful woman like Billie Cox doing coming to this charlatan?* I wondered.

The big-haired blonde bustled out the door into the hallway, and Dr. Dorin turned to me. A short, heavyset woman wearing a flowing, flowered skirt and a black knit top, she had startling brown eyes, playful beneath heavy brows. Her hair was dyed a severe nun's-habit black, but half an inch of stark white roots trimmed the center part. "Are you here to make an appointment?" she asked. "I don't have anything available until the end of next week, but I'm sure we can work something out then, if you'd like."

"My name is Lieutenant Sarah Armstrong," I said, pulling back my gray blazer to reveal my badge with the lone star in the center pinned on my white button-down shirt. Dorin must have also caught a glimpse of my rig with my Colt .45 in the holster riding low on my black Wranglers. She gulped.

"What can I do for you?" she asked, sounding decidedly less friendly.

"I'm investigating the death of Elizabeth Cox," I said. "Her sister, Faith Roberts, tells me that Billie was coming to you for counseling."

"Ah," she said. Apparently my response eased her fears, as Dorin's smile quickly returned. "I'm glad to hear someone is taking Faith seriously and looking into Billie's death. I've never believed that she took her own life. Come in my office, and tell me how I can help you. I have forty-five minutes before my next patient."

"So you see, there was no reason for Billie to have fired that bullet," Dr. Dorin concluded, stirring green tea growing cold in her pink-flowered china cup. The room looked more like a quaint English parlor than a therapist's office. Rather than a couch, Dorin had an overstuffed recliner for her patients, one I was cuddled up in with a similar nearly empty cup of tea balanced on the arm. On the table beside me was a half-eaten slice of poppy seed bread. It was good, but I was still thinking about that barbecue sandwich.

"Would you like more tea?" she asked.

"Yes, thank you."

For the previous half-hour, Dr. Dorin had described her sessions with Billie Cox, explaining what she knew about the dead woman. Yes, she said, there had been an affair with a married man, but Cox never revealed the man's name, only that he was married to someone close to Billie, an old friend Dorin thought, which made the liaison risky.

"The man didn't end it. Billie told her lover it was over," Dorin insisted. "Through our work here, she came to understand that in her many past lives she habitually chose the wrong mate, and that she was doing it again. This time, in this life, she said she wanted to wait for a true match."

As Dorin explained it, we all have multiple lives. Each time we die, we are reincarnated and come back to work out our failures from our previous lives. Throughout time, we are surrounded by the same souls only in different bodies. Our brother may have been our husband in another life, and our mother might have once been our son or our sister. "We're all branches on the same tree," she said. "And each of us has a single person we are meant to be joined to for eternity, a partner we're intended to spend the hereafter with."

The identity of that soul mate isn't always apparent, she said. Billie Cox, through hypnosis, had traveled back in time to discover that in previous lives, including one as an Indian warrior and another in the 1700s as a daughter of a wealthy Swiss shipbuilder, she had made bad choices. "We discovered that Billie consistently chose someone convenient rather than waiting for a mate with whom she had a real bond," said Dorin. "Through our work here, Billie made the decision not to repeat that mistake in this life. She broke off her relationship with the married man and, at our last meeting, sounded determined to wait to find the one person she truly loved."

Dorin, who had a doctorate in psychology from Ohio State on the wall, explained what she called "the process," a journey under hypnosis into the dark recesses of our beings, where we keep the knowledge of previous lives. In sessions, she took patients first into their childhoods, then further back, into their mothers' wombs. From there, they traveled to a place of peace and solitude, where souls wait between lives. Through the wombs of their mothers, these souls were reborn again and again in new bodies.

The therapist refilled my cup and offered sugar and lemon, as she rattled on about past lives and souls traveling through time. I like to think I'm pretty open-minded, but despite Dorin's apparent enthusiasm for her work, all I could think of was that it made about as much sense as folks who bring snakes to church, believing if they're holy enough God won't let the fork-tongued reptiles bite them. Heck, they're snakes. They're genetically engineered to bite humans. It's even in the Bible. Reincarnation? It sounded like self-delusion, about as possible as Billie Cox's ghost turning on ceiling fans and computers. When you thought about it, how did Cox know that under hypnosis her subconscious didn't replay old movies she'd watched about Indians and a Swiss shipbuilder? In my opinion, there could be lots of reasons folks under hypnosis saw themselves living in teepees or wearing hoop skirts.

I thought I had on my best poker face, but Dr. Dorin shook her head, frowned, and said, "You don't believe a word of this, do you?"

"No," I said. "But that's not important. What's important was whether or not Billie Cox believed it."

"She did," Dr. Dorin said. "Absolutely."

"And you can't tell me anything about this man, the one she had the affair with?"

"Just that he's married to someone close to Billie, and that he was furious over the breakup."

When I left Dorin's offices, a pale-skinned, balding man in his forties wearing a business suit was seated on the waiting room couch. As I pushed the elevator button, I wondered what he'd been in previous lives. My guess was that most folks opted for something glamorous, not a fishmonger but Henry VIII or Cochise. I figured if I got to pick, it would probably be Sherlock Holmes. Rangers don't get to have partners. Most of the time, we work alone. I've always thought it would be comforting to have a Dr. Watson.

As I walked through the parking lot to my car, my cell phone rang, and it appeared I might be getting my wish.

"Lieutenant Armstrong," Janet said. "We've had a hitch in the subpoenas for the Collins case, the ones I wrote to get records on the e-mail accounts Argus uses."

"What kind of a hitch?" I asked.

"Jurisdictional," she said. "Unless we can prove Argus is operating out of Texas, the district attorney's office tells me that we don't have jurisdiction to subpoena the Internet information."

"Now, that complicates matters," I said. "Have you talked to the captain? Did he have a suggestion?"

"I did, and I think he's already solved it," Janet said. I wondered why she hadn't said that up front, but then I knew. I wasn't sure how I felt about the news when Janet said, "The captain decided to get the FBI involved, figuring they have methods of getting at the information. He called the Houston office, and Agent David Garrity is on his way over. He'll meet you here, at the office, to discuss the situation at two o'clock."

Eleven

I'd left my hairbrush somewhere, probably at home or the office. It wasn't in the Tahoe or my purse. Squinting into the visor mirror, I ran my fingers through my frizzy mane a couple dozen times. My only tube of lipstick was used flat down, but I scraped it over my lips and turned them a faint but somewhat alluring Sunset Mauve. Then, driving to the office, I felt ridiculous for fussing for David Garrity. After all, where had he been? I hadn't seen him since the end of the Lucas case. That wasn't totally true. He'd called a couple of times, wanted to get together, but at that point things were still rocky at home, especially with Maggie. I thought David would hang in there, give us a little time to repair. I thought he and I had something, maybe it was too early to define what exactly, but something. Instead he just stopped calling. It was disappointing. I hadn't pegged David for a quitter.

So instead of rushing back to the office, I stopped at a hole-in-the-wall barbecue joint where the ceiling was cured black from decades of grease and smoke. The tables were battered, the chairs rocky, and the only napkins torn from paper towel rolls. Famished,

I ordered a chopped beef sandwich smothered in barbecue sauce, and when it came on a sheet of butcher paper, I lovingly cradled it in my hands to the self-serve counter, where I ladled on pickles and chopped onions.

Why not? I thought.

Seated at the table, I wished I'd taken the sliced onions. They would have been easier to ditch, once I reconsidered greeting David with dragon breath. After inhaling lunch, I thought about stopping at a drugstore for more lipstick. But by then I was running late, so I took a clean paper towel to the women's room. In front of the chipped mirror, I used the paper towel to scoop out the remains from the base of the tube, dabbed the little I scored on my chapped lips, and rubbed it on with my finger. My reflection stared back at me unimpressed. It wasn't great, but I looked passable. Considering the potential benefits of base and mascara, I thought, *Tomorrow, I'm buying real makeup, along with new shampoo and conditioner.*

A little while later, at ten minutes after two, I walked into the captain's office, where the walls and bookshelves were covered with ranger memorabilia, old badges, patches, books, and vintage photos from the Wild West days. Leaning back in his oak desk chair, Captain Williams was talking to David. As soon as the captain saw me, he grinned, I thought perhaps a bit mischievously. "Sarah, look who's riding to your rescue again," he said. "I made one call, and Agent Garrity came right over."

Standing up and turning around to greet me, David didn't look a lick different. His hair, a soft brown graying around the temples, still bunched around his neck and ears, and his gray suit hung vaguely rumpled on his athletic frame. I thought he might be a little apprehensive at first, but if so that quickly washed away, and he couldn't have appeared more pleased. To my surprise, I felt anxious shaking his hand. I'd always liked David's hands. Actually, there was a lot of David I found appealing.

"You look great, Sarah," he said. He still had that rugged look that attracted me a year earlier. I got a whiff of aftershave and wondered if he'd fussed, as nervous about seeing me as I was about seeing him.

"Thanks," I said. "It's been awhile."

I didn't mean for that to sound like a dig, but it must have, because David frowned. For a moment, he appeared pensive, as if considering a response. If so, he decided against it, and the captain took over the conversation.

"Agent Garrity figures he can get those subpoenas for you without too much red tape," he said. "Tell Sarah what you've got in mind."

"I'm not surprised your subpoenas ran into problems. Jurisdiction is a persistent problem with the Internet," David explained. "But the Bureau has tackled this before, and we've found that sidestepping county and state courts and getting a federal judge to sign the paperwork cuts through the red tape. I called ahead, and we're meeting with an assistant U.S. attorney at the courthouse in half an hour. Why don't we discuss this on the way downtown?"

I thought about being alone with David, wondered what he would say. Maybe he'd explain what had happened. "Sure," I said. "My Tahoe's in the lot and the engine's still warm. Let's go."

Ten minutes down the road, David hadn't said a word. I kept my eyes on the freeway, but occasionally felt him looking at me. Maybe he was waiting for me to start the conversation? The way I figured it, that chore was his.

"How's Maggie and your mom?" he finally asked.

"Great," I said. I asked about his son, who lives with David's ex-wife in Denver. "And Jack?"

"Good. Really good," he said. "I just saw him last month. We went skiing."

Silence again. There was a time when I enjoyed our silences, impressed that David wasn't the type who felt compelled to fill every moment with senseless chatter. This was a different quiet, uneasy, like a gaping yawn between us, one that grew wider every moment the silence endured.

"You going to take Memorial Drive downtown?" he asked.

"Thought I'd shoot over on I-10," I answered.

"That'll work," David said.

With the exception of commenting on the exceptionally warm winter day, little more information was shared in the car. I pulled into a parking lot across from the federal courthouse, in the middle of downtown Houston. It had to be one of the ugliest buildings on the planet, a gray box with rows of small square-framed windows. Minutes later, David and I were in a third-floor room going over the Collins case with a young prosecutor and the judge he'd convinced to sign our subpoenas.

"How hopeful are you that this will actually get you anything useful?" the judge asked as he signed each page.

"We have to start somewhere, Judge," I said. "This is our only lead."

Outside in the hallway, the prosecutor handed us the subpoenas. "Good luck," he said. "Let me know how it works out. My thirteen-year-old daughter loves that Collins girl."

"Be afraid," I said, straight-faced. "Be very afraid."

The lawyer looked as if he couldn't decide how to take my warning, but he laughed. If he met Collins in person, or even over the telephone, he might not have found my words funny.

"I hope this helps," I said to David in the car. He'd just called his office to let them know that we had the documents signed and they could notify the Internet companies to start gathering the information. Thinking again about the likelihood of any of it being useful, I asked, "As computer savvy as this stalker is, what's your guess on how successful this will be? Think it'll lead anywhere?"

"Probably not," David said. He looked at me, and again, for a brief moment, I thought he'd say more. Instead, he turned away and stared out the window. This new David wasn't exactly what I'd hoped for in a Dr. Watson. But I had to admit; I wasn't really stirring up conversation myself. I wondered if maybe I was the problem, that I'd been too distant, given him the impression that I wasn't interested. It felt strained, uncomfortable, and at first, I was relieved when my cell phone rang. But when I saw it was Mom, my relief turned to worry.

"Bobby and I noticed it this afternoon. Emma Lou's waxing up," Mom said when David and I arrived at the ranch. *Waxing up* meant that the milky discharge released before foaling was coming in. I'd filled David in on the situation during the drive. He seemed to understand the seriousness, but he didn't ask many questions. There'd been no time to drop him at the office, and I regretted that we hadn't taken separate cars. His silence made me increasingly uncomfortable.

"That's not good," I said. "How long do we have?"

"Doc figures less than a week," Mom said. "But it's not all bad news. If Emma Lou makes it just two more days, until Friday, the foal has a chance. From the date of breeding, that's three hundred and one days."

"If it comes sooner?" I asked.

"Let's hope that doesn't happen," Mom said, shaking her head. "Doc gave the mare oral meds, but said we should get ready, just in case, and have the shed set up for birthing. Bring in a heating lamp and double the straw matting, make sure it's clean."

Feeling helpless to do anything else, I sighed and said, "Okay, let's go."

A good sport, David helped out, taking off his suit jacket and putting a pair of old rubber boots over his dress shoes. When Maggie walked up from the school bus, we didn't have to tell her the bad news. She took one look at what we were up to and knew. She didn't even say hello to David, acting as if she didn't notice him pitchforking the shed straw.

"How long?" she asked.

"Soon," I answered.

Twelve

"Somebody named Mike Davis called for you, and the captain wants you in his office ASAP," Sheila said the next morning, Thursday. Then she whispered, "He's agitated about something."

I decided to postpone calling Mike and find out what had the captain in a flap. When I walked in his office, he was visibly uptight. "I told them you couldn't do this, Sarah," he muttered, his face flushed. "We're just getting you back after that mess last year, and the last thing I want is to throw you into the middle of this thing, send you off to Dallas."

"Dallas? I don't know, Captain. Emma Lou is getting ready to deliver, and there's a good chance the foal won't make it," I said. "Maggie will be devastated. And I'm still walking on eggshells at home, trying to convince everyone, including myself, that I won't be sucked into another situation like that Lucas mess."

"I know, and I wouldn't ask you. But this is coming directly from the governor," the captain said. "Cassidy Collins's people called Austin and asked for added security at her concert in Dallas."

"The local guys can cover that," I said. "I'm more valuable

here. I thought I'd have that Justin Peterson, their prime suspect, staked out."

"We can take care of Peterson. Doesn't appear it's him anyway. Collins requested you by name, said she's not doing the concert if you're not there," he said, shaking his head, as if confronted with a bizarre turn of events. "She seems to think you can help her, Sarah, and the kid's plumb scared. She wants you with her, as kind of a personal bodyguard throughout the evening."

"How long will I have to be gone?" I asked. "I do feel sorry for the kid, but if Emma Lou gives birth while I'm away and there are complications, Maggie may never forgive me."

"Now there, I pulled rank," the captain answered, offering up a small wink and a self-satisfied nod. "I've got a DPS helicopter lined up to fly you to Dallas Saturday afternoon, about one, in time for Collins's rehearsal, and it'll fly you home as soon as Collins gets on her private jet after the concert. You should be at the ranch a little after one A.M. on Sunday morning. Until then, you can coordinate security from here. In addition to Dallas P.D. and the arena's security force, the governor is bringing in state troopers as backup, and I talked to David Garrity. He's going along."

"Why David?" I asked.

"Because he offered," he said, shooting me an exasperated glance. "And I wasn't about to turn down any help. Sarah, if we lose that girl, if that stalker manages to carry out his threats, we'll be second-guessed forever. This isn't one where we want to take any unnecessary chances." The captain narrowed his eyes and sized me up. "Why don't you want Garrity along on this? I thought you two got pretty tight last year."

"No matter," I said, with a shrug. "That's fine. Like you said, we can use the help."

"Okay, then," he said. "It's all set? I can tell the governor you're on this?"

"It's all set," I agreed. "I'll be there."

The morning evaporated on the telephone. I talked with Rick Barron about Collins's usual security measures. She had a staff of four regular bodyguards who accompanied her on the road. All were former police officers and licensed to carry concealed weapons. Afterward, I called the American Airlines Center in Dallas, where Collins was scheduled to perform. I brought the facility's head of security, a guy named Mack McDougall, up to speed on the situation. By the time we hung up, I had McDougall bringing in every security guard the arena employed, a third more than usual, for Saturday night's concert, and he'd agreed to forward us a schematic of the complete stadium.

"There's no way anyone can infiltrate our system from outside the arena," McDougall insisted. "Collins's people will plug their sound equipment directly into ours. To break in, your stalker will have to do the same or hack into the frequency. Either way, he has to be on-site to do it."

That, of course, left no room for what had happened in San Diego, where Argus's voice fed directly into Cassidy Collins's earpiece. San Diego P.D. hadn't found an explanation for the breach in what is supposed to be a closed system, other than to surmise that Argus was in the arena and used some type of new high-tech equipment to tap into the frequency.

Once I had McDougall preparing, I reached out to Dallas P.D. They were aware of the situation and promised to add a second layer of protection outside of the arena, along with additional officers near all the entrances and exits. Metal scanners would be in place at all the doors, and an officer would be assigned to stand by each, watching the screen and searching anyone who looked suspicious. With some prompting, they also agreed to bring in dogs two hours before the concert, to comb the arena and the backstage area, looking for anyone hiding in the shadows, behind a curtain or in the rafters.

Despite his solid alibis, I e-mailed Justin Peterson's driver's license photo to Dallas P.D., Rick Barron, and McDougall. It never hurts to be prepared.

It promised to be a grueling couple of days, organizing what would most likely be a strange evening. Since I preferred a Carrie Underwood or Tim McGraw concert, I briefly wondered if I could get away with earplugs. Instead, I asked Barron to have in-ear monitors for David and me, so that during the concert, we could hear what Collins heard, and to set up a recorder to tape everything that came through her earpieces. If they'd taken that step in San Diego, we would have had Argus's voice recorded.

With so much to do to prepare for Saturday night, I'd forgotten about Mike Davis's phone call until Sheila buzzed me about one that afternoon and said he was on the line again. I picked up, and before even saying hello, Davis blurted out, "Listen, there's no way that Cox woman wrote this suicide letter. Absolutely no way."

"I take it you're certain about that?" I said, not surprised by Mike's vehemence. One of the things I liked about the guy was that he spoke his mind. "You want to tell me what you really think?"

Mike chuckled. "Listen Sarah, you're right, this is my field, but I wouldn't have to be an expert to tell you that Elizabeth Cox didn't write this suicide note."

"Print or fonts don't match?" I asked. "What's the problem?"

"No, it could have come off her printer, all right," he said.

"Then what are we discussing?"

"Everything," Davis said. "There are the small details. Like everything we know for sure that this woman typed had two spaces between sentences, after the periods. The suicide note has one. That's an automatic thing, not the type of detail people change."

"Interesting," I said. "Tell me more."

"I've got plenty more," Davis said. "Cox's letters have a totally different syntax, no fragments, no random capitalization, clearly more refined. She was a careful woman, and the random capitalization is not consistent with her personality."

"Okay," I said. "But maybe she was just upset? Maybe she wasn't as careful as usual because she was about to shatter her skull with a bullet?"

"I can tell you this," Davis said. "I've been analyzing suicide notes for forty years. Yes, planning to end one's life can cause a person to write differently. Most suicides are frightened and in a lot of mental anguish, that's true. But they don't become a totally different person. This note wasn't written by Cox. It was written by someone else."

Well, now, that was interesting.

"Any thoughts about the author?" I asked. "Any hints that might help me zero in on the right suspect?"

"Based on the note, I suspect you're looking for a man," he said. "This reads like a man writing the way he thinks a woman would write, overly emotional and fragmented. That's the opposite of the facts, since women's notes are usually more carefully written than men's. When they reach this point, most men just want to go off into the woods with a gun and do the deed, while women more often take their time and write something to soften the blow for the family and friends they leave behind. They almost always mention loved ones by name, telling them that they love them. You don't have any of that in here."

"Okay, Mike," I said. "I'm going to talk to the captain about getting payment for you on this. Can you put this in writing, just a few pages? I'd like to share it with the folks in my office and H.P.D. homicide."

"Sure, I'll get to it this afternoon and have it to you tomorrow morning," Mike said, chuckling again. "Glad this turned out to be a paying job. My government pension gets a little tight. Told the wife, I'm going to have to start freelancing to keep up."

"I'm sure with your resume you don't need references," I said. "But if you decide you want a few, be sure to include me."

"Will do," Mike said. "And good luck with this. I don't know anything else about Ms. Cox's death, but I don't think there's much doubt that you're looking at a homicide."

I hung up, thought about what Mike had just told me, then picked up the receiver again and dialed the Harris County morgue. The ever-jolly Dr. Joe took awhile to get to the telephone. "I'm busy, Lieutenant," he said. "What can I do for you?"

"I was wondering about the GSR test on Billie Cox's right palm," I said. "You must have results by now."

"I phoned that in to H.P.D. the morning after you were here," the physician said, sounding irritated as usual. "Haven't they told you?"

"No. I gather you talked with Detective Brad Walker?"

"The same," he said with a sigh. "You know, I've got bodies waiting for me. Now it's true they don't complain, but I'd like to tell you people things once and be done with it, so I can get out of here at a reasonable hour at least once a week. I told that detective you'd requested the test and asked him to make sure you heard about the results. Why didn't he tell you?"

I knew better than to interrupt when Dr. Joe expounded on the shortcomings of law enforcement. But once he finished, I still needed to know the test results. "I'll be sure to convey your disappointment to Detective Walker," I said. "Now Dr. Joe, if for no other reason than to get me off the telephone, what did you find?"

"GSR," he said.

"You found gunshot residue on the palm that held the gun," I said. "That shouldn't have been there."

"Exactly what I told that detective," Dr. Joe said. "There should have been gunshot residue on the back of the hand, because that was exposed. But the palm was closed around the grip. I shouldn't have found GSR on it."

"So what are we thinking now?"

"I don't know what you think, Lieutenant," he said, grudgingly. "But my best guess is that Cox wasn't holding the gun at all. I figure she had her hands out, palms up, maybe in a defensive position, trying to stop the killer."

Faith Roberts and Mike Davis were right. Cox was murdered. "I gather you'll change the manner of death in the autopsy?"

"If I ever get off this telephone and find a free moment," he growled. "Elizabeth Cox's death is now officially a homicide."

Thirteen

Something wasn't right. Walker should have called me. It was only professional courtesy. I'd never worked with the detective, but another ranger in the office had, Sergeant George Fields, more commonly known as "Buckshot." Fields had investigated a murder case with Walker the previous year. I'd heard through office chatter that it hadn't gone well. Maybe it was Walker's reputed tendency to see every case as black or white? Maybe not.

Figuring it was time to find out, I walked three doors down to Buckshot's office. A large, square man with a thick mustache, the sergeant was on the telephone, and he motioned for me to sit. I moved his Stetson off the extra chair and did as instructed. A wire frame on his desk held a small glass vial containing a dozen or so round lead pellets, buckshot recovered out of the rear end of a thief. A decade ago while working a case in north Texas, the sergeant decided to do a little deer hunting. Shotgun in hand, Fields happened upon a rustler pilfering someone else's prize-winning bull. The guy kept running after Fields warned him to stop. That was a mistake. When he took the rustler to the local emergency room, supervised the removal of the pellets, and then put them on his desk as a souvenir, Sergeant Fields became forever known as "Buckshot."

"What can you tell me about Detective Brad Walker?" I asked, when I had the sergeant's full attention.

"Guy's a malcontent," he sneered. "He's up for retirement in about a year, I think. Just lazy."

I told him about the case and Buckshot nodded, as if he understood.

"So with all the great homicide detectives at H.P.D., and they've got a bunch, I get somebody who's just putting in time?" I said.

"I'm afraid so," the sergeant growled, impatiently tapping his pen on his desk, as if annoyed by the memory of old frustrations. My guess? Buckshot's short tenure with Walker had left the sergeant irritated. "If that case is in Walker's closed file and you reopen it, I guaran-damn-tee that he's not going to be happy. Based on my experience, I suggest you sidestep him and work it on your own. Walker won't object, and he wouldn't be any help anyway. I'll guaran-damn-tee that, too."

Most investigators hover over their cases like momma birds guard their chicks, so I had my doubts. But I put in a call to Walker as soon as I got back to my desk. Since we'd never officially met, I introduced myself and then asked if he'd heard from Dr. Joe.

"My guess is that you already know I did," he said. "What's the point?"

"The point is that you now have a homicide to work," I said. When he didn't respond, I offered, "If you're too booked up, Detective, I'm willing to investigate Billie Cox's murder, but it is your case. If you'd prefer, I'll step back and let you and your partner run with it."

I didn't think less of Walker for making a mistake by writing off the murder as a suicide. Anyone can be fooled. There's an old ranger story about Colonel Jack Hays during the Texas war for independence. Believing he was one step ahead of the Mexicans, Hays left San Antonio with his men to scout for approaching enemy troops only to discover when he returned five days later that a Mexican military force had used his absence as an opportunity to move in and take over the river city.

So it wasn't Walker misjudging the situation that bothered me; it was that he didn't fight for his investigation, that he didn't insist on working his own case. Instead the detective fell silent, perhaps considering if he could get away with turning it over. If Buckshot was right about Walker's attitude, it had to be tempting. There was no way the Cox case was going to be easy, with the killer's trail already a week old. Walker must have settled on a way to explain my commandeering the investigation to his lieutenant, because the next thing he said was, "I'll fax you a copy of the case file. I know you've seen it, but you might want it, now that you'll be the lead."

"Sure," I said. "Fax away."

I hung up, and then, rather than wait on the paperwork to arrive, I put in a call to Faith Roberts and brought her up to speed on the coroner's new findings. When I told her Billie's death was now officially a homicide, I heard her sobbing. Sometimes, even when folks believe a loved one's been murdered, hearing it's real comes as a shock.

"Faith, I need more information on Billie," I said. "Do you have other family, anyone else I should talk to?"

"Just myself and my husband, Grant. We're Billie's only family," she said. "Like I told you, our parents died young, our father first and then our mother when we were still kids."

"Then I'd like to talk to you and your husband," I said. "I need to know everything either of you can tell me about your sister."

"Of course, anything we can do to help," she said. "Grant's a

Realtor, and he offices near the house. I'll call him, and he'll come right home. We'll be waiting when you get here."

"I'm on my way," I said.

"Lieutenant Armstrong?" she said.

"Yes?"

"Thank you."

I put down the phone and grabbed my rig out of the drawer, strapped on my Colt .45, and pulled on my blazer. I was heading toward the door when David Garrity walked in.

"You look like you're prepared to do some business," he said. "Did I catch you at a bad time?"

"Kind of. Looks like I've picked up a murder case. I'm on my way to interview the victim's family," I said. "Do you need something?"

"If it's okay, I'll tag along," he said. "Slow day at the office, and I'd like to talk about our plans for Saturday night."

"Saturday night?" I repeated, clueless.

For a moment, he just looked at me with a bemused smile. "Unless we have other plans, I'm talking about the Collins concert," he said, obviously finding my stumble entertaining. I felt myself blush, but decided to ignore it and head for the door. Quickly, David returned to business. "I'd like to go over the arrangements, to make sure we've covered all the bases."

"That's what's set up so far," I concluded on our drive to the Robertses' home. "We're doing a full-court press on security, but if you've got other ideas, I'm all for expanding."

"No, that's great," he said. "You've got everything in motion."

"How about those subpoenas?" I asked. "Any results yet?"

"It's looking tough," David admitted. "Looks like the e-mails went through a web of resenders, those forwarding services that hide the identity of the source. To get access to the records, we have to write more subpoenas at every level. In the meantime, the lab guys are tracing back the text messages that came in on Collins's cell phones, but that looks like another dead end."

"Bouncing off towers all over the country, I bet," I ventured.

"Don't you know it," he said. "This guy, whoever he is, knows how to scramble the towers of origin. The lab guys say he's clued into the latest technology, new equipment that funnels through phone networks to scattered towers. They're impressed."

"I'm happy your lab guys are enjoying this, but it's making a mess of work for us," I said. "And all these roadblocks sure aren't moving the investigation along."

That conversation ended and, like the day before, there was an uncomfortable silence between us. To fill it, I recited the basics on the Cox case, since David would be at the interview. He asked only a few questions, probably because I left out all of Faith's assertions about the haunted television and computer.

"How's Maggie's horse?" he said, changing the subject.

"Emma Lou seems a little better, but we're not sure about the foal yet. Today's day three hundred, so if she doesn't give birth before tomorrow, Doc says there's at least a prayer that the foal has a chance."

"That's good news," he said. "Maggie looked upset when I was there yesterday. Poor kid's been through a lot."

"Well, we've had a rough spell. First losing Bill, and then that mess last year," I said.

Then, again, silence.

I thought about David and me, what we'd been like and his unexplained retreat. I wondered if he was waiting for me to make a move, if he'd gotten tired of knocking on a door I never opened. I glanced over at him. Heck, I'd never been in favor of wishing and hoping. Seeing him again, well, it made me remember how much I enjoyed the brief time we'd spent together.

"You know, when you stopped calling, I was surprised," I said. "I'd thought that maybe we'd—"

"I did, too, Sarah. I really did," he interrupted. I glanced over, and he was staring at me. He looked sad, distant, yet I had the sense he wanted to reach out, to touch me. And there was something, something on the tip of his tongue, waiting to be said. But what? I considered pulling the car over, but we were right around the corner from Faith and Grant Roberts's house, and they were waiting.

"If there's something you need to tell me, you should just say it, David," I said.

"There's nothing I can tell you, Sarah. I wish there were," he said, quietly. "Sometimes, what we want isn't as easy as it should be. Sometimes there are other people involved."

"What does that mean?" I asked, but he said nothing, only shook his head, still staring at me. "David, I'm a grown woman. There's no need to mince words. If you found someone else or changed your mind about how you feel about me, that's something I can understand. I know I wasn't particularly available."

"It's not as clear cut as that," he said, as I pulled into the driveway of a square, box of a house, two stories and redbrick, in a quiet middle-class neighborhood, the kind with tree-lined streets and sidewalks, where neighbors pick up each other's newspapers and mail when they go on vacations.

I turned off the engine, but didn't get out of the car. I wanted an answer. When he went to open the door, I flipped the locks.

He looked startled at first, but then smiled. "What is this? Am I being kidnapped? You know that's a federal crime."

"Time to fess up," I said. "I need to understand where we are, what changed."

He turned toward me in the seat and skimmed his hand gently

over my shoulder, then slowly up to my cheek. It felt so good, just to feel his touch again. I turned toward him, and then cupped my left hand over his. "Tell me, David," I said. "Tell me where we are and how we got here."

I wanted and didn't want to know, but David smiled, the crooked, warm, aggravatingly charming smile I'd thought about so many times since I'd last kissed him. But again, he shook his head and didn't answer. I could see it in his eyes, something, a parcel of truth he wanted to tell me. I thought about brushing back the hair that had fallen over his forehead. I thought about what his skin felt like when we'd made love, warm and firm.

"Now's not the time," he said, resolutely turning away and unlocking the car door. As he swung it open, he said, "Let's go talk to the victim's family."

"The truth is, we really don't know of anyone who'd want to hurt much less kill my sister," Faith said. "I've been thinking, maybe it does have something to do with that man she was seeing? Maybe she broke it off with him, and he couldn't bear it? Maybe he was angry? You read about things like that in the newspaper all the time, some spurned boyfriend who kills a woman just because she doesn't want him anymore."

"But you can't put a name on this mystery man?" I asked. "Any information about him at all would help, Faith. Anything Billie mentioned would be a start."

Faith shook her head no. Beside her, Grant Roberts, not a bad-looking guy, a little thin for my taste, but tall and just a bit stooped, with short saddle-brown hair and tepid blue eyes, talked for the first time in our interview. "I heard that he was someone she worked with or in a company she had dealings with. A business relationship," he said. "Billie mentioned it one afternoon, when she was here having Sunday dinner."

His wife looked at him, surprised. "Billie told you about him? She never said anything to me."

"She waited until you were out of the room. Billie knew you wouldn't approve, Faith," he answered. "The man was married. She was your little sister. You know that she always wanted you to think well of her."

Faith dropped her head, and wiped her eyes with an already soggy tissue she clenched in her right hand. "I guess that's true," she said. "Billie was always concerned about the way I saw her. After our mother died, I was as much mother as sister."

Something about what Grant Roberts had just said rang wrong for me. Not the part about Billie being reluctant to tell Faith about her lover, but that Billie would confess something so personal to her brother-in-law. So I asked a question I would have anyway, only sooner, "Please don't be alarmed. We ask this of everyone in an investigation. Just for our records, where were both of you on that Friday, say from four to six, the afternoon Billie died?"

Faith shrugged, unconcerned. "We discussed this," she said. "I was home, picking up a few things around the house. Then I watched that show. You know, when the television just suddenly—"

"Was anyone else home?" I interrupted. The haunted TV episode was something I really didn't want to share with David. I wasn't too sure how he'd interpret a victim communicating from beyond the grave.

"No," she said. "I was alone."

"And you, Mr. Roberts? Where were you?"

Grant Roberts didn't immediately answer. Instead, he looked at David and me, as if wondering what to say. He'd now piqued my curiosity twice. Finally, he said, "I was at the real estate office around six-thirty that afternoon," he said. "Before that, I was driving around Houston previewing houses for a client, but by six-thirty, I was in the office. I left there at about quarter to seven, and came directly home for dinner."

"Grant's office is only a mile down the road," Faith said. "I remember him coming in before seven. I noticed the time because I was still watching television. It was an hour program, just ending, and I didn't have dinner ready, as I usually do by then."

"Write down your office address and phone number for me, Mr. Roberts," I asked, handing him my pad of paper and a pen. "Just so we can contact you when we have news on the case."

Grant Roberts did as requested, but I noticed his hands trembled, ever so slightly.

Fourteen

"Do you mind stopping at Grant Roberts's office with me?" I asked David in the Tahoe.

"You sensed he was lying, too," he said. "Something is off there. You can hear it in his voice."

"It shouldn't take long," I said. "Promise this isn't like yesterday. I'll get you back to your car before dark."

"Unless you decide to kidnap me again," David responded. When I looked over he had a roguish grin.

"I only attempt one federal crime a day. Here on out, I'll wait until you're ready to talk," I said, figuring I might as well. It was obvious he wasn't in any hurry to come clean. "But I do think you owe me an explanation, and now you can't say I didn't try to get to the bottom of this."

"This?"

"Us," I clarified.

His smile had disappeared, and David said nothing, but looked again as if he wanted to. I considered reneging and ordering him to spit it out, but restrained myself and drove to Grant's real estate office. I had work to do. I pulled into the parking lot, turned off the Tahoe, and got out without asking David any of the questions that wouldn't stop bombarding my mind.

"Yes, Mr. Roberts was here last Friday," April Sims, a shapely young woman in high heels and a red dress said, when we inquired. Long dark-blond hair falling about her shoulders, the office manager was tall with a wide smile and arrestingly inquisitive almond-shaped green eyes. "I'm sure he was here until three-thirty or so. He left, saying he was going to preview houses, and he returned by six-fifteen or shortly after, maybe six-thirty. Why?"

"We're just checking on a few things," I said, being as vague as possible. "Do you know where he was that afternoon? Any record of what part of the city or what houses he previewed?"

"Well, not really," she said.

"Don't the agents tell you where they're going?" David asked. "It seems to me that they would want someone to know where they were, who they're with, when they're showing houses."

"*If* they're showing houses," a voice behind us boomed. We turned and saw Grant Roberts walk through the door, blisteringly angry. "Why are you here? I told you I didn't have a client with me. I was previewing."

"Grant, these officers are asking about last Friday."

"It's all right, April," Roberts said. "It's nothing. In fact, they were just leaving."

"Mr. Roberts, I think perhaps it would be a good idea to talk to us in private, in your office," I said. "Obviously, we still have questions."

"I'd rather not," he said. "We already spoke, and I told you where I was."

"Mr. Roberts, you need to listen to the ranger. This is one of those we-can-do-it-the-easy-way-or-the-hard-way things," David explained, focusing a cold, dry stare on the man. Instinctively, Roberts shuffled back a step, putting more floor space between them. His brow knotted, as if angry, David cocked his head to the side and let Roberts sweat a moment, before adding, "You can talk to us now, or, and this is a promise, in the very near future the lieutenant will escort you to her office."

Furious, Roberts glared at both of us, but blandly asked the pretty blond office manager, "Is the conference room free?"

"No," she said. "Missy has a client in there. Use my office."

"Thanks," he said, and David and I followed him down a hall-way, toward a back corner office with a window overlooking a parking lot.

"I told you where I was," Roberts said. "I wasn't with anyone. I was alone, in my car, driving from house to house all that afternoon, figuring out what to show an out-of-town client who came in that Sunday. There's no more to tell you than that."

"Is there any way to prove your whereabouts?" David asked. "Any records kept that show what houses you saw when?"

"No, why would there be records?" Roberts said. "Like I said, I was alone. But that's exactly what I did that afternoon. You'll have to trust me."

"Mr. Roberts, when there's been a murder, trust isn't on the table," I said. "Can you tell me, who inherits your sister-in-law's estate?"

"Faith is Billie's only living relative, as, I'm sure, she told you. But why are you asking that? You don't think she or I could be responsible?"

"I'm not implying anything," I said, coolly. "I'm asking basic questions that have to be answered in any investigation. Who has motive? Who profits?"

"I think you'd better leave," Roberts said, looking more agitated with each passing moment. "Now, before I do something I'll be sorry about later."

The man was squirming like a worm pulled out of the earth and exposed to the sun. "Are you sure you haven't done that already?" I asked. Roberts fumed but said nothing, as David and I turned and left.

On the drive back to the office, David said, "You know, when I moved to Houston, the Realtor who took me house-hunting used a computerized device of some sort, to open the lockboxes holding the keys."

"That's interesting, but is this headed somewhere?" I asked.

"Maybe. If those devices are monitored, there's probably a central tracking office. If so, they have records of what houses a particular Realtor enters and when," he explained. "If Grant Roberts was previewing houses at the time Billie Cox was murdered, those records would prove it."

"That's good. I'm impressed," I said, and looked over to see David grinning, quite pleased with himself. "When we partnered last year, did I ever tell you about my Dr. Watson fantasy?"

He laughed. "No, I don't remember talking about fantasies, but if we did, I think that's one you left out."

David was on his way back to his office, when I tracked down Houston's central booking office, responsible for making appointments for Realtors to see houses. They had no such records, but I was told that the security company that monitored the computerized lockbox system might. I called that number, and the woman I spoke with verified that the company kept records on which homes an individual Realtor entered, and at what time. I gave her information on Grant Roberts, including the name of his real estate company, and we agreed that with a subpoena, I could have the information the following morning. As soon as I got off the telephone, I asked Janet to draw up the paperwork. By then, it was nearly three. My agreement with the captain had been for half-days at the office, but I hadn't made it home by one once since I'd returned.

An hour later, after sending the subpoena to the Houston D.A.'s intake division, to get it signed by a judge, I left the office for home, then, I had another thought. I reached for my cell phone.

"Mom, everything okay at the ranch?"

"Yup," she said. "Bobby finished up at the office early, so he's here helping me make desserts for his barbecue cook-off party tomorrow night."

With Emma Lou and work, I'd been so busy, I'd forgotten about the cook-off. On the weekend before the rodeo opens, the parking lot outside Reliant Stadium fills with smoke-belching barbecues. Teams of folks, many whom routinely man desks and computers, slow-cook briskets, ribs, chickens, shrimp, even buffalo and alligator, over smoldering hickory and pecan. In the end, the best efforts win trophies. Like everything else, Bobby takes the event seriously. The Barker Oil tent is as big as most folks' homes with a smoker the size of a restaurant kitchen, a bar, a catered buffet, and a twanging, strumming country western band.

"How's Maggie?" I asked.

"She's up at the shed with Strings, tending to Emma Lou. The horse had a good day. That antibiotic has kicked in, I think. She's looking healthier all the time. Doc stopped in around noon, drew more blood, and said he thinks we've got a chance of coming out of this with both horses."

"Good news," I said, feeling relieved. "Mom, if you don't need me at home, I'd like to work a couple more hours. I've got one more stop to make."

"That's fine, Sarah," she said. "You do what you need to do. We'll all be here when you get home."

Century Oil officed on the eighth floor of a mirror-skinned office building on the I-10 energy corridor, home to oil companies big and small, west of downtown Houston, just off the Sam Houston Tollway. I prowled around for an hour or so after I arrived, interviewing Billie's employees, including her assistant. Her coworkers told me how Billie had worked her way up in the business and been personally chosen as president by one of the two founders, Carlton Wagner, a wildcatter who'd started out speculating in the fields sixty years earlier. The old man treated Billie like a daughter, they said, and was so devastated by her death that it led him to put the place up for sale.

No one I questioned at Century admitted knowing anyone angry with Billie or any reason someone would take her life, and all said she meticulously kept her personal life out of the office. None knew the identity of the man she dated in the months before her death. I needed an official to sign a consent-to-search form for Billie's office and tracked down one of the vice presidents. When I told the man that Billie's death was now classified a homicide, he appeared shaken but had no more answers for me than the other employees I'd questioned. He did, however, sign my paperwork and unlock Billie's office.

Billie lived well. Like her home, her large corner office was decorated with antique furniture, a heavily carved desk and credenza, and ornate Oriental rugs. I thought about how she must have swelled with pride every time she walked into the place. Cox was a young woman who'd risen quickly to a place of prestige in Houston's powerful energy circle. How heady that must have felt. How quickly and sadly it ended.

There were no family photos or personal items, but then Faith had already told me about her trip to claim them. I went through the files on Billie's desk, wishing a forensics team had searched the office immediately after the murder. How many others had been in that office during the previous week? What had they taken with them? Evidence leading to the murderer could have walked out the door.

I shuffled through the drawers and found nothing that jumped out at me, until I spotted a folder marked PROSPECTUS: STANHOPE FIELD. On a Post-it note, white with her initials and the outline of an oil well in red, Billie had written: "Withdraw offer. Call B. Barker on Monday to explain details and tell him to do same." That struck me as odd. I wondered if this could be the East Texas oil field Bobby mentioned, the one he and Billie were working the deal to buy. Yet Bobby talked as if he and Cox were ready to make the offer. Perhaps, he didn't know she was backing out, since she hadn't lived until that Monday to call him?

I opened the file and saw lists of numbers. They could have been in Russian for all the figures meant to me. In the back of the file, I paged through brightly colored charts, with layers of different colors, but no explanation of their meaning. So I put the file on the corner of the desk to take with me.

The desktop computer screen was dark and none of the indicators were lit, so I turned it on. A log-on screen came up asking for a password. I hacked around for a while trying Faith's and Grant's names, Billie's birth date and her Texas driver's license number, but couldn't get in. Giving up, I turned the computer off, watched the screen go black, and then concentrated on the credenza, finding only more files, nothing that caught my attention. Finally, I sat in Billie's desk chair for a full fifteen minutes, simply letting my eyes randomly scan the office, looking for something, anything that looked out of place. Nothing. I looked at my watch. It was going on six, and Mom and Maggie would be waiting.

I grabbed my purse and took two steps toward the closed office door, when I heard the computer click on. Startled, I looked around for someone else in the room. But there was only the one door, still shut, and I was alone. Feeling more tentative than entering a crime scene with my .45 drawn, I walked back to the computer.

"This some kind of a joke?" I muttered.

To my astonishment, Billie's log-in screen booted with the Century Oil logo. I didn't touch the computer, but watched mesmerized as this time six black dots appeared in the password slot. In an instant, Billie's opening screen flashed on and then off, replaced by a photograph.

I again looked around the office, convinced someone had to be orchestrating the events. I thought about Faith's six-o'clock experiences, including the one with this same computer that had offered up the suicide note.

"Oh, I don't think so," I murmured. I thought about turning and leaving but couldn't. No matter how it was happening, I figured it was best to pay attention, so I surveyed the photograph on the computer screen. The image was dark, of a field at night. In the photo, three men stood near the shadowy silhouette of an oil well. One had his back to the photographer, but the two whose faces were visible looked up in years. The stars were shining in the night sky, and across the bottom of the photo, someone had handwritten: "Stanhope Field, East Texas."

"Okay," I whispered, "I don't know what's going on here, but I gather this is important."

I printed the screen, picked the copy up, and slid it in the file with Bobby's phone number on the Post-it note on top. I tucked all of it under my arm. Now I really had to leave.

But I hesitated, thought for a minute, and whispered, "Anything else?"

I waited, but only silence. The place was starting to give me the chills.

Back in the reception area, I told Billie's assistant, "I need thick tape, and the key to Miss Cox's office door."

The meticulously dressed young man, who appeared young enough to be right out of college, searched through his desk, took out a roll of clear strapping tape, and handed it to me along with the key. I pulled Billie's door shut, locked it, and then slipped the key into the top front pocket of my black Wranglers. Then I peeled off long strips of tape and slapped them down, crisscrossing the door. When I finished, I said, "Now I need a black marker."

He handed me a Sharpie, then stood back, watching as I printed POLICE LINE, DO NOT CROSS, over and over again on the strips of tape. I left him there, staring at the makeshift crime-scene tape, and stepped out in the hallway, near the elevators, most importantly out of earshot, and called Janet. I was lucky to find her working late.

"I need a search warrant for Billie Cox's office at Century Oil," I said. "When can you get a judge to sign it?"

"Not until morning, by the time I round up a prosecutor to draft it and get everything in order," she said.

"Okay," I said. "I've got a signed consent, but I'd like a warrant, just to be sure we're covered. I'll pick it up first thing. Schedule a couple of forensic guys to meet me at Century Oil around nine, including a computer specialist. Get a search warrant for her house, too. We'll go there second."

Finally, I ducked back inside Century Oil's offices for one last piece of business. I returned the Sharpie to Billie's assistant and shot him one of those looks, the kind that says, "Don't mess with me."

"Are you here until lockup tonight and back first thing in the morning?" I asked.

"I can be," he said, his voice faint. He cleared his throat. I figured the stare I had focused on him was making it tight. "Almost every-one's already gone for the night, but I can wait until the last ones leave."

"No one, and I mean *no one* goes in Billie's office," I said. "I hold you personally accountable."

He nodded, and I turned and walked back toward the elevators with the file on the East Texas oil field tucked under my arm.

Fifteen

I was puzzled to see Doc Larson's old green Chevy pickup block-ing the driveway, when I pulled up to the ranch. He'd already dropped in once that day.

"So, what do you think?" Mom asked Doc as I walked into the shed. Maggie and Strings held on tight to the mare, expressions of utter worry crowding their young faces. They'd braided the horse's white mane, and I wondered if that made Emma Lou feel any bet-ter or only the kids. Bobby stood nearby, more than a bit somber.

"I'm glad you called. You're right, Nora. It's looking more and more like we haven't got much time," Doc said, inspecting the horse's bulging girth. Just since morning, Emma Lou's belly appeared sunken around the base of her tail, a common sign that foaling is near. "Could be tonight."

"Too soon?" I asked.

"I hoped for at least another day or two. This is right on the edge," he said, shaking his head. "I don't know, Sarah. Could be a rough one. Someone needs to sleep within earshot of the horse to-night and call me if her contractions start."

"I'll do it," Maggie said.

"Maggie . . ." I started to argue, but then I thought better of it. Emma Lou was her horse, and this was no time to pull rank. "Okay, but I'll be out here with you."

"Now the important thing is to keep the mare comfortable," Doc said. "And don't rile her up. Let Emma Lou handle it without help, if she can, until I get here."

"We know what to do, Doc," Mom said. "We've birthed a few foals at the ranch over the years."

"This time's different, Nora," Doc said. "This little one is going to need every bit of luck to make it through."

That evening, we had a quiet dinner at the picnic table under the corral elm tree, the lights blazing, Mom, Bobby, Strings, Maggie, and I. Afterward, Maggie and I set up our cots outside the shed, and then I went inside to talk to Bobby. I still had work to do, and I found him helping Mom with dishes. She was washing the pans and he was drying.

"I've got some questions on the oil business, Bobby," I said. "Could we sit down and look at some papers together? It's for a case, and I need your help."

"Of course, Sarah," Mom said. "You go now, Bobby. I'm almost through."

"No, let me help you finish, Nora," he said. "Only a few more to go."

"Don't be silly. Sarah needs your help. I'll finish these up."

He kissed her tenderly on the cheek, which made me think of David. I shrugged it off, and Bobby and I sat down on the living room couch, where I put Billie Cox's file with the Post-it note on the cocktail table in front of us. I didn't have to say anything. Bobby took his rimless reading glasses out of his pocket and put them on, picked up the file, and started slowly working through it, digesting each page. As he did his smile dissolved, replaced by a scowl, and pretty soon his brow grew heavy and his eyes formed angry slits. When he finally put the file down, he folded his hands on his lap.

"Explain all this to me," I said.

"Not much to explain, Sarah," he said. "But I think you just saved Barker Oil close to fifty million, maybe more."

"How'd I do that?" I asked.

"Looks like I was about to buy a bunch of dry holes," he said. "Looks like those oil leases in East Texas aren't as lucrative as Billie Cox and I were led to believe."

"Show me," I said. "I need to understand what I'm looking at."

"Just a minute," he said, getting up and walking back to the kitchen. A minute later, he returned with a pad of paper and a pencil, and again sat next to me. He pointed to one line of numbers on the list inside the folder and copied it onto the top sheet of paper. Then he flipped through to the back of the folder and pulled one page out of the stack of colored charts.

"This is well number one-forty-four of the Stanhope Oil Fields," he explained. "Stanhope is the field Billie and I wanted to acquire in that joint mineral-rights purchase I told you about the other night."

"I thought that was probably the case," I said. "Now, tell me what the numbers mean."

"Well, the first is the number of the well, one-forty-four. The second is the year it last operated, and third the number of barrels per month produced during its final year. The fourth number is the date the well could be operational again, basically how long it would take to get it in working order, and the fifth is the projected number of barrels the well is expected to produce per year. The final is a projection of the number of years before the well plays out."

"What's the chart, the colored drawing you pulled out?" I asked.

"That's part of a study on a section of the field, the section that includes well number one-forty-four. The company that analyzed this report used that study to predict how much oil was below the ground," he said.

"Did you know this was being done?" I asked.

"Not a clue," he said. "My guess? I can't be certain, but I'd bet Billie had doubts about how much the wells were really worth, some reason to question the figures we'd been supplied. She must have brought someone in to study the wells, to verify the expected profits from the field."

"And the important thing about all this is?"

Bobby sat back against Mom's old sofa and resolutely folded his arms across his chest. "I don't like to say this," he said. "But it sure looks to me like we were being bamboozled. Must have to Billie, too, based on the note. We'd been given other numbers, much higher ones for this field. These wells, they ought to stay abandoned. No reason to drill, because they're verging on dry holes."

"With crude prices so high, why would anyone have to run a scam to make money?" I said. "These days most of us are bleeding money for oil. Every time I go to the pump, gas has gone up. The price for a tank is plumb crazy."

"That's why they're doing it. The price is so high, companies like mine are buying old wells up right and left, planning to use all the new high-tech equipment to recover more oil," he said. "When oil prices were low, no one could afford to invest enough to pull the hard-to-get-to reserves out of the ground. But with prices sky high, it's worth the cash, even if the well's not the gusher it once was."

"But these particular wells . . . ?" I asked.

"They're not worth shelling out the investment it would take to try," he said. "Anyone in the business can look at these figures and tell you this field is played out, probably thirty years ago."

"Who owns the fields?" I asked. "Who's running the con?"

"Don't know," he said. When I looked skeptical, he explained,

"Mineral rights are complicated, lots of layers of ownership over many generations. We were told that it's some kind of partnership that wants to remain anonymous, that they bought the rights up years ago when oil was cheap and want to cash in now that it's high. We were proceeding based on a prospectus presented by their attorney. He's the one we were dealing with."

"I need his name," I said. "And anything else you can tell me about all this."

Bobby reached into the back pocket of his blue jeans. "By the way, you shouldn't blame me for the price of gas," he said, as he rifled through his worn-out black leather wallet. He flipped through a stack of business cards and pulled out one, white with black print.

"Aren't you oil tycoons the ones making all the big profits?"

"Well, yeah," he said, with a reluctant shrug. "I guess you could say that."

"Why wouldn't I blame the folks cashing in?"

"Most of the oil in the world is owned by nations, like Venezuela and Saudi Arabia, not companies or individuals. They're the ones setting the price and limiting production, not us," he said. "And you need to talk to the developing nations, like India and China. They're fueling the demand. Couple that with our own government, that's blocked drilling in most of the nation. America's playing in a world market now, Sarah, and we don't control the action. War in the Middle East, prices climb. Third World needs energy to develop, prices climb. Just last year, no one wanted our oil. The price of a barrel was bargain basement, and we couldn't afford to invest enough to drill. No profit in it. We couldn't control the price then and we sure can't control it now."

"Okay," I said, taking the lawyer's business card from him. "But that's probably not going to make me any less annoyed next time I hit the gas pumps."

"Sarah, you are something," Bobby said, with a guttural laugh.

"Well, I'm not going to tell you oil isn't making a lot of folks, including me, richer, but it truly is a bunch more complicated than the way it sounds on the evening news."

"I'll try to keep that in mind," I said.

"I'd appreciate that," he said. "But let's get back to this Stanhope Field. I've got a question to ask."

"Sure," I said. "What?"

"We're talking about all this because now you don't think Billie Cox killed herself. Billie was murdered, right?"

I paused for a moment, wondering how to answer that. Then figured he needed to know. "Yeah," I said. "The folks at her office know, so it'll get out soon, but keep it as quiet as you can for now, okay? I need some working room."

"Sure," he said. "So, who killed her?"

"I don't know," I said, "Could have something to do with this scam, or it might not. It could be totally unrelated, like maybe that married man she was dating. But there is something else you can look at for me."

I opened the file to the back, where I'd paper-clipped the computer photo. I handed it to Bobby, and asked, "Can you tell me anything about this?"

Bobby eyed the photo, and then flipped through the chart inside. "Well, it's the Stanhope Field all right. See, the number on the oil well in the picture is on your list. And that's Clayton Wagner, one of the owners of Century Oil," he said, pointing to one of the elderly gents. "Crazy old man. Lives larger than life. The guy's made fortunes and lost them, then made them and lost them again. A real speculator, but he has always had a knack of betting on the wrong horse, if you know what I mean. Until Billie, that company was constantly in the red. She was the best thing that could have happened to that old codger."

"Who are the other two men?"

"This is Ty Dickson," he said, pointing at the other man whose face was visible. "Dickson is Wagner's partner and just as explosive as he is. But I thought he was sick, and that he'd retired. Strange that he'd be involved in any of this."

"Any ideas on the identity of the man with his back to the camera?" I asked.

Bobby sized up the man, taller than the other two, younger, an awkwardly built man. "Maybe he looks familiar, but from the little I can see, I'm not sure," Bobby said. "Sorry."

"That's okay," I said. "You've been a big help."

"So Sarah, one more question," Bobby said, peering at me over the tops of his glasses. I realized that he looked worried. "If someone did murder Billie over these wells, and I was her bidding partner, am I in danger? Since Billie died, I'm in negotiations to buy this field solo. The deal's supposed to go through late next week."

Perhaps I should have thought of that, but I hadn't.

"I'm not sure," I admitted. "If Billie died because of this scam, I think it's because she figured it out. The best advice I can give you is not to say anything about any of this to anyone."

"But I've gotta pull out of the Stanhope deal, and maybe the Century Oil buyout," Bobby said, alarmed. "If Wagner's involved in all this, I'm dealing with a crook, maybe even a murderer."

"Don't pull out. Stall," I suggested. "Say you're running into some issues at Barker Oil, freeing up the cash. Make something up. Delay but stay in the deal, so no one guesses that you know what's going on. At least until I have Billie's murder sorted out."

"Okay, I can do that," Bobby said. He considered it all for a moment, and then slapped his palms on his knees and stood up. "Now I'm going to see if that beautiful mother of yours needs any more help with those dishes."

Before long, Bobby had left for his home in Houston, while Mom got ready for bed. Meanwhile, Maggie and I got wrapped up in our sleeping bags on the cots. It was a cool night, predicted to drop into the high forties by morning, but our gear was thick and warm, and we wore our clothes inside. At ten, as they do every night, the corral lights clicked off, and the night turned a rich dark with the stars piercing brightly overhead. The world was quiet, while inside the shed all was ready. Emma Lou had fresh straw and everything needed in place for the delivery. Now, all we could do was listen and wait.

"Mom, are you seeing Mr. Garrity again?" Maggie asked, as I flirted with sleep.

It took me a moment to answer, mostly because I wasn't expecting the question. "No, I'm not," I said. "We're just working a case together. Why?"

"Do you want to see him, like date him?"

"What makes you think that?" I asked.

"No reason," she said. "I was just thinking that you used to act like you liked him. Sometimes, you looked pretty happy when you were with him."

It's amazing how easily a kid sees through a parent. Poor Maggie. She had Emma Lou to worry about, but she was still trying to figure out David and me, a relationship even I couldn't make sense of. I unzipped my sleeping bag, and pulled my legs back out, got up and stood over her. Squatting on my haunches, I looked into her hazel eyes, so much like Bill's. I briefly wondered what she'd look like in thirty years, if she'd have crow's feet around those eyes. I had a hard time remembering being so young.

"Let's not worry about anything tonight, Magpie. Emma Lou's peaceful, and it's beautiful out here. Look up at the stars, say your prayers, and sleep," I said, giving her a soft kiss. I pushed her sleeping bag in tight around her, the way I swaddled her in blankets when she was a baby. "I'll be right here with you, listening for Emma Lou if she needs us."

"Okay, Mom," she said. "But about Mr. Garrity, I—"

"Shush now, Maggie," I ordered. It had been a long day, and we both needed sleep. "There's no reason to be concerned about David Garrity. I don't want to talk any more about him. Right now, all I want to hear is you sleeping."

Maggie still looked worried, but I gave her a hug, and she nodded. Fifteen minutes later, she slept softly, and I stared up at the canopy of stars above me, closed my own eyes, and drifted to sleep.

Sixteen

At first, I wasn't sure where I was. I woke in the darkness, to the sound of Emma Lou stirring in the shed. I found her lying on the straw, restless and agitated. She stood up, then immediately lumbered her bulging body back down. Contractions rippling her belly, the horse got back on her feet and stomped at the floor. This wasn't good.

I shook Maggie, and when her eyes opened, handed her my cell phone. "Call Doc and wake Gram," I said. "Emma Lou's foaling."

"Now?" Maggie said, her voice rising.

"Calm down," I warned. "The worst thing you can do is spook that mare."

Eyes wide, Maggie nodded.

While Maggie ran to the house, I slipped a blue nylon halter and lead on the horse, and then walked her toward the yard, talking softly, soothing her. Mom and Maggie rushed out, but slowed before reaching us.

"Something's not right," I said.

"Doc's on his way," Mom said, warily looking over Emma Lou.

"I'm going to keep walking her. You talk to her, Maggie," I said. "Keep it calm."

Maggie nodded, swallowed hard, and then said, "It's okay, Emma Lou. It's all going to be okay. You and your baby will be just fine."

We stayed like this, pacing the yard, comforting the horse, until Doc's pickup pulled in. "Give her to me, Sarah," he instructed. "I need light."

Relieved, I handed over the lead. We followed as he walked the horse to the shed. After examining her, he said, "She hasn't dilated. Contractions, but unproductive."

"Is the foal okay?" I asked.

"As far as I can tell," he said. "Let's leave the mare alone and see what she does."

Doc slipped off the gear and stepped back. Emma Lou grunted once, twice, and then lowered her bulging body onto the thick blanket of straw. One, two, three contractions, then they subsided. As each wave hit, the mare instinctively panted.

Maggie's arms tight around my waist, we watched, waiting. Soon the edge of the milky placenta could be seen, and then delicate front hooves, followed by spindly front legs. We held our breath as Doc coaxed the foal out with a firm yet gentle tug. Once he'd freed it from the placenta, the fragile, all-black creature lay on the straw, alarmingly limp.

"Is it all right?" Maggie whispered. "It's not breathing."

"Shush," Mom scolded. "Maggie, let Doc do his work."

Absolute quiet. So quiet I heard the beating of my own heart.

Finally, the soft rustle of the foal's breath ruffling straw. I smiled at Maggie, and she and Mom laughed, the first crisis past. All the while, Emma Lou lay on her side panting, as if recovering from a long run.

"Isn't the foal beautiful, Mom?" Maggie asked. "She's so tiny."

"Not a she a *he*, Maggie," Doc said, down on his knees, inspecting the newborn. "You know, he looks all right, skinny but all right."

"A colt?" Maggie said with wonder.

"So, he's healthy?" I asked.

"I can't say for sure, Sarah," Doc cautioned. "We won't know for a while yet."

The colt was more delicate than any I'd ever seen. So thin, its legs appeared little more than bone, too lean to support even its meager weight. Yet, Emma Lou stood and nuzzled him, and the foal stirred. The newborn pulled his head up and gazed at his mother, then about the shed, inspecting the disheveled crew gathered to welcome him into the world.

"That's good that he's popped his head up, Mom," Maggie said. "Isn't it?"

"It is," I said. Yet weak, the tiny horse quickly lay back down. Emma Lou prodded again at her tiny offspring, alternately nudging it with her nose and licking it. But the foal lay still. "Do you have a name for him?" I asked Maggie.

She'd picked Glory for a filly but never announced a colt's name. Faced with the task, Maggie stared down at the little creature. Breathing softly, he looked like a preemie, with a silky, thin, and short coat, his ears floppy. A funny little animal, but a precious one.

"Give him a courageous name, Maggie," Mom said. "One that sounds like a survivor, because that's what he needs to be."

Maggie nodded. Emma Lou pushed against the colt's head, still resting on the straw, urging it up, as Doc grabbed a towel. "Get the wheelbarrow, Nora," he ordered as he worked the towel over the creature's thin frame. "I don't want him suckling off the mare until we're sure she's kicked the infection. We need to move him."

Mom did as instructed, but as we lowered the colt into the

wheelbarrow, Emma Lou let loose an insistent whinny. That was her colt, she seemed to say. Where were we taking it?

"Let's put him in a stall and bring the heat lamp," Doc ordered, covering the little guy with a clean beach towel. "Put it on low. Just enough to warm him."

As Mom and Doc wheeled the colt away, Emma Lou's dark eyes flared and she reared up and snorted.

"It's all right," Maggie cried out. "Warrior will be okay. I'll watch him for you."

"Warrior?" I repeated.

"Like Gram said, Mom, something brave."

I reached the stable with a baby bottle of defrosted and warmed first milk, high in antibodies, that Doc had supplied, just as the little guy raised his head, peering about his new quarters. I gave the bottle to Maggie, and she cautiously put the nipple near his mouth. Disinterested, Warrior turned his head to look at us.

"Brush the nipple over his lips, Maggie," I suggested. "Let him smell the milk."

She did, but nothing. The colt made no attempt to latch on. At least ten pounds below a healthy foal, our new charge didn't appear to have the desire to feed. Doc shook his head.

"What's next?" I asked.

"We wait and watch," he said. "The colt should stand soon and eat. If not . . ."

Doc didn't finish the sentence, and none of us asked him to. Maggie, Mom, and Doc stayed with the colt, while I returned to Emma Lou. I thought about how empty she must feel, after giving birth and watching as her firstborn was whisked away. I sat on a chair, right outside the shed door, where she could see me, and before long fell asleep. When I awoke, the sun wasn't yet up and Maggie peered at me. She had tears in her eyes.

"Oh, no, Magpie," I said. "Is it Warrior?"

She nodded, and I thought the worst, but she said, "He's standing, Mom, and feeding, and Doc says he's small, but he thinks he'll be all right."

Seventeen

At the ranch the following morning, Maggie slept in. There wasn't any talk of school. She was too exhausted. Considering how the previous night could have turned out, all was relatively well. Tired and fidgety, Emma Lou paced in the shed, no doubt missing her colt. Meanwhile Warrior hungrily slurped a full bottle of milk. The colt's vital signs, at least so far, were promising.

As I drove into Houston, David called from his office at the Federal Building, to update me on his efforts on the Collins stalking case, following up on leads generated by the subpoenaed Internet records. He offered no more hope than the day before. Each lead the FBI traced brought them to yet another Internet resender, a Web site set up to process and forward e-mails. Each new resender had to be served with a separate subpoena, and each resulting lead took David and his computer forensic team to yet another shadowy link in a long chain. Argus had done his homework. He knew how to use the Internet to hide his identity, and he hadn't made any rookie mistakes to help us find him.

David said he'd keep following the trail, and report in later that day.

The tape on Billie Cox's office door appeared undisturbed when I arrived midmorning with a signed subpoena and a two-man crime-scene team. A full week after her death, we now knew she'd been murdered, and I had a couple of potential motives: one, love gone wrong; the other, a complicated oil well scam. Which, if either, would lead to the murderer? I didn't have a clue.

My best shot at moving the murder case forward was finding evidence in either Cox's office or home. Gilberto Torres, our office's resident computer geek, went right for Cox's desk. There was no plan to examine Cox's computer on-site. Everything we collected would be taken to the lab adjacent to our offices. He got busy unhooking the printer and the keyboard from the desktop computer. "Make sure you bag and fingerprint the keyboard. And take everything, including the printer," I told him. "We'll want to verify that the suicide note was printed here."

Torres nodded. Then, something else occurred to me. "While you're checking that computer out, try to figure out how it turns itself on," I said.

"Turns itself on?" Torres repeated, giving me a questioning look.

"Yeah," I said. "It has a habit of doing that."

"Oh, okay," Torres said, looking just a little doubtful. "We'll take a look, Lieutenant."

Meanwhile crime-scene specialist, Kerry Adkins, an angular woman with dark brown skin and a shaggy wig that sat just the slightest bit off-center, giving her an unbalanced look, photographed, bagged, and collected anything that looked vaguely like evidence. She and I searched Cox's desk, hoping for something important I'd missed the day before. I instructed Adkins to watch for anything associated with the Stanhope Field, along with calendars or business diaries, anything that would document Cox's schedule. She had to be meeting with the mystery man sometime, and she might have included something, anything on her schedule to point us in a direction.

In the back of my mind, I mulled over what if any involvement her brother-in-law, Grant Roberts, had in the murder. Early that morning, the subpoenaed information had come in from the real estate lockbox company, showing that his computerized key wasn't used the entire day of Billie's death. As soon as I finished executing the warrants at Cox's office and house, I planned to drop in for a follow-up with Faith's husband. I was curious to find out how he'd maintain his alibi, that he'd previewed houses up for sale all that afternoon, when he didn't access a single key to get inside one.

"Over here, Lieutenant," Adkins called out. A meticulous woman with a reputation for being as tenacious about gathering evidence as a squirrel stockpiling for winter, she held a black loose-leaf binder in her hands.

"Copies of Cox's expense reports," she said.

"Log them in. They're going with us," I said. While Adkins worked on the desk and Torres boxed up the computer, I inspected the credenza behind the desk, pulling out books, a few office supplies, and a pair of worn running shoes. I held them up, looked at the soles, and saw dirt wedged into the tread.

"Bag these, too," I instructed Adkins. "Get the dirt analyzed."

Two hours later, we left Cox's office with seven brown paper bags and six boxes full of potential evidence. On our way to Cox's River Oaks mansion, I called and checked on Maggie and the horses. Mom said all three were resting well. At least for now, everything at home was under control.

Figuring it had already been a week and not wanting to get the entire neighborhood gossiping, I hadn't sealed Cox's house with crime-scene tape the night before. If anyone was going to clean up evidence, they'd already had plenty of time. Instead I called Faith that morning and asked her to meet us there with the keys. When I rang the doorbell, she answered.

"This is the search warrant I told you about," I said, handing it to her.

"Lieutenant, you didn't have to do that," she protested. "I would have let you in. I want you to find Billie's killer."

"I know," I said, not mentioning I was less sure of her husband's motives. "This is just easier, since we were already getting one for her office."

Faith nodded, and we walked inside the house.

"I want you to show us Billie's bedroom," I said. "Where she died."

We followed Faith across the white marble floor and up a winding staircase with an ornate metal banister to the second floor, where we took a walkway that overlooked the two-story entry on one side and the living room on the other. When the passageway split off, Faith turned to the left and took us to the first door, then removed a key from her pocket and unlocked the door.

"You've had the bedroom locked?" I asked. "How long?"

"Since the evening Billie died," she answered. "I didn't know why I wanted everyone to stay out, but maybe I knew even then that she'd been murdered and there could be evidence."

"So no one has been in there?"

"Not that I know of. Not since the paramedics and police left," she said. "I have the only key."

"Thank you," I said. "This will help."

After putting on shoe protectors, a cotton mask, and latex gloves, Adkins went in, while we waited in the hallway. She had the video camera, and she made her way around the room slowly, recording everything as she found it, zeroing in on anything that on first blush smacked of being potential evidence. The floor was a dark oak with Persian rugs scattered about, so there was no thick pile and nothing visible that resembled a footprint. Still, she video-taped the floor, using oblique lighting, a flashlight held at an angle. She found no footprints.

That done, Adkins videotaped the dressers and an antique ar-moire, with a big-screen television hidden inside, even the tissue box next to Billie's bed. When she'd finished videotaping, she shot digital stills of the room. Lastly, she focused on the bed, still covered by the tapestry bedspread, speckled with blood. Facing the bed, the headboard to the right bore a fanlike pattern of high-velocity blood spatter and brain matter, caused by pressure from the gun's explo-sion forcing gas through the wound track. After sitting for a week, the spatter had aged brown, barely visible on the dark wood. When Adkins finished, she searched the perimeter of the bed. After a few moments, she motioned toward me.

"Take a look at this, Lieutenant," she said.

Similarly suited up, I walked in. Adkins had sprayed the floor a foot from the left side of the bed, about three feet from where the body lay, with a colorless liquid, Fluorescein, a chemical that detects latent bloodstains. We put on orange goggles, and Adkins set up the ALS, the alternative light source, a device in a square aluminum box, the size of a DVD player, with a 400-watt, high-intensity bulb at the end of a long flexible wand. She then set the meter on the ALS, turned on the light, and pointed the ALS at a small Oriental rug, all in shades of beige.

"Notice anything?" she asked.

With the goggles on, it didn't take long before I saw a bright yellowish-orange glow on the rug. But not on all of it. One section appeared clean. "You found a void?"

"Yup. Nothing in this section right here. Someone was stand-ing there, I bet," she said, aiming the flashlight at the point closest to the bed frame.

"Make sure you photograph that before we move anything," I said. Thinking about Cox's body at the morgue, I added. "The entry wound was on the victim's right side. That's the angle."

Adkins nodded, and I walked back out to the hallway, careful where I stepped. Fifteen minutes later, she'd bagged the rug and marked off a section of floorboards without spatter. Later, we'd send someone in to cut that area out of the floor. "Okay, you can come in now," she called out.

I entered Cox's bedroom again, this time with Torres beside me, and all three of us began searching for evidence. The first thing Torres did was bag the bloodstained bedspread. When I saw Faith about to walk in, I stopped her.

"Have you been in here since Billie's death?" I asked.

"No," she said. "I locked it from the outside and left. Except for the police and paramedics, the only one who has been in the room since Billie's death is Lena, the housekeeper. She found the body, but hasn't been in the room since she called police."

"Is she here now?" I asked.

"In her quarters over the garage," Faith said, offering, "I can go with you, introduce you."

"No," I said. "I'd really prefer that you waited outside, on the front porch. I don't want you to leave, in case we have questions. But it's better to keep a distance, and please don't touch anything."

"Of course," she said. "Anything you say."

Lena Suarez was a tall woman, heavy-boned with a long nose and graying hair pulled into a bun. Her apartment over the four-car garage had its own kitchen and a small sitting area, and she invited me in, although rather reluctantly.

"I only went looking for Miss Billie because she asked me to wake her," Suarez said. "When she get home, she said, 'Lena, wake me at six-thirty. I have dinner at home tonight.' And I said, 'Yes, Miss Billie.' I was disappointed. Friday nights are my time off, so after work, I came here to my room, but then I remember that I need a gift for my nephew's birthday. So I leave my room and drive to the store. I buy a game for his computer, so expensive those games are, and go right home to fix Miss Billie's dinner. When I get back, I hurry and put a plate in the microwave for Miss Billie, tamales I made on Wednesday. They are her favorites. Then I go to wake her for dinner."

"Had she said what her plans were for that night?" I asked.

"She tell me that she will have dinner at home and stay in," the woman said. "Miss Billie young and very pretty, and she went out a lot the last few months. Before that not so much, but lately, all the time. Until the last few weeks, then she stay home again."

"When she went out, do you know where she went?" I asked.

"No," the woman said, shaking her head. "She never tell me where she go or who she go with."

"So what happened after you put the plate in the oven?"

"Six-thirty, like she say, I go upstairs to wake Miss Billie," Suarez said. "I knock on the door. No one answer. I knock again, two more, maybe three more times. No one answer. I think she's sleeping, but I am afraid to go in. Maybe she not want me to. So I wait in the hall and try to think what to do. Then I say to myself, 'Lena, Miss Billie say to wake her, so you should do as she tell you.' I open the door."

"Did you notice anything odd in the hallway, anywhere in the house, before you went into the bedroom?" I asked.

"No," she said. "Nothing."

"Did you see anyone? Anyone at all?"

"No, no one," she said.

"Go on," I said. "What happened next?"

With this, the woman lowered her face and rubbed her eyes. Her voice grew weary. "Like I say, I open the door," she recounted.

"The shutters are closed. It is dark in the room. No lights on. So, I turn on the light switch. I say, 'Miss Billie, it is the time you say . . .' But I don't finish, because I see Miss Billie. I see the blood, so much blood, and her face, her beautiful face. What that bullet did to her. *Dios mio*. I look hard to make sure it's her. It is Miss Billie."

Lena Suarez stopped talking and wrapped her arms around herself, appearing troubled. I felt sorry for her, but I needed the woman to talk. "What did you do next?" I asked. "Did you call the police?"

"No," she said. "I stand there for a while, and I just look, wondering if maybe my eyes not tell me the truth. Then, I think, I must get help. So I call for ambulance on nine-one-one, on the telephone down the hall, on Miss Billie's desk. They ask me to help her, to do CPR. I tell them, it is too late."

"Did you wait for them in the office?"

"No," she said. "I go downstairs to the front porch. I sit on the steps and try not to think about what I see. And soon they come in the ambulance with the siren. I point to the room, and the ambulance people go inside. But they come back in a hurry and say there is nothing they can do. Miss Billie is dead, and the medical men, they called police."

From that point on, Lena Suarez told me of waiting for the police to arrive, without going back in the house. She'd never entered the front door, not since that afternoon. Instead, she stood on the porch and watched as the officers and a coroner's assistant made their way upstairs. They lingered, undoubtedly sizing up the scene, and then filed slowly down. Late that night when the police were finished, a detective, probably Brad Walker, told her that the medical examiner was removing the body.

"That detective say Miss Billie kill herself, but I couldn't understand why she do that," Lena said. "She seem happy, not upset. And she's so proud of the way she looks. Why would she do that to her face?"

"I don't think she did," I said.

The housekeeper looked just momentarily surprised, then nodded, as if she'd suspected.

"Have you seen any men here, anyone at all that Miss Billie appeared to have a relationship with? Anyone she was dating?"

"No," Suarez said. "The only ones who visit Miss Billie are Miss Faith and Mr. Grant. Miss Billie very busy at work. She work all the time."

"But you said she'd been out more lately," I pointed out. "You said she'd been going out over the past few months."

That made her pause, and she thought. Then she said, "Yes, I don't know where she go, but she go out more. Maybe with a man."

"Miss Suarez, what was Miss Cox's relationship like with her brother-in-law, with Mr. Grant?" I asked.

Her eyes grew round and she stared at me, and then cautiously said, "They seem to like each other very much."

"How much?" I asked.

The housekeeper lowered her eyes.

"I need to know," I said. "It's important."

"I don't think they do anything wrong," she whispered. "But sometimes, I think maybe they like each other too much."

"Did you ever see them together?" I asked. "Without Miss Faith?"

"Only once," she said. "That time, he bring Miss Billie home. She said her car broke, and she called him for a ride."

"What did you see?" I asked.

"Nothing," she said. "Only I think, maybe Mr. Grant like Miss Billie more than he should. He kissed her on lips, a little kiss, and she look happy. I worry that Miss Faith will get hurt."

By the time I made my way back to the main house, Torres and Adkins were carrying evidence out to the crime-scene-unit's van. Adkins had collected the bedding, everything she could out of the bedroom, while Torres gathered up Cox's home computer, a laptop.

"I found these in her home office," she said, handing me a pile of credit-card statements and receipts. "Maybe they'll help."

"Maybe they will," I said.

As we got ready to leave, Faith stood on the porch.

"I need your sister's keys," I said. "This is a crime scene now, and we need to make sure it's secure."

"Of course," she said.

She watched as we strung yellow tape over the front and back doors, and then drove out the driveway and onto the street right before us in her Subaru SUV. I thought again about Grant Roberts and wondered if Faith had any idea of the pain that might wait ahead.

Eighteen

After I left Billie Cox's place, I called Janet from the car and asked her to subpoena Grant Roberts's credit card and cell phone records. I also asked her to track down an address for Carlton Wagner, Billie's boss and one of the two identifiable men in the Stanhope photo. It turned out that Wagner lived nearby, so I tabled Roberts for the time being and made a U-turn, drove less than a mile east, and parked in front of the biggest mansion I'd ever seen. The darn thing took up half a block, all gray granite with ornate black-iron balconies. I parked the car, walked up to the massive oak doors, and knocked. I expected a butler or a maid, but a rickety white-haired man with a back humped by age and a full white beard answered. Carlton Wagner.

"I'm glad you finally decided to introduce yourself," Wagner mumbled, glaring at me, when we sat in his parlor. He had a thick East Texas drawl and a frown as crooked as his posture. "I heard about your tomfoolery at the Century Oil offices this morning. I was surprised. Since it's my company, I thought you'd have the courtesy to contact me first. Getting my employees all upset hurts productivity. They end up spending all their time at the water cooler, gossiping. Is this your usual overbearing way of looking into a suicide?"

A feisty old guy, Wagner's faded denim-blue eyes bristled with contempt. He may have invited me into his home, but he put on no masquerade. The old man was blatantly angry about the intrusion. His entire manner suggested annoyance at my very presence.

"No. It's the way we investigate a murder. The medical examiner has changed his ruling, Mr. Wagner," I said. "Elizabeth Cox's death is now a homicide."

"That's about as likely as a hurricane in Detroit," he snarled. "Damn Yankee-town's too far away from the ocean for that to ever happen."

"How can you be so sure Billie wasn't murdered?" I asked.

"Who'd kill Billie?" he scoffed. His beard flapped when he talked, and he toyed with the edge of the lace cloth on the small table between us, rolling it between his thumb and index finger. I'd never met Wagner before, but my bet was that the old geezer had a stomach full of nerves as he rattled on. "Everybody, including me, loved that woman. Why she was beautiful and smart, and had the best business sense of any oil company exec I've ever had on my payroll. Plus, she wasn't old enough to make an enemy, not one that hated her enough to commit murder."

With that the old guy exhaled a short laugh. "Now take me, for instance," he bragged. "I've been around long enough to step on toes, some mighty big toes at that. Stirring folks up to get my way, for me, that's a big part of the fun. But not Billie. She was a good sort of person. And even if she had teed somebody off, that woman could've charmed him into figuring that he was the one who was wrong. She had it all, beauty, money, brains, a darn good personality, everything but happiness."

The old guy shook his head, as if in disbelief. Something about his act, however, I wasn't buying, principally that I would have used that exact word to describe it, an *act*. If Wagner hadn't cashed in working the oil fields, he could have made a living playing Gabby Hayes parts in Westerns. The old wildcatter was a natural performer.

"Why would she be unhappy? Why would any woman with so much chuck it all?" I asked.

Wagner sucked in his thin upper lip in disdain. "I don't like to spread gossip," he said. "Ain't in my character."

"This isn't gossip," I assured him. "This is cooperating in a police investigation into a murder."

He paused, studied my face, and appeared to consider that for a moment, before going on. "Well, I still disagree about the murder part. But I guess either way it's an investigation," he said. "Billie was smart every way but in matters of the heart. When it came to love, that woman was an utter fool. She threw herself at men. It wasn't a pretty sight. And when they were done with her, she fell to pieces. I feared one day she'd take a dead-end romance too hard. I figure that's what happened here."

"You do, do you?" I asked. "That's interesting."

"Thought you should know the truth, if you're doing a real investigation," he said, looking up at me from under eyelids that hung as loose as wrinkled curtains. "I figure I knew Billie as well as anybody. I don't care what that third-rate doc down in the morgue says. I've got no question that she killed herself."

"Who was this man, the one who broke her heart so badly that you believe she shot a bullet through her skull?" I asked.

Wagner sucked in again and let out a long breath. "Well, don't really know," he said. "I hear he was married. Some man she hooked up with she shouldn't have."

"How about a name?" I asked. "How about anything that would narrow the field down from every married man in Texas?"

The old man scowled, and then said, "Listen, I knew Billie

well, that's for sure. But I'm not in the habit of asking about my employees' personal lives. You're the detective. The way I see it, you need to figure that out."

Some might have found Carlton Wagner's performance amusing, but I had a case to solve. "What I have figured out is that Elizabeth Cox didn't kill herself. This case is, as I said, a murder investigation."

Looking increasingly uncomfortable, Wagner fidgeted in his chair. The old man was a bundle of unspent energy. "You're sure of that?" he asked, still sizing me up with a skeptical stare.

"As sure as I am that I'm sitting here in this fine mansion with you," I said. "No doubt about it."

"Hmmm," he said. "Well, I'm sure you'll understand if I continue to disagree, but what do you want from me? You should be busy finding out who that man Billie dated was. My guess is that he's the only one with a motive."

"I appreciate the advice," I said, thinking that Billie Cox picked one squirrelly old geezer to work for. "The reason I'm here is that I'd like you to tell me about the Stanhope Field acquisition."

Looking unconcerned, he said with a shrug, "I can't tell you a thing about it. That was Billie's deal. I wasn't involved."

"Not at all?" I asked.

"Lieutenant Armstrong, I've closed multimillion-dollar deals on a handshake. When I tell you something I mean it. I wasn't involved in any of Century Oil's business for the past two years. When I turned the company over to Billie, I told her to charge ahead and not worry about waiting for this old man to limp along behind her," he said. "I know I'm over the hill, and it was time for me to get out of the business."

"So you had nothing to do with the planned acquisition? You weren't involved in any way?"

Wary-eyed, Wagner responded as if I'd just suggested he donate all his money to Greenpeace's global-warming, anti-oil campaign.

"Isn't that what I just told you?" he said, at the end of his patience. "You need an interpreter for English?"

"When's the last time you were at the Stanhope Field?" I asked.

Again, Wagner paused, sucking in a deep breath that fanned out his brittle, old chest, as if reining in great frustration. "I don't know that I've ever been there," he said. "But if I was at Stanhope, it must of been close to a decade ago."

"You feel pretty certain about that, Mr. Wagner?"

"I wouldn't have said it if I weren't certain," he said, arms folded tight across his chest.

With that, I unzipped the black cloth folder I'd brought and took out the photo from Billie's computer. "Please, tell me about this then. When was it taken?" I asked.

Again the churlish frown. I had no doubt that Wagner had been candid about at least one thing, that he'd stepped on plenty of toes during his career and managed to make more than one enemy.

"Where'd you get that?" he asked.

"That's not important. Just answer my question. When was it taken?"

Wagner shook his head. "I'm not sure, but at least eight years ago. Matter of fact, I'm pretty sure it was right before my old partner, Ty Dickson, retired. It was in December, right before Christmas, because we'd made some plans to go to Florida that year for the holidays. We couldn't go because Ty's wife, Emily, died unexpectedly a few days later. I'd forgotten about that night, when you asked me earlier."

"Why were you there?" I asked.

Wagner shook his head, as if I were the most incompetent woman asking the most ridiculous questions. He sighed and then said, "Ty and I still ran Century Oil back then. We were looking at buying the mineral rights to the field. At the time, oil was dirt cheap and it cost too damn much to get it out of those old wells."

"You're telling me, and you're sure about this, that you haven't been to the Stanhope Field since?"

"Nope. Not unless you've got another picture in that case of yours to jog my memory," he challenged.

"Tell me why Billie kept this photograph on her office computer," I asked.

"Beats me." He shrugged. Then he looked at me and flashed a wizened smirk. "The girl did like me. I was kind of a father figure to her. Maybe it was out of deep affection."

When I said nothing, just stared at him, he said, "We about done here? It's time for my afternoon nap."

"Almost," I said. "One more question. Where were you the afternoon Billie Cox died?"

"The way this conversation was going, I figured you'd get around to asking that," he said. "I was at my doctor's office. I'll give you the man's name and phone number, if it'll stop your inane questions. You get as old as I am, you spend a lot of time tending to your body. Not that it does much good. No matter how much you patch it, the damn thing keeps falling apart."

At four that afternoon, it felt like a long day. I hadn't had much sleep the night before, but I drove to Grant Roberts's real estate office. The beautiful Miss April Sims was just heading out the door, with her oversized gold lame purse under her arm. She let me in, gave me a rather cold stare, pointed at the back of the offices, toward Grant Roberts's cubicle, and turned to leave. Then she started to stalk out the door. I grabbed it before she could open it.

"I just need to get your recollections of that afternoon on tape," I said. "For my records. When you saw Mr. Roberts at the office the afternoon his sister-in-law died."

She looked at me, tilted her head a bit and frowned, then shrugged. "Okay, but make it quick."

Glad to cooperate, I held up my small digital recorder, pushed the record button, and said, "This is Lieutenant Armstrong investigating the Billie Cox homicide. I'm with April Sims. Miss Sims, can you please tell me when you saw Grant Roberts on the afternoon of his sister-in-law's death?"

Sims bent down to get close to the recorder, and then said, in a matter-of-fact manner, "Mr. Roberts was in the office earlier that day and then out previewing properties late that afternoon. He returned here at about six-thirty and left shortly after. That's all I know."

I clicked off the recorder, and she turned and left, not appearing at all concerned that I'd just recorded her statement for posterity.

About then, Roberts walked into the lobby. He must have heard me talking to Sims, because he glared at me and shook his head. "Haven't you got better things to do?" he asked.

"That's funny," I said. "At first, Miss Sims looked less than happy to see me, too. Is there some reason for that? Have I unintentionally hurt someone's feelings?"

"What do you want?" he asked.

"I just need to get your whereabouts at the time of the murder," I said, showing him the recorder. "I need it on tape so the secretary can transcribe it and put it into the case file, when I get back to the office."

"I've told you where I was once," he said. "Why do I have to explain again?"

"I'm sure you have forms to fill out in your job," I said. "This is something I have to do for mine."

With that, I clicked the recorder on and held it up to my mouth. "This is Lieutenant Sarah Armstrong of the Texas Rangers, and I'm speaking with Mr. Grant Roberts in his offices regarding the investigation into the murder of his sister-in-law, Billie Cox," I said. "Mr. Roberts, please tell me where you were on the afternoon of Miss Cox's murder."

At first, I wasn't sure he'd answer. Roberts appeared wary and angry. Finally, he bent down toward the recorder and said, "I spent that afternoon from about three or three-thirty on previewing houses, narrowing down the possibilities of what was on the market for an out-of-town client who came in that Sunday. I was back at the office about six-thirty, and left not long after, arriving home sometime before seven."

"When you preview houses, you look them over inside and out?" I asked, with a smile. "You want to find something similar in floor plan to what your client has expressed an interest in?"

"Of course," he said. "You have to go inside, see what they look like, what kind of condition they're in, or you end up taking the client into something totally unsuitable and wasting a lot of time. That's why I spent the time working on it, to narrow down the choices."

"Then why didn't you enter a single house that afternoon?" I asked, still smiling, the tape recorder rolling.

"What are you talking about?" he said, looking stunned, glancing nervously at the recorder. "Of course I went inside the houses. I went into a bunch of houses."

"The folks who monitor the lockboxes for all the real estate agents in Houston gave us copies of their records. Your computerized keypad wasn't used to access a single house that entire day," I said. "Where were you really?"

Looking up at the tile ceiling and fluorescent lights, Roberts remained silent for a few moments, as if trying to decide what to say. When he spoke, he said exactly what I'd expected: "I'll hire an attorney. You can talk to him. Now, please leave."

I looked at Roberts, turned off the recorder, and smiled.

"Now that I have your lies recorded, so they can be played in a courtroom at the proper moment, you need to come clean," I said. "No sense in continuing to lie. We'll figure this out. We'll find out what you're afraid of."

"I said, 'Leave,'" he repeated. "Now."

With no warrant for his arrest, no real evidence, I didn't have a choice. I couldn't take him in. Instead, I said, "Mr. Roberts, I promise you that I am going to find the person who murdered your sister-in-law, and if it's you, you're better off working with me than pissing me off."

Flushed with anger, he opened the office door and held it. I walked through, and he slammed it behind me.

Nineteen

I made one stop on the way home, at a convenience store, chugged gas into the Tahoe, watching the cost climb on the digital display, all the time thinking about oilman Clayton Wagner's mansion, and bought myself a Dove ice cream bar, the kind with crispies mixed into the chocolate. On my way out the door, I spied the magazine rack and made a detour. Cassidy Collins was on the cover of nearly every teen magazine. I peered at the options for a few minutes: "Cassidy at Home!" "Is Cassidy in Love?" "Can you kiss like Cassidy Collins?"

Geez, it was worse than I thought. I bought them all and then headed out the door munching on the Dove bar.

David's government-issue, blue, four-door sedan was in the driveway when I pulled into the ranch. I figured he'd called my office and heard I was on my way home. I assumed he wanted to finalize the details for our trip to Dallas the next day. In the house, Mom had every available countertop and the stove covered with cheesecake ingredients, more desserts in the making for Bobby's barbeque cook-off party that night. I thought about the years Mom baked for us like that. She used to all the time, until she went pro and it became work. Now she only gets the bug when something's needling her. I guess having Bobby around had settled her down, because I, despite the now-consumed Dove bar, started to long for the days when dinner ended with homemade apple cobbler.

"David Garrity is up in the stable with Maggie," Mom said, when I walked in.

"David's in the stable?" I asked. "Never realized he was into horses."

"It was Maggie's idea," she explained. "She wanted him to meet Warrior."

"How is the little guy?" I asked.

"Small, Sarah. Can't remember when we've had such a little one," she said. "But strong. I think the name Warrior fits that horse."

"Hope you're right," I said.

Mom nodded, and I tunneled my finger though a bowl of whipped-cream frosting dyed green to top her armadillo cheese-cakes. She feigned annoyance and slapped at my hand, missing as always. When I got to the shed, David and Maggie were petting Warrior. He was chatting it up with the colt like they were old buddies.

"You're a handsome guy, aren't you?" he said, his voice gentle. "Beautiful black coat. One day you'll be a real ladies' man."

"I don't know," I said. "Seems to me that Warrior has more sense than that."

"Ah, the voice of reason," David said, with a small laugh.

"Hi, Mom," Maggie said, glancing up. "Mr. Garrity and me were just keeping Warrior company."

"Mr. Garrity and *I*," I corrected.

Maggie grimaced. Math, not English, was her subject. "Mr. Garrity and I," she repeated.

"How's he eating?" I asked.

"He didn't finish his afternoon feeding," Maggie said, worried.

"But Gram says maybe Doc will give the okay and he'll be able to feed from Emma Lou tomorrow, if the blood tests are all right."

"That would be good news, Maggie," David said. He looked at me and smiled. "You look tired."

"Thanks, that always makes a girl feel beautiful," I said. "A long day, and I'm worn out after last night."

"Are you up to talking about tomorrow?" he asked.

"Sure," I said, sincerely glad to see him. As much as I didn't understand what had happened between us, I missed being with him. "I'll grab a couple of beers and meet you at the picnic table."

Nursing our beers, we spread the plans for Dallas's American Airlines Center out on the picnic table under the corral elm tree, the one with Maggie's lights strung on every limb. "I think we've got the arena covered," David said, pointing to the massive stadium's perimeter and motioning at the doors. "Per the plan you discussed with them, Dallas P.D. is bringing in enough extra men to guard every entrance and exit, public and private, along with scanners for the doors. Even the workers will be checked. And you've got that sweep with the dogs you set up for two hours before the concert. That should uncover anyone hiding inside."

"So what are we forgetting?" I asked.

David shook his head. "Nothing," he said. "But let's face it, there's no way to ensure that kid's safe. If someone really wants to, they'll find a way to get a weapon in."

"Unfortunately, that's true," I agreed. We sat there for a moment, and then I said, "Nice of you to talk to Maggie like that. I didn't know you liked horses. That's something you never mentioned last year when we were—"

"Yeah, we were, weren't we?" he said with a chuckle. He shook his head, as if recalling an old memory. "Last year was one heck of an investigation, in more ways than one. We were something else, weren't we, Sarah? Traveling all over the state, chasing a killer."

"Yeah, we were," I said, glad to see his wide grin and the bit of mischief in his eyes. I'd missed that. "That's a good smile, David. Where've you been hiding it?"

"Sarah, you can be absolutely exasperating," he said, followed by another small laugh.

"Glad you still think so," I said, meaning it. "Seems to me that's something."

"It is. It certainly is. You know . . . ," he said, but then he stopped, looked at me, and as quickly as he'd let his guard down, it was back. "We've got a tough day ahead of us," he said, motioning at the diagram. "Anything else we can do? Anything at all to get ready for tomorrow?"

Deciding yet again that somewhere inside the man sitting across from me hid the old David, waiting to burst out, I figured I'd better follow his lead and concentrate on work. At least that was something I had a chance at understanding. Unlike men, especially this one. So I considered the ways Argus could smuggle a weapon into the arena. There had to be a bunch, but maybe I was just too tired to think of them. I'd just have to stick to that kid like a second skin to make sure nothing happened.

"Did you follow up on having the arena's sound equipment inspected?" I asked.

"Everything has been checked and double-checked," he said. "They've run circuit tests on every system, from the audio to the headphone systems used by the security people. They didn't find a thing."

"So, if the guy finds a way to break into Collins's headphone and talks to her again, what are the possibilities?"

"The folks at the arena say none of their systems cover beyond the inside of the arena," David said. "So if he manages to break in like he did in San Diego, he's on-site, in the audience or behind the stage, somewhere in that arena."

"Okay," I said. "Let's make sure they're videotaping the entrances and exits and that they scan the audience in the auditorium with the cameras. We could get lucky and get this guy on tape."

"Good idea," David said.

"What if he is there?" I asked. "How do we respond?"

"With twenty-thousand screaming fans, mostly kids, we can't close the place down," David said. "Our best option is to man the exits, search anyone leaving who looks the part, a man, maybe carrying a large bag, something that could hold audio equipment."

"Okay," I said. "We're all set then. One o'clock tomorrow, I'll meet you at the airstrip."

"One o'clock," he said. I walked him to his car, and then watched him drive away. It made me feel lonely. I went inside and found Mom spreading whipped cream over her last armadillo cheesecake.

"You look like you're down in the dumps," she said. She stood there for just a moment, sizing me up, I'm sure able to see as clearly as she could in grade school that I was upset. With that, she cut a wide slice of the cake on the counter. "Try this. It always works for me. As a matter of fact, I'll join you."

Mom cut herself a piece, I grabbed two forks and two napkins, and we went out onto the porch, sat in the rockers, and ate. Late afternoon, there was a briskness in the air. The cheesecake was made with crème de menthe, and it tasted like the old grasshopper drinks my pop used to make after dinner.

"You need to talk to the man," Mom said, as if reading my mind.

"I've tried," I said. I closed my lips around the fork and peeled off another rich bite. "The man isn't talking."

I took another forkful, skinned it off with my teeth and let it dissolve in my mouth. This probably wasn't a good food day nutritionally, but for pure comfort, it's hard to beat a Dove bar and cheesecake. Yet as good as Mom's cake tasted, it didn't make up for what was missing in my life. That I knew. I wondered about how the world was set up, if folks really ever get second chances at happiness. My pop died, but now Mom had Bobby.

"Is it the same with Bobby as it was with Dad?" I asked.

"Well, it's good," she said. "But in a different way."

"How different?"

"Different because I'm different, older and wiser," she said. "Different because we're not kids, and we've both been batted around by life."

"But different is good?" I asked, sincerely wanting to know.

"Sure," she said. "We don't have the heat of a younger love. But maybe it's sweeter, because we know we don't have all the time in the world to enjoy it."

I nodded. That made sense. I'd been head over heels with Bill from the day we met, and he'd been the same way with me. Maybe I expected too much to hope for that again. It had been different with David. An early attraction, but I was more cautious. Maybe that wasn't bad. Maybe it was even understandable. But maybe that was why I'd lost him. The truth was that I'd never stopped thinking about David, but I had to accept that maybe the kind of love I had with Bill only comes once in a lifetime. The thought tasted bitter, but the cheesecake went down smooth and sweet. For just a little while, it masked the pain of remembering David driving away.

Twenty

Maggie wound her way upstairs to bed about nine, after we spent the evening rotating between Emma Lou's shed and Warrior's stall. Mom and Bobby were at the barbecue cook-off on the rodeo grounds, most likely mingling with friends, and, I hoped, working in a few swings across the dance floor. Mom had worn a denim skirt and a suede top with fringe. She loved to two-step. Thinking of the old days, I closed my eyes and imagined the feel of Bill's arm around my waist, the sway of our bodies across the dance floor, in unison yet apart. At its best, love was like two-stepping to a strong-beat country song. When the dance was good, two folks had someone to lean on and hold onto, someone who knew when the other needed space and when all a person wanted was to be loved.

I closed my eyes and thoughts of Bill faded as I remembered David's embrace, the smell of him, and the heat in his touch.

"Oh, heck," I thought, and minutes later I rooted through the fridge, where I discovered a second slice of armadillo cheesecake. "Gotta love Mom," I whispered. I grabbed a fork and the file on the top of the stack we'd seized from Billie Cox's office and made myself comfortable at the kitchen table. The lab had called earlier in the day, and the dirt on Billie's shoes was common in the Houston area, leading nowhere. I hoped the boxes of records proved more helpful. It turned into a long night. I combed through the files, inspecting each, skimming every page, without finding anything that appeared the least bit like evidence. Finally, I made my way down to Billie's expense reports and credit-card bills. I passed up the older docu-ments and started six months earlier, two months before Lena Suarez said she noticed "Miss Billie" going out more than usual.

What hit me right off was the size of the balance on Cox's plat-inum American Express card. It was paid off every thirty days but had a new balance in the twenty-thousand dollar range every month. Twenty grand a month on a credit card? When I thought about my paycheck, I felt embarrassed. For what must have been the tenth time that day, I thought about the price of gas and shook my head. Somehow I felt pretty sure I was getting ripped off at the pumps.

First, I took out a sheet of paper and charted where all the money was going. Judging by what she wore in the crime-scene photos, I wasn't surprised that a bunch went for clothes, at least three grand a month at Saks and Neiman Marcus. Maybe the woman didn't wear anything more than once? Then there were the classy restaurants, little French bistros and the fancy steak houses I'd read about in the newspaper but never been to. When it came to travel, Billie made short hops to Dallas, San Antonio, and Austin, a two-day trip to Midland and three days in Amarillo. She, of course, stayed at the best hotels. Many, I figured, were business expenses, reimbursed by Cen-tury Oil. I wondered what the captain would say if I used my expense account to hit a steak house in Dallas on Saturday, while I was there on the Collins case. I'd order a thick porterhouse, one of those wedge salads, asparagus, and a good glass of cabernet.

Nah, I thought. *That bird won't fly.*

A couple of hours into it, I had Cox's credit cards charted, and I pulled out her expense reports and bank statements. As I'd suspected, much of the Amex card was paid for by Century, including most of Billie's clothes, which surprised me. Maybe when one is the head of an oil company a chichi wardrobe is a fringe benefit? Since the company was privately owned, it wasn't illegal. If anyone had a right to complain, it was Carlton Wagner, but he'd approved and signed all the reports.

One check in Billie's bank statements caught my attention, written a month earlier to a geological consultant. For some reason, Billie had paid fifty grand to the guy out of her own money-market account, and I couldn't find an entry for it on any of her expense accounts. Why would Cox lay out those kinds of funds to pay for what appeared to be a business expense and not be reimbursed, unless she didn't want anyone, even Wagner, to know she'd hired the company?

I made notes on everything and put it into a file folder. The grandfather clock in the hallway struck midnight, and I decided to check on the horses and then go to bed. In the shed, Emma Lou was still awake, her eyes drooping and sad. She must have been exhausted. Mom said she'd hardly slept, just paced back and forth in the shed. I ran my hand over her long, muscular neck, and pushed her white mane to one side, then nuzzled up against her. "He'll be here soon, girl," I said. "You'll see. Warrior will be here soon."

In the stable, Warrior looked small and fragile. Maggie had fed him right before bed, but when he woke up and whinnied at me, I went inside, fixed a bottle, and sat with him while he slurped it up. He was undersized, that was true, but if the colt had as much thirst for life as he did for that bottle, he'd make it, I decided. I planned to go up to the house to bed, but instead I sat with the colt, on a pile of straw, thinking we'd keep each other company. Before long, his head lay on my lap, and we both drifted to sleep.

The next thing I remember I woke up and found David standing over me. It must have been morning, because daylight filled the stable, but Warrior was still asleep, his narrow head on my lap.

I thought at first that I might be dreaming, but then David knelt down, pulled a piece of straw out of my hair, and dropped it on the shed floor. He had the saddest look in his eyes, as if he saw me from very far away. He gazed at me longingly and brushed his hand over my cheek. Then he leaned forward and pulled me close, wrapping me in his strong arms. He felt as inviting as I remembered. His lips gentle, he kissed me long and hard, hungry, and the feelings I remembered from a year earlier, the ones I'd fought so unsuccessfully to bury, stirred.

"I shouldn't have done that," he said, when our lips finally parted.

"No? Why not?" I said. "Tell me why not."

David said nothing, and I pulled him toward me, and this time I kissed him. His body responded, yielded. He held me and returned every bit of my passion. Then, suddenly, Warrior jostled awake, and David pulled away, jolting up to his feet.

To my disappointment, he ran the back of his hand over his lips, wiping away all evidence of my kiss.

"Doc Larson is up at the house with Maggie and your mom. They'll be here any minute," he said, his face flushed. Why did he pull away? "They were looking for you. I said I'd check the stable."

"Lucky you found me," I said. "Lately, I've been wondering if you saw me at all. It's good to know that I haven't disappeared."

"Sarah, you are without exception the most . . . ," he started but didn't finish. Instead he grabbed my hands and brought me to my feet. As soon as I was upright, he let go and concentrated on removing the bits of straw that covered his pant legs and shoes. He brushed at his clothes, and said, "We can't let them find us like this."

My jeans and T-shirt were covered, and I picked off the larger bits, just as my family and Doc Larson bustled into the stable.

"We were looking for you, Sarah," Mom said. "Why did you sleep out here?"

"Just keeping Warrior company," I said. Maggie stared, first at me, then at David. Attempting to distract her, I asked, "So, what's the verdict?"

Doc had a grin that gave away the news before he spoke a word. "It's high time Warrior's momma gets to know the little fella," he said. "No more of that damn bacteria. Let's introduce the colt to Emma Lou. Let them spend a bit of quality time together."

Minutes later, we had Warrior moved into Emma Lou's shed. The colt was done with the bottles and enjoying the real thing, courtesy of the mare who looked, if a horse can, proud as a new momma. As we stood and watched, I slipped my hand into David's, but, to my disappointment, he pulled his away.

"I have a summary of the Internet reports on the Collins case I'd like to share with you," he said. "Let's take them to the picnic table, and I'll show you what our lab guys sorted out."

Trying to hide my disappointment, I nodded. On the way to the corral, I ducked into the kitchen, poured two cups of coffee, grabbed a breath mint, and then met him at the picnic table.

"Are you going to explain to me what's going on?" I asked, once we were alone again. "That wasn't the kiss of a man who's lost interest."

David took a long sip of his coffee, and then frowned at me. "Sarah, we made a mistake last time, allowing ourselves to mix our personal lives in with our work," he said. "I don't want to make that mistake again."

"Is that really it?" I asked. I wasn't convinced. Last time, during the Lucas case, we'd never let our attraction to each other get in the way of the investigation. It never became an issue. What was different now?

"That's it," he said, looking me squarely in the eyes. "Now, let's talk about these Internet records."

An hour later, he'd walked me through a complicated maze of e-mail addresses and text message records that traced a pattern across the country, leaving no clues to where they originated. "This Argus knows how to work the Web," David said. "Our computer lab guys have been working on this night and day without a break since I joined the case. They haven't uncovered a single clue to where the text messages and e-mails are coming from."

"Pretty disappointing," I said.

"Yeah," he said. "I know."

"Well then, we go ahead as planned," I suggested. "We leave for Dallas this afternoon and do our best."

"What about Justin Peterson?" he asked. "Have you totally ruled that kid out as a suspect?"

"No," I said. "The captain has two undercover squads on duty tonight to keep track of him. Since he's our only suspect, I'm not ready to walk away yet."

When I'd poured the coffee, I'd also retrieved the bag of teen magazines I'd bought at the convenience store. "David, we've got four hours before the chopper takes off, and I've got some research to do," I said. "If there's nothing more you're ready to talk to me about, I guess you'd better leave. I'll meet you at the airport at one."

He looked at me for a moment but said nothing. Got up and left. Afterward, I thought about that kiss. I didn't believe for a minute his reluctance was about work. Something was going on with that man, but I had too much on my plate at the moment to spend a bunch of time trying to figure it out.

Twenty-one

Our chopper landed at a heliport in downtown Dallas late that afternoon, on the roof of the convention center. Dallas P.D. had an unmarked squad car waiting, and David and I were at the redbrick-and-granite American Airlines Center minutes later, where we were summarily ushered through a side door. To my great frustration, the only thing I'd accomplished on the Cox case before leaving the ranch that morning was a quick phone conversation with the geologist who'd run the study. He confirmed that Billie paid for the work personally.

"It was kind of a strange deal. Am I going to get in trouble for this?" he asked. "I knew I was on someone else's land. Cox told me, but she was paying a bucket of money for such a small study. I've got a kid in college, and I couldn't pass it up."

"I'm not interested in a trespassing charge," I assured him. "This is a murder investigation. Just tell me how Miss Cox explained paying for the study on her own."

"I offered to invoice the company, but she said not to. She said she didn't want anyone to know about the work I'd done," he said.

"I thought it was really strange when she said especially the folks at her company, Century Oil. Part of the money was payment for keeping my mouth shut."

I couldn't help wondering, *why?*

Outside the arena, I'd noticed a tour bus near the freight entrance, bright pink with butterflies and Cassidy Collins's name scrolled across the sides, surrounded by uniformed Dallas P.D. officers. Inside the lobby, our heels clicked on terrazzo floors, and sweeping arched windows framed the city's ultramodern skyline. We had four hours until the concert, and in the arena proper all remained dark except a stage in the center of what was usually the Mavericks' basketball court.

"Where's the superstar?" I asked the Dallas P.D. sergeant who guided us in.

"The kid's on the bus," he said. "She's supposed to be here any minute for a sound check. That Barron guy, her security head, said to wait here."

With that, the sergeant left to make sure the equipment was in place for the door searches. Despite our instructions to stay put, David and I trekked down an aisle toward the stage, into a frenzy of activity. We'd already been informed that since she was playing in a sports stadium, not a traditional theater with all the equipment, Collins couldn't put on her whole show. The arena didn't have trapdoors to raise her up from below the stage or rafters to anchor her flying harness, so, both here and in Houston, there'd be no gold cocoon or Peter Pan act. Instead the Dallas set consisted of a rather spartan round stage ringed with footlights and a canopy of spotlights. Still, there appeared to be a lot to do, and last-minute checks were being done by a crew who all seemed preoccupied with the smallest details. As we drew near, we were abruptly stopped.

"Stage passes?" a man in a golf shirt and jeans with an identification card dangling around his neck demanded. The guy must

have been six-foot-five, the muscles in his arms bulging like a professional bodybuilder's.

I opened my black suit-jacket, flashing my badge, while David
flipped his wallet open to display his, and the guy nodded. "Mr.
Barron is expecting you," he said. "I'll let him know you're waiting."

"Boss, that Texas Ranger is here," Muscles said into a walkie-
talkie the size of a cell phone. "The one you said to be on the look-
out for, and a guy with an FBI badge."

"On my way," the answer crackled back.

"Show me how the audio's fed into Miss Collins's earphones," I
asked. Muscles nodded and led the way as we circled below the re-
volving stage. All around us workers double-checked electrical con-
nections and repositioned props. Muscles stopped in front of three
black tents set up on one side of the stage. Flaps were open, and inside
I saw the kid's wardrobe changes lined up on metal clothes racks and
a fully stocked hair-and-makeup station. In the third tent, Muscles
pointed out the mixer desk, a black panel the size of a small pickup
truck bed, lit up like a passenger jet cockpit.

"Meet our audio guy, Jake," he said. Jake, a kid adorned with
silver earrings, two chin piercings, and a backward baseball cap,
nodded, paying no more attention, everything focused on what he
heard through his headset. Just then another mammoth of a man
walked toward us, as immense as Muscles but dressed in a tie-less
suit with narrow-framed sunglasses dangling from his unbuttoned
shirt collar. He had one of those tanning-bed tans, unnaturally even,
and brown hair bleached blond at the tips.

"Rick Barron," he said. We shook hands, and I introduced
David. "We're glad you both came. Cassidy has been frantic waiting for you, Lieutenant. She should be here in a few minutes," Barron said. "But I want to review things with you first. Is everything
set up, all the arrangements we discussed on the telephone?"

"Everything," I said. "The search dogs are on their way to sweep the arena. The scanners are all in place at the doors. I assume you have the monitors I requested, to allow us to listen in on Miss Collins's audio feed?"

"Yes," he said. "And the recording device you suggested is hooked into the sound system, to record Argus's voice if he breaks in again."

"Great," I said. "My understanding is that David and I will be positioned in this tent with your audio person."

"Yeah," Barron said. "It was Cassidy's decision. She wants to be able to see you from the stage."

"That's right, because I want you close," a young voice said from behind. I turned and found Cassidy Collins, looking younger in person and without makeup than she did on the magazine covers, walking toward us. "I want to know you're there, because if that Argus dude makes a move, you need to be close."

"Cassidy, I was just explaining . . ." Barron interrupted.

"Yeah, I heard," she said.

"As I gather you know, I'm Lieutenant Armstrong," I said, holding out my hand to greet the kid. Whether or not she was going to show some manners, I was. "And this is Agent Garrity, with the FBI. They're assisting us on this case."

"That's great," Collins said, not even acknowledging my extended hand. "I don't care how many cops you need. Bring in everybody. It's cool with me. I want to get out of this stupid state alive. You need to get this creep outta my face. Understand?"

"That is, of course, our goal," David said. At the moment, I was too annoyed to speak.

"Great, then we're all in sync," she said. "I'm headed onto the stage for the sound check. Lady Cop, when I'm done, you come with me to the bus. Make sure you've got your gun."

"It's right here," I said, patting my blazer. I didn't tell her who I

fantasized scaring with that gun, but instead said what was bound
to be the first in a long line of such corrections, "But the name is
Lieutenant Sarah Armstrong, not Lady Cop."

"That's great," she said. "I'll call you Sarah."

"I'd rather you didn't," I started.

"Be here when I get back, Sarah," she said. Ignoring my objec-
tion, she turned her back and quickly clambered up the wooden
ramp that led to the stage.

Frowning at David, I put on a headset Jake handed me, and the
audio started. David did the same, and within a few moments
Collins's backup band kicked in. They ran through a few bars of a
song I didn't recognize, and then Collins began to sing. All I could
hear through the headset were the drums and backup singers. I motioned for Barron.

"Something's wrong," I said. "I can't hear everything."

"You're hearing what you asked for, what Cassie hears. That's a
feed off her monitor," he said. "Jake can plug in anything she wants,
but all she likes are the drums and vocals, to keep her on time and
in tune."

"Oh," I said. "Got it."

David nodded at me and shook his head, and I figured he felt as
out of place as I did. By then the dogs had arrived, and we could see
them circulating with their handlers through the boxes and seats.
"You can live your life, just do it right," Cassie sang.

Sure, I thought, my mind sarcastically adding, if right is to be a
spoiled brat. I gave up on that thought, concentrating on the dogs
scouting the American Airlines Center and keeping track of the goings on around the stage. I didn't know any of the folks in the arena,
but everyone seemed comfortable, like they belonged. The sound
check went without a hitch, except for one time, for some unknown
reason, when Collins snarled at the prop manager. He groaned and

whispered a rather colorful string of expletives as he walked past me. Moments later, Collins clomped down from the stage, motioning toward me. I sighed, handed my headphones to David, and we were off.

Inside the bus was dressed to the nines, as Mom likes to say, posh furniture covered in taupe suede and granite countertops in the small kitchen. Collins had a bedroom at the rear, which she lost no time in disappearing into the moment we entered the bus, slamming the door behind her. A plump woman dressed in black leggings and a big sweater introduced herself as Germaine Dunn, Cassie's stylist, and apologized for the kid.

"Cassie's been under a lot of pressure," Dunn said. "Don't take it personally."

"To take it personally, I have to assume she realizes I'm a person," I said. "That doesn't appear to be the situation."

Dunn let loose a hoarse, gruff, cigarette laugh. Her red-and-banana-yellow-streaked hair seemed to fit her come-what-may demeanor. The woman was so laid back, I figured it would take an elephant crashing through the trailer roof to surprise her. Still, her face was well lined, like she'd experienced more than her share of life's disappointments.

"That girl always so polite?" I asked.

"No," Dunn said. "She's got on her best manners because she likes you." I laughed, and then she went on. "Cassidy's really not a bad kid, Lieutenant. I think most of the tough stuff is an act. She can be really sweet. She's just been kicked around a lot in life, and she's scared right now, more than she'd admit."

"I can understand that," I said. "So what happens now?"

"Cassidy rests for about an hour, gets up and eats a burger and fries, and then the dressers come in and get her ready for her performance," she said.

"Okay. You're secure here with the guards outside. I'm heading back to the arena. I'll pop in later to escort her to the stage."

"No," Germaine snapped, looking alarmed. "Like I said, Cassie's scared. She'll freak if you're not here. The kid may act tough, but she really is spooked. We promised the world to get her here. We told her that you and the other cops would protect her, no matter what."

That's great, I thought. *No pressure here.*

I considered what had to be done inside the stadium and reasoned the others had it covered. To make sure, I called David. Once he reassured me that everything was on schedule, I took my jacket off, claimed the seat opposite the stylist's, slumped back into the chair, and stretched out my legs, one gray lizard-skin cowboy boot propped up on the other. With all the commotion at the ranch, I hadn't had a bunch of sleep lately. There was enough security in the surrounding area to protect a president, so I figured I was entitled. That was before I looked over at Dunn and thought maybe there was a better way to spend my time.

"So tell me about the superstar," I said. "Anything you think I should know."

"Well, since you asked, like I said, you have to give the kid a break, Lieutenant," she said. "Cassie acts tough, but she's just a sixteen-year-old who's lived the life from hell."

"Yeah," I scoffed. I'd read all the celeb rags, with pictures of the mansion and Cassidy standing in her closet, the size of my living room. "I guess a fortune to spend any way she wants and the adoration of millions can be tiring."

The woman smacked her lips in disapproval. "That may be how she's living, but that's not Cassie. I don't know a lot about the kid, she keeps her past to herself, but my impression is she came from nothing, no money, no one to rely on. I know her mom died, and I haven't heard her mention a father," Dunn explained. "The only thing that made a difference was that Cassidy could sing. No one gave that girl a free ride. She's had to scrape for everything. That tends to make most kids a bit harsh."

"Tough breaks," I said. "Hard way to grow up. So she doesn't have any family?"

"I don't think so. If she does, I've never heard about or met any of them," Dunn said. "I guess all of us, the crew, we're the closest she has to a family, but even with us, she keeps a distance."

I nodded. "Have you got any theories about this stalker, this Argus?" I asked.

"Wish I did," she said. "Cassie's hard enough to work with on a good day. All this going on, she's a volcano."

"Have you ever heard his voice? Seen any of the text messages or e-mails?"

"Never heard him, but Rick showed the e-mails to me," she said. "At first I wasn't too worried. I figured he was just another kook. But the guy hasn't given up. He's obsessed with her."

"Where'd Cassidy grow up?" I asked.

"Somewhere in northern California, I think," Dunn said. "She told me once that when her mom died, she took the little money they had and grabbed a bus for L.A., figuring she'd get a job singing. She was eleven. Somehow she made it to the city with a couple of hundred bucks that some teenage thug stole from her. She lived on the street until a woman figured out the kid didn't have a home and took her to CPS. From there, she went to her first foster home, and then on to the next. That's pretty much the whole story."

Listening to Dunn, I was starting to feel my disdain for the kid melt away. Maybe I was being too harsh. Still, she'd do well to work on her attitude.

About then, there was a knock at the door and Barron came in.

"Looks good out there," he said to me, and then he turned to Dunn. "Germaine, we've got a group of kids from one of those special schools who want to see Cassie. Five girls, oldest about fourteen. I'm going to keep them outside. When she's up, shout at me."

"Will do," Dunn agreed.

Barron left, and I picked up a magazine and leafed through it. I called home and checked on everyone at the ranch. So far, so good. Warrior was eating well and Emma Lou had calmed down now that she had her foal close. Strings was over with his guitar, and he and Maggie were in the shed singing for the horses. Wish I'd been there. That must have been a sight.

Ninety minutes before the concert, a delivery service brought Cassie's hamburger and fries, and Dunn knocked on the kid's bedroom door. She did that twice, then went in and woke her, reminding me of trying to get Maggie up on a Saturday morning, when she figured she could sleep in.

Cassidy came out with her long blond hair piled on top her head wearing a torn-off T-shirt and jeans, and plopped down in an armchair. She said nothing, just tore into the burger and fries like she hadn't had a meal in a month.

"Have a good nap?" I asked.

"Sarah, I don't really like to talk when I'm just waking up," she said. "So cool the questions, okay?"

"We discussed this. I prefer being called Lieutenant Armstrong," I said, giving the kid one of my narrow-eyed stares.

"Yeah," she said, with a disinterested shrug. "I remember you said something about that, Sarah."

Figuring it was a lost cause, I let it go. I'd be on my way soon and the kid would be someone else's problem. No percentage in arguing. As soon as the hamburger was devoured, Germaine went to the door and called out for Rick Barron. The kids had been waiting outside, on a cool day, two of them without jackets, for nearly an hour. They were so excited that I bet they hadn't even felt the chill. One of the girls appeared to have Down's syndrome, and the others looked as if they had various degrees of cerebral palsy. I thought maybe there was hope for Cassidy Collins when she got up to greet them, an I'm-excited-to-see-you grin spread across her face.

"I'm so, so sorry I kept you waiting. You need to come inside where it's warm," she said, and the girls did, climbing into the bus, where they stood shyly, most with hands folded behind their backs. One of the girls tried to talk, but her speech was too broken to understand. The woman who accompanied them translated: "She'd like you to know that they're all big fans, Miss Collins."

"I'm so honored that they like my music," Cassie said. "I don't get a lot of chances to meet other kids. It's really fun to have them here."

"Fun for us, too," the girl with Down's syndrome said. "Wait til we tell our friends. They won't believe us."

"I can take care of that," Cassie said, winking conspiratorially. As if on cue, Dunn handed Cassie five copies of the same head shot Barron had sent me with her file. She asked each girl's name, and wrote a personal message, finishing off with swirled autographs and hand-drawn butterflies. When they left, Cassie stood at the doorway and waved at them. I thought maybe she wasn't such a bad kid after all, until the door slammed behind her and she stalked back onto the bus.

"Glad the freak show's over," she said. "Okay, Germaine. I'm ready for hair and makeup."

If I'd had any right to, any at all, at that point I would have straightened that kid out. A month or two on house arrest, time to reconsider her attitude, would have done wonders for her.

"Great," Dunn said. "Take your shower, and I'll get everything ready."

———

For the next hour, Cassidy Collins was the center of everyone's attention, especially Germaine and a clutch of assistants. Once the kid emerged from the shower, she was powdered and dressed, her hair curled and arranged.

"How do we get into the arena?" Dunn asked me.

"I've arranged to have a Dallas P.D. officer in a limo drive us through the freight entrance and up to the gangway," I explained. "Even though this is a secure area, we can't take any chances."

Dunn nodded. "That'll help with the paparazzi, too. They swarm around Cassie like mosquitoes sucking blood. But when the right photo or video, especially one embarrassing to the kid, can fetch up to a million bucks, you can't keep them away. Sometimes I think every minute of that kid's life is recorded by someone for a fast buck."

"A million bucks?" I repeated.

Dunn nodded and her chemically enhanced mop bobbed with her.

Everything from that point went off as scripted. The limo showed up with an officer who immediately asked for Cassidy's autograph for his daughter. Smiling sweetly, she complied, and we were escorted into the arena. We headed to the sound tent where David waited. He handed me my headset, and we listened, while on the stage, fireworks exploded and Cassie sang her opening song dressed in a pink sequined minidress, black boots, and leggings.

In the audience, young girls, a smattering accompanied by one parent or another, screamed, some crying, dancing and singing along. Others reached out toward their idol. The stage rotated, giving everyone a view of the superstar, and Cassie sang and danced, accompanied by three backup singers and four male dancers. Every couple of numbers she rushed back down the ramp past us and into the wardrobe tent, and while the band covered for her, the dressers swarmed around her. She emerged once dressed like a cheerleader and another time a hippie from the seventies, in a flowered minidress and platforms. An hour into the show, David and I hadn't heard or seen anything alarming. Then, while Cassie was singing a pop ballad with the verse *"livin' the dream ain't all it seems, when at heart you're a regular girl,"* the sound system in the entire arena died.

"What's up?" David asked.

"Jake?" I said, turning to the sound guy.

Panicking as he looked at his dark panel, not a single light glowing, Jake shrugged.

I turned back to find Collins peering down at me, trembling with fear and looking as vulnerable as a little kid. I motioned for her to come down, but she stood there, frozen. I ran up the ramp, and, just as I reached the edge of the stage, a man's voice boomed throughout the arena. Without hesitation, I grabbed Collins by the arm and pulled her toward me.

"Cassidy, I'm here," the voice said, sounding tinny, unnatural. "I promised I'd come for you, and I have."

She stopped, searched the auditorium, staring out into the crowd.

"Come on," I screamed, urging her forward. "Let's go! Now!"

The audience laughed and twittered. Few appeared frightened, and I saw no panic, no one running. The girls in the front rows reached out, grabbed at us and screamed out Cassie's name.

"I'm here for you, Cassidy," the man's voice warned, booming through the stadium sound system, and then a horrible, taunting laugh. "You know what I'll do."

I yanked Cassie harder, this time getting enough of her

attention to force her down off the stage. We ran toward the gang-way where the limo waited as the horrible voice jeered, "You're mine, Cassidy Collins. Anytime I want you, you're mine."

David followed. He pushed Cassidy into the limo, while I watched, gun drawn. We jumped in with her, and the limo took off, gunning the engine to speed us away from the arena. When the driver started to circle back to Cassie's bus, she panicked. "That's the first place he'll look for me. Get me out of here."

"Ms. Collins, we're here to protect you, until we can get you to the airport," I started.

"No!" she screamed. "He's here. Get me out of here, now!"

"Drive us downtown, to the convention center," I told the uni-formed officer behind the wheel.

"Where are we going?" he asked.

"The heliport," I said, as David shot me a questioning glance. "We have a helicopter waiting."

At the convention center, we drove into the back service en-trance and then ran inside where we took an elevator to the roof. We jumped aboard the chopper, and the pilot started the engine. Within minutes we hovered over Dallas, the vast city lights glow-ing beneath us.

"Where now?" David asked, looking more than a little con-cerned that I'd taken an unwise detour. "You do realize that we can't fly her to Los Angeles?"

"I'm not going home," she said. "I can't. He knows where I live. He'll be there."

"You have a whole security force to protect you," I said.

"Yeah, and it hasn't helped. That guy knows where I am every minute. He knows who I'm with, even if the drapes are closed on my bedroom at night. He knows how to find me, anytime he wants me," she said. "I'm *not* going back there. I need to disappear. Sarah,

I'm staying with you until you cops make sure I'm safe. I'm not leaving your side, until that guy's in jail or better yet dead."

"Whoa, now. Let's take some time and figure this out," I said. Having the superstar attached to my hip didn't sound like a particularly good idea. I'd been looking forward to our parting. "While we're thinking, we'll head to the airport in Houston. You're safe for now. The best option is for us to get you a private plane, or wait with you there for yours to fly in."

"No!" she screamed, tears streaming from her eyes. "I'm telling you, I'm not going home. I won't be safe. I won't."

This wasn't going particularly well, not as I'd envisioned it. I was up for getting the kid out of Dallas, but not for living with her for the duration.

"We could bring her to a hotel room, keep her there," I suggested.

"Too many people," David said. "You've got desk clerks, maids, waiters, probably a hundred employees, plus all the guests in a big hotel. Everyone knows her face. Word will be out in no time."

"We need someplace secluded," I said. "Quiet. Someplace we can keep her while we figure out where to stash her and give ourselves time to catch this guy."

"That's what I'm saying," Collins pleaded. "Just until I'm safe. I can't go home. I really can't. I don't know who this creep is. Maybe it's that Peterson dude, but maybe it's not. Argus could even be someone on my crew. All I know is he wants to kill me."

I thought about it, but I didn't want to. We'd been through enough, and I didn't need to drop this mixed-up teenager with the big mouth on Mom and Maggie. But I honestly didn't know where else to go. "Okay, give me everything electronic you have on you," I said, holding out my hand.

"Why?" she asked.

"Because this guy is into technology. That's how he's stalking you, and maybe that's how he's tracking you."

She took off her earphones and mike and handed them to me. She wore her getup from the last number, a skimpy white gauze top and skintight jeans, yet she'd somehow managed to conceal an envelope-thin cell phone in a belt.

"You carry a phone on stage?" David asked.

"Just since that schizo started stalking me," she answered. "I thought, well, I was afraid I might need it."

"Anything else?" I asked.

From another pocket, she pulled out a small device with a keypad. "For text messages," she said. "I figured it was backup, in case I didn't have the phone or he found someway to make it not work."

I nudged the pilot's shoulders, and he looked back. He worked for the department of public safety, and he'd flown me before. My guess is he was used to my bizarre requests. "Can I open a door or window?" I asked. "I need to dump these, in case we're being tracked."

He nodded. "But we're going to have to slow way down. We don't want anything sucked into one of the rotors."

"Okay," I said. "Tell us when."

We were south of Dallas, traveling about a hundred mph, and the pilot pulled back until we hovered over the lights of what appeared to be a small town, and then over near-total darkness, most likely a farmer's field.

"Okay, quick, or I'll lose lift," the pilot said. "Seat belts on?"

We all double-checked. "Yeah," I said. "All buckled in."

He hit a button, and the window on the door next to me eased open, stopping when I had a clearance of a few inches. The cold night air swept through the chopper's cabin. Winter cold. I dropped Cassie's phone, text device, and everything else out the window, but one earpiece flew back in. I threw it out again and watched it fall, disappearing in the shadows.

"Hang on," the pilot said. The window shut, and he built up speed, pulling up.

"Okay. Now, where are we going?" he asked.

"My ranch," I said. "It's north of Houston. I'll give you directions when we get close."

"Sarah, I'm not sure that's a good idea," David said, shooting me one of his worried glances.

"Unless you've got another idea, I can't think of anyplace else," I said. "Let's just keep her there overnight. We'll figure out what to do and have her out by morning. I'll call the captain and have the ranch flooded with state troopers and rangers before we set down."

"Okay," David said, still looking uncertain. "But just until morning."

The kid, uncharacteristically, said nothing, only stared out into the night, perhaps wondering where Argus was and if he'd find a way to follow.

I called the captain at home, woke him up out of a dead sleep to fill him in, and he said he'd get right on it, sending three of my fellow rangers and a squad of DPS troopers out to the ranch to guard us for the night. By morning, he promised, he'd figure out another plan and make the spoiled superstar someone else's problem.

Two hours later, we circled over the Rocking Horse's back pasture, the pilot looking for a place to put down. When we finally landed, he turned off the engine, and made us wait until the blades stopped before opening the door. Once he did, David jumped out, and then I did. We turned to help Collins from the helicopter, while the small crowd that peered at us from the dark perimeter ran toward us. Mom, Maggie, our stable hand, Frieda, the captain, and three rangers, including Buckshot, quickly surrounded us.

"Sarah, what's going on?" Mom asked. "The captain only told us you were on your way, not why."

"Cassidy Collins?" Maggie shrieked, her face a mixture of shock and excitement. "Is that Cassidy Collins?"

I braced myself for the kid to spout a smart retort, figuring that her brain had to be flipping through a list of tart comebacks, but all she did was nod at Maggie, and then start to cry, the tears flooding her cheeks. I put my arm around her, and we all walked back to the house together. It had been one heck of a night. All I kept telling myself was that the morning would be better.

Twenty-two

I fell asleep on the living room couch and woke up at daybreak to find David and the captain on their cell phones pacing Mom's dining room, the scent of jasmine in the air and her white lace curtains fluttering in the breeze from an open window. I ran my hands through my hair, wiped the sleep out of my eyes, thought about a shower but hung around long enough for the captain to get off the telephone to ask, "What do we know about where Justin Peterson was last night?"

"He's not our guy," he said. "We had him under surveillance all night long. He did his usual, dinner at a place near the university and then home early. His lights went out about ten-thirty, and we had two cars on him the whole time. Neither saw him leave. Of course, by then the concert was over anyway."

"What did Dallas P.D. and our guys find at the American Airlines Center? What kind of clues do we have?"

"Struck out there, too," David said. "The sound folks insist Argus had to be in the arena to do what he did. He had to cut into the frequency to take over the sound system. But anyone who looked the least bit suspicious was searched exiting. Nothing was found. And his voice was electronically distorted. It's useless."

"Great," I said. "Any more good news?"

"Your mom's baking," David said. "It was a rough night."

Sighing, I shrugged and shook my head. I stumbled like the living dead to the kitchen where I found Mom, just as David described, wrist deep in bread dough, kneading it like she could beat down all our problems. Every inch of counter was covered with cake pans, muffin tins, cookie sheets, and all manner of fresh baked goods. If Bobby Barker calmed Mom down enough to keep her from heading to the ovens, my shenanigans had driven her to the spatulas, eggs, nonstick baking spray, and flour. Luckily, I wasn't the only one on the premises to feed. We had a battalion of cops patrolling the property, all dressed in civvies and acting like ranch hands, tending to the stock. Still, if anyone looked too closely they might see gun bulges under their work shirts.

"I have blueberry, cranberry, and banana-nut muffins, iced coffee cake, and four kinds of bread, including your favorite cheese and jalapeño," Mom said, whacking the ball of dough in her hands back down onto the wooden cutting board. "You can have any and all for breakfast. Right now, I'm working on braided egg bread for lunch. I'm thinking chicken salad sandwiches."

"You don't have to feed everyone, Mom," I assured her. "The captain will send out for food. He doesn't expect you to do this."

"They're our guests, Sarah," she said. "Besides, you know this helps me settle down when things are, well, stressful."

"Okay," I said. "Hand me a cranberry muffin, and I'll put on fresh coffee. I have no doubt that if we've accomplished nothing else, you've done enough work here to get nominated as Ranger Mother of the Year."

"There's an award like that?" Mom said. She looked at me, and then broke into a nearly hysterical laugh. I slipped my arms around her and gave her a long hug.

"I love you, Mom," I said.

"I love you, too, dear," she answered, but then she frowned, a look I knew only too well. Mom was far from happy. "Sometimes being your mother brings adventure into my life. I have lady friends who yearn for excitement, but a lot of this I'd pass on if anyone gave me the option."

"That I can't argue," I said. "But we'll have the superstar out of here this morning and you can go back to baking cheesecake for the paying customers."

"Sounds good," she said, but then she thought about that and said, "You know, I do feel sorry for that girl. Where will she go?"

I wasn't surprised. Mom's heart was always a bit too soft. Plus, I didn't have an answer. The captain walked in and it appeared he did, but not one I was going to like. "We've kind of hit a wall there, Mrs. Potts," he said. "Agent Garrity and I have been working on it all night. That kid's face is too well known. We're afraid to move her. Someone's bound to spot her, and once that happens, the paparazzi will swoop in and we don't have a heartbeat's chance of hiding her. Sarah's decision to bring her here was a good one. It's our best option."

That wasn't what I wanted to hear. "Captain, may I talk to you in the living room?" I asked. He nodded and followed. David was still in the room, and I didn't mince words. "You can't keep that kid here. Absolutely not. This was a stopgap measure to cover last night. Nothing more. Having her here puts Mom and Maggie in danger. Cassidy Collins needs to leave."

"We understand that, Sarah," David said. He looked tired and worried. "But the captain's telling you the truth. We've talked with everyone at the FBI and ranger headquarters who could help, and they've all come up dry. We don't have a safe house we can get her to without her being noticed. It's too risky. Her face is too well known. If we move her, someone is going to recognize that kid. We can't take that chance."

"You're not listening to me," I said. "I will not have my family in harm's way. It's not an option."

"Now hold on, Sarah," the captain said, putting up his hands as if blocking a blow. "We're not suggesting you do that. We've come up with another alternative."

"Another alternative, other than sending that smart-mouthed kid somewhere else? You expect me to believe there's another option, one that doesn't put my family in jeopardy?"

"Yes," David urged. "Give the captain a chance."

Doubtful, I put my hands on my hips and waited. "Okay," I said. "You've got my full attention."

"We're moving Maggie and your mother to another location," the captain said. "All the arrangements are already made. They're getting a vacation, kind of, all at the taxpayers' expense."

"Tomorrow is Monday. Maggie has school, and Mom has the ranch to run," I said. "Where are you planning to send them? Disney World?"

"Just through tomorrow evening, Sarah, and this will all be over. Collins will be on her way back to California," he said. "Right after the girl performs at the rodeo."

Now that really threw me. I couldn't believe anyone thought Collins would be appearing in Houston anytime soon. "You think anyone will come to see that kid at the rodeo, knowing some whack job might show up and try to kill her?" I asked. "After what happened in Dallas? It must be all over the newspapers."

"It is," David said. "And on the Internet. But Collins's public relations machine stepped in and spun it, started rumors that what happened was part of Collins's act, a publicity stunt to get the kids in the audience stirred up. It worked so well that a Houston radio station started a 'Find Cassidy Collins Contest' with tickets to her rodeo concert tomorrow night as the prize. Unfortunately, that wasn't exactly what we were hoping for. We didn't particularly want teenagers all over Houston looking for the kid, hoping to be the first to post her location online."

"The PR folks convinced the press that this whole thing is a game?" I scoffed. "How could anyone believe that, when she ran off the stage and didn't finish the act?"

"Well, we caught a break. It all happened near the end of her performance. The timing worked," David said. "With a little prodding from her spin guys, yeah, her fans and the press believe it was all a ruse, just an exciting way to get Collins off the stage and start a worldwide publicity campaign."

"Okay, so the fans will come. I understand. But you can't think that kid's going to perform? After last night?" I asked.

"We're hoping to have the SOB in custody by the time the kid's supposed to walk on the stage at the rodeo," David said. "If that doesn't happen, we need her to perform to draw him out in the open. Our plan is to use Collins's rodeo performance to lure him and we're hoping he'll drop his guard. This time, we'll be prepared."

"What are you going to do that we didn't do in Dallas?" I asked.

At this point, it appeared neither one of the two men wanted to take the lead. I had a feeling they didn't want to admit they hadn't planned that far in advance. "We've got a mess of people looking into that," the captain said. "When the time comes, we'll be ready."

"That's fine, but don't involve my family," I protested. "I want that girl out of here this morning. I won't disrupt Maggie and Mom. I can't. Not after last year."

"It's okay, Mom," a small voice said behind me. When I turned around, Maggie stood listening, and I figured she'd heard much of the argument. "If Cassidy Collins needs help, Gram and I can move for a couple of days. Only thing is, Captain, I can't go to Florida, even if it is Disney World. I need to take Warrior and Emma Lou with me."

"No, Maggie," David said. He shook his head, and moved toward her, reached out and put his hands on my daughter's slim shoulders. She looked up at him, as he smiled reassuringly down at her. "I'm sorry, but there's no way you can take the horses," he said. "That's just not possible."

An injured look flashed across her young face, and David didn't appear surprised. He must have understood that for Maggie, leaving Warrior was unthinkable. "I know this is difficult, but we're in a bad situation. Our priority is to keep Cassidy Collins and you and your grandmother safe," he explained. "The best way to do that is what we've worked out for the next couple of days, keeping Cassidy here on the ranch and checking you and your grandmother into a suite at a downtown hotel. You'll be registered under assumed names, as our guests, until Cassidy Collins leaves for California."

"But what about Warrior? He needs us right now," Maggie said. "He's so little."

"Most of the rangers helping out on the ranch have horses, and they'll help your mom watch over him. And in a pinch, we can call Doc Larson," David said, his manner calm. "Maggie, it's really for the best. Warrior is so young, barely two days old. You wouldn't want to risk moving him, would you?"

"David, I don't think this is a good idea," I interrupted.

"No. He's right, Mom," Maggie said, being very brave. She looked up at David again, this time with a sad acceptance. "You'll all be here to take care of the horses. It'll be okay. And the hotel could be fun. Gram and I could get room service and watch television and movies."

"Tomorrow morning, you'll call her school and tell them Maggie's sick," the captain said. "We can get her teachers to give us her books and the day's assignments. Tuesday morning, she'll be back in class."

"It's all right with me, too," Mom said, standing in the doorway. "That Collins girl needs help, Sarah. Maggie and I will be all right. Frieda will help you look after the horses."

"Frieda should go to the hotel, too," the captain said. "It's safest if she's with you and Maggie at the hotel."

"Are you sure?" I asked Maggie, and then looked over at Mom. "Are you positive you're both okay with this?"

"I'm sure," Maggie said. "I don't want anything to happen to Cassidy. I really don't. And I trust you and Mr. Garrity to take care of Warrior."

"I'm sure, too, Sarah," Mom said.

"It's settled then," the captain said. "Can you be ready to go in an hour?"

"I'll get the car packed," Mom said.

"No, the chopper is still out in the pasture. It'll take you," he said. "Just pack your bags. We'll tell Frieda to pack hers, and we'll fly you out of here, so we're sure you're not followed. You'll land in downtown Houston, and there'll be a limo waiting. We're hoping to spoil you ladies a bit, to try to make up for the inconvenience."

"What'll I tell Bobby?" Mom asked. "We were going to the barbecue cook-off again this afternoon."

"Call and tell him you had to go visit a sick relative, Mrs. Potts," the captain suggested. "It's safer if no one knows where you are. We booked a large, three-bedroom suite, and you'll have two officers with you at all times. We're not taking any chances."

"Okay," Mom said. "I'll call Bobby right away."

"No," the captain said. "Not from the ranch. From here on out, no one uses the house phone or your old cell phones. We have new cell phones for all of you, just for the duration."

Mom looked at me, alarmed. "Well, is that really necessary? Can't I make a few phone calls?"

"Not if we're doing this, Mom," I said. "You and Maggie are under guard and secluded until it's over. Just call Bobby on the new cell phone and give him that number as your contact. Don't call him on any other phones, including from your hotel room, and don't tell him where you are."

Mom nodded. "Okay," she said. "If it'll help that girl, it's okay."

"One more thing, Mom. You need to call Strings and tell him to stay away, that Maggie's illness, whatever it is, is contagious," I said. Maggie looked for a moment like she was going to protest, but then stopped. "If we don't, he'll drop in like usual, and he'll know something is going on."

"Okay," Mom said. "I'll do that, too."

"We're getting Sarah a new phone, too, one you can safely call her on," the captain said. "She won't be answering her old one until this is over, and we don't figure she'll do well not hearing from the two of you, even for two days."

"That's a smart decision," I said. "Even a day could be a problem."

"We need to move quickly, while it's still early and most folks are asleep," the captain said. "We don't want anyone to notice the helicopter taking off from the ranch."

The captain gave Maggie, Mom, and Frieda an hour to pack, but they were ready in thirty minutes. Everyone was gathered at the chopper in the pasture but Maggie, and the luggage was loaded, just a few small bags.

"Where's that granddaughter of mine?" Mom asked.

"I'll get her," I said. I didn't have to guess. I knew where she'd be. When I walked in the shed, Maggie was patting Warrior with Emma Lou watching.

"It's time, Maggie," I said. "Everyone's waiting."

"Okay," Maggie said, her voice cracking ever so slightly.

"I'll do my best to watch over him. I promise," I said. "And if anything at all looks wrong, I'll call Doc Larson ASAP."

"Yeah," she said, hugging me. "I know you will, Mom. I'm not worried."

"Then come on, Magpie," I said. "You've got an adventure ahead. Your first helicopter ride!"

Maggie smiled, while I fought back a wave of overwhelming anxiety, one I knew nothing but finding Argus and getting my family safely home could ease.

Twenty-three

"Y uck, look at all that fat and sugar," Cassidy Collins said when she finally made her way downstairs about eleven that morning, sizing up Mom's baking binge still covering the kitchen. Even a squad of rangers and state troopers hadn't polished it all off. "Thanks, but I don't eat sweets. Someone needs to hit Starbucks. I want my usual, a venti, nonfat vanilla latte, two shots, extra hot."

"Not exactly health food," I commented. Without looking up from the report I was reading, a faxed rundown on what Dallas P.D. discovered by searching the American Airlines Center the night before—basically nothing—I said, "There's coffee in the pot on the counter. Shouldn't be too bad. It's just four or five hours old. And there's milk in the refrigerator, unless my mom used it all baking. We don't buy skim. Sorry."

Collins put her hands on her hips. She wore one of my old T-shirts as a nightgown. It came down past her hips with DON'T MESS WITH MAD COWGIRLS stenciled across the chest. It was a gift from Bill, wrapped in a bow and handed to me the morning after our first argument.

"Hey, Lady Cop. You listening?" the kid said, clearly questioning my sanity. "I need a Starbucks."

"I heard you," I said. "I'm just not doing anything about it. There's coffee on the counter. If you want some, help yourself. I've got horses to check on."

"Horses? Am I on a farm?" she said, her words dripping in distaste. "Is that where you live?"

I sighed. Last night the kid clung to me like a raft in a shipwreck. Sadly, it appeared that her humility washed away in daylight. "Kind of. You're on a horse ranch, and, yes, this is my home," I said, perturbed. "My daughter and mother were uprooted out of here early this morning so that you could stay, to keep you safe. There are more than a dozen state troopers and rangers patrolling the property to protect you who'd rather be at home with their families or at church this beautiful Sunday morning. Some haven't slept since they were rousted out of their beds last night to rush here to help. Perhaps you could stop grousing and appreciate the sacrifices everyone is making on your behalf, so we can make this as pleasant as possible?"

"You want grateful? That's their job," she challenged. Her eyes were rimmed in black eyeliner, and stage makeup from the night before was smeared across her face. I thought about the mess that must wait on my pillowcase. Maybe I should have hauled out a cot for the kid and slept in my own bed. She didn't appear particularly appreciative. "Isn't that what cops do? They protect people?"

"We don't move our families out of their homes to put folks up. So this is above and beyond. And I'm not pleased with the situation," I warned. "So if I were you, I'd try to get along. Otherwise, I might decide you're not worth the trouble, and send you packing."

I stared at the kid for what must have seemed an eternity. She squirmed a bit, and then said, "This is crap, Sarah. You think I want to be here?"

"No, I don't. But last night, you sure didn't want to go any-where else, particularly home. One more thing, as far as you're con-cerned, my name is Lieutenant Armstrong," I said, thinking about how my mother would have reacted to the superstar kid's behavior, if she were here to see it. I had no doubt that by now Mom would have had Cassidy Collins scrubbing out the stable. That would have been worth watching. "My family and friends call me Sarah. You're not either one."

"Yeah, well," she said.

"Yeah, well, *who?*"

"Lieutenant Armstrong," she said, clipping off each syllable. Unfazed, she sneered back at me. I figured there was no sense wast-ing my time with the kid. I planned to put it to good use. If no one else had bothered to, I was teaching the brat manners.

"I'll be in the shed, checking the horses," I said. "Then, Miss Collins, we're going to sit down together, and you're going to an-swer all my questions. Every single one. I need to know everything, absolutely everything about you and this lowlife who's stalking you, so we can figure out who this Argus is, stop him, and get you the hell out of my life and my home."

This time the kid smiled. "Great," she said, contemptuously. "Believe me, this dump is no Ritz-Carlton."

"Very true. This place is better. This is my home," I said. "And unfortunately, it's your only safe place. But keep in mind, no one can force me to allow you to stay here. If I get too ticked off, you're on your way."

Outside, the sun was high and the sky a pale blue dotted with cotton-ball clouds. I brushed both the horses down, and then de-cided to give them a few hours in the front pasture. It wasn't a long walk, but the colt was slow, picking his way on the uneven earth. David showed up, and I thought I must look a sight. I'd showered and washed my hair, tied it back in a ponytail, thrown on jeans and a T-shirt, but that was it. I had too much to do to fuss over my looks, even if he was on the premises. Besides, he'd done every-thing but file a restraining order to keep me away. It no longer seemed to matter.

"I'm sorry about this, Sarah," he said. "The captain and I did try. It was all anyone could figure out to do. It just didn't seem safe to move her."

"So you said," I answered. "Somehow having that kid around hasn't helped my disposition."

He laughed. "I can understand that," he said. He had on an old pair of Bill's jeans and a denim work shirt, both of which hung loose on his athletic frame. My husband had been dead for two years, but I still hadn't given his clothes away. Another one of those things on my permanent to-do list. Maybe I just didn't have the heart for it.

"Here," I said. "If you're going to stand around gabbing, help me with the horses."

I handed him Emma Lou's lead, and he nudged her along. She was lagging, waiting for her foal. Warrior was so tiny, I could have picked him up and carried him, but he needed the exercise to build strength in his wobbly legs. As we neared the gate, Cassidy walked up.

"Boy, that's the smallest horse I've ever seen," she said.

"He's just two days old and a preemie," I said. "He's got some growing to do."

"Can I touch him?" she asked.

I looked at her, and figured it couldn't hurt. "Sure," I said, stop-ping our little parade to the pasture. "Gently."

The girl moved cautiously forward. She looked wary of the horses, probably never been near one before. She'd thrown on a pair of my shorts and a clean T-shirt I'd left out for her. She had on her shoes from the concert the night before, navy blue flats with sequins. It made for a strange combination. As she sidled up to the foal, Emma Lou threw her head back and let loose a warning grunt, worried.

"Hold her," I told David. "Pull her in."

He did, and Collins got close enough to reach out one tentative hand to rub along the foal's back. "He's soft," she said. "Are all horses this soft?"

"Just the young ones, like all babies," I answered, watching a smile edge across Cassidy's face. Sometimes horses can get to folks that other folks can't, fix them. I figured, why not try? "If you want to, you can follow us to the pasture. It's Warrior's first outing."

"Is that his name? Warrior?"

"Yup," I said, and then I decided to add, "If you want, you can help care for them while you're here. Foals, especially preemies, need a lot of attention."

For a moment, Cassidy appeared to consider my offer. Then she shrugged. "Nah," she said, the word laced with a heavy dose of condescension. "I'm no farmer."

The girl had a chip on her shoulder the size of Texas. "No problem. I'd hate to interrupt your nap time," I said. "But if you're not helping, go up to the house and wait. We'll be right there to start work."

With a smirk, Collins walked away.

"You said last night that you wondered if Argus is someone in your crew," I said to Collins, when we sat together in the living room. The kid was spread over Mom's favorite chair, a red corduroy recliner. The arms were worn, and Cassidy picked absentmindedly at fraying threads. "Let's start with that assumption. Do you have anyone in mind?"

"No," she snapped. "I just kept telling Rick that the creep knows more about me than my friends."

"What do you mean?"

"He knows where I live in L.A., and what I do, who I'm with. His e-mails sound like he's watching me or like he knows where I'm supposed to be," she said. For a minute, she looked tentative. There was something else there, something the kid wasn't eager to say.

"There's more you're not telling us, isn't there?"

The kid said nothing, just stared at me, thinking.

"Cassidy, this guy is threatening to kill you," I reminded her. "This isn't the time to hold back any information that could help us."

For another moment, she paused and frowned, thinking that through. Then she said, "Sometimes I wonder if he knew me before L.A."

"Why?" David asked.

"In one e-mail, he said he liked the freckles on my nose when I was a little girl," she said, with a puzzled look. She shook her head slightly and shrugged. "I haven't had those freckles since fifth grade. They faded. How would he know that?"

"I don't know. You've got a fair complexion. Maybe he just guessed you had freckles as a kid? I didn't see that e-mail in the packet Mr. Barron gave me," I said. "Why not?"

"I deleted it," she said, with a shrug. "It was one of the first ones I got, before I was really scared of this jerk. I thought he was just another nut. I get them all the time. I didn't think he'd threaten to . . ."

Her voice dwindled off.

"Did you show that to anyone, the e-mail I mean?"

"No, but it was the same guy. He signed it Argus."

"Are there other e-mails you didn't tell Barron or anyone about?"

"A few," she admitted more than a little reluctantly.

"Did they contain anything else surprising?" I asked.

"Yeah," she said. "I guess, maybe."

"What?" David asked.

The kid wrinkled up her face in disgust. "The morning after the concert in Atlanta, that was a week or so before we played Caesars Palace, that Argus dude e-mailed and claimed I winked at him," she said. "He said our eyes met, and he knew that we had some kind of special bond. Yuck. Really sick."

"What did he mean by that, the bit about the special bond?" I asked.

The kid grimaced and shrugged. "Nothing, okay? Nothing I know of anyway."

"He could have meant anything," David said. "These types of stalkers often fantasize that they have a relationship with their victims."

"Yeah. That's true," I said. "Okay, talk about Atlanta. Do you remember anyone you saw that night? Is it possible that he was telling the truth, that you saw his face in the crowd?"

"That was a big show, full-stage show, with the fly harness and the cocoon. Sometimes, up on the hoist, over the audience, I kind of see people, but I can't see faces," she said. "It's more shapes. Girls and moms, a few dads. I don't focus on anyone, and no one ever stands out."

"Did you respond to those e-mails?" David asked.

"No," she answered. "Like I said, I did what Rick says to do with garbage. I trashed them. But that Argus jerk, his e-mails had those things, where you click and it tells the sender that I opened it. So he knew I got them."

"What else did this Argus know about your past?" I asked.

"That my family was dirt poor," she said. "And that's something I don't tell anyone."

"What do you mean?" I asked.

Collins looked wary, guarded about saying any more.

"What's the problem?" I asked.

"What I tell you two goes nowhere?" she said. "You don't flap about it? Like to reporters?"

"No," I said. "We won't tell anyone."

"Sure?" she prodded.

"Sure," David said. "Absolutely."

"Well, okay. I don't ever tell anyone about my past. I don't want the press to dig around, find out where I grew up," she said. "The truth is that Mom and I lived in a trailer park. My mom was a drunk. I don't know my dad, not even his name. The thing is, I have no privacy. Anything anybody finds out about me gets splashed all over those grocery store rags."

"Okay, Cassidy, let's go with that," David said, ever so patiently. "Let's assume this guy *is* someone out of your past. Tell me about people you knew growing up, anyone who'd know about your life before Los Angeles."

Her eyes dropped, and she layered her hands on her lap, looking young and frightened. The kid was tough but hurting. She'd been through a lot in her short lifetime, but now someone wanted her dead. That was beyond all her experience.

Of course, that didn't give her the right to be rude, I told myself, but . . .

"I changed my name when I hit L.A. I'd thought of Cassidy Collins when I was a little kid, liked it, so I gave that to everyone, even the social worker who stuck me in those foster homes. I made up a name for my mom, too. Said she was dead. That's the only true thing I told anyone," she said. "I never talk about being trailer park trash. I don't talk about my mom drinking herself to death, either. Once I got to L.A., I wanted to be a different person."

"We understand, Cassidy. But think back, before Los Angeles," David instructed. "Whom do you remember?"

Again she hesitated. Quiet. "Not anyone much. Mom and me kept away from other people. Mom didn't like strangers. She always said we had to be careful. I don't know why, but sometimes she seemed scared," the kid said. "I went to school, but I looked really different. My hair was darker, and I wore big glasses. When I started singing and made money, I bought contacts. And before anyone in L.A. knew much about me, while I was still a kid, I dyed my hair blond. Like I said, I don't look like I used to."

"But this person, whoever it is, he recognizes you?" I said.

"I guess so," she agreed, with a shrug. "I don't know, but sometimes I think maybe he does."

"Why didn't Rick Barron tell us this?" David asked. "It's at least a lead."

Again, the girl's voice got small, defensive. "Rick doesn't know. I didn't tell him," she admitted. "People who work for celebrities sell stories to the tabloids for millions. I didn't want even Rick to have anything personal on me, anything about my past. It's a lot of bad memories."

"Germaine Dunn knows you've had a tough time," I said. "She told me about your mother dying while you were still young."

"Germaine's my only friend," Collins said. "But even she doesn't know my old name or where I came from. She didn't know what I looked like before I was Cassidy Collins."

"Well, you're going to have to trust us," I said. "You've got no choice."

She nodded, as if perhaps she understood. "What else do you want to know?"

"First off, your real name and your mother's name," David said. "Then we need the name of the school you went to, the town, the trailer park, and the names of anyone you remember from the years before you arrived in Los Angeles."

Cassidy nodded.

"I'll get a pad of paper, and I want you to sit here and write down everything we've asked for and more," I said. "Anything that could, in any way, help us find and stop this Argus. This is your shot, Cassidy. You help us get this guy now, or you pray that he doesn't find you before we find him."

Twenty-four

Okay, so Cassidy Collins is really Angela Jane Eckert, and her mother was Claire Eckert," I read to David off of Cassidy's list. "The trailer park is called Wooded Acres, in northern California. That could help, but the kid has no memory of the full names of anyone she knew there. There are only four people listed, first names and no last names. Three old women, Sharlene, Sherry, and Sue, who Cassidy calls 'The Ss,' and describes as women in their late seventies with blue hair who sit around clacking their dentures and playing afternoon quarter poker at a picnic table. There's only one guy on the list, a Jack somebody, who hung around the trailer park off and on, the son of one of 'The Ss.' She's not sure which one. Cassidy doesn't know where he lived or anything else about him, just that she saw him sometimes, and he gave her the creeps."

"So, how do we investigate that?" he said, with a slight laugh. "Not much help."

"That's an understatement," I said. I thought for a while, and then said, "Maybe this Argus person has been in trouble before?

Most of these guys have been, even if it's only little stuff like peeping or exposing themselves in public."

"That's true," David said. "At least it's a place to start."

"Let's ask your San Francisco office to interview these three old women, find out if they know of anyone in the area who appeared overly interested in young girls," I suggested. "And we need a list of all the sex offenders known to reside in the vicinity of the trailer park during the years Cassidy lived there with her mother."

"Sure. We'll give it a shot," David said. "Anything else?"

"Not that I can think of," I said. The info could take up to a few hours to come in, and I wondered if sitting around waiting was the best use of my time. "Anything I can do? Do you need my help?"

"No," he said, understanding where I was headed. "You might as well get something else done while we check this out. Now that the Peterson kid's been cleared, the California link is our most likely scenario, and our offices on the West Coast will take it from here."

"Okay. I'm going to check on the horses," I said. "And then, I've got that other case I'm working, Billie Cox's murder. I'd like to have sit-downs with a couple of folks this afternoon, while you watch over Collins. Truth is I could use a break from that kid."

"That I can understand. I'll call if we discover anything," he said.

"Thanks," I said. "I'm counting on it. I want this over, fast."

I turned to leave, and David said, "Sarah?"

"Yeah," I said. "Did we forget something?"

"You look great sleeping," he said, eyeing me a bit sheepishly.

At first, I was surprised, even flattered, but quickly angry. "Glad you think so," I said. "But I don't think you get to tell me that. Not when you won't explain why you're pushing me away."

David thought for a moment and then said, "I guess that's true."

For a moment, I hesitated, in case more was to come, but David put his hands in his pockets and just looked at me, his eyes sad but resolute, so I left. I had Billie's murder to solve, and the way my life was currently unfolding, I figured that might be easier than either finding Argus or decoding David.

Ty Dickson, Clayton Wagner's old partner, was a small man, about the size of an average woman. Of course, at seventy-nine, most folks shrink, but he had the look of a fellow who'd always been dwarfed in a crowd. We talked for nearly an hour in his walnut-paneled office on the first floor of his mansion, perhaps not surprisingly right across the street from Wagner's palatial spread. The butler had escorted me to the room and then left us alone. The guy might as well have stayed for all the information Dickson offered. All he'd tell me about either the Stanhope Field or the photo sounded like a recorded copy of Clayton Wagner's story from two days earlier. Not surprising since Wagner had probably prepped Dickson.

"Yeah, ya see, the reason I can tell you for certain about that photo is my wife, Emily, died soon after," Dickson said, for the fourth time, each time emphasizing it, as if this point alone should erase any doubt about the photo's time frame. "That's why it's all so fresh in my mind, that it was in December and all, 'bout eight years ago."

Getting nothing new that might help solve the case, I figured I didn't have much to lose. Why not say what I was thinking? "You know, Mr. Dickson, you don't look any different in this picture than you do today. Hard to imagine eight years have passed."

The old man smiled, displaying long, narrow, crooked teeth discolored by age and smoke, evidenced by ashes and cigarette butts, the filters yellow from saliva, in an ashtray cut from a hollowed-out steer horn on his desk. Throughout the interview, Dickson had hacked away, a loose, hairball cough, the kind that usually means people aren't aging particularly well. Guess he didn't consider that a problem. "You know," he said, with an impish grin, "folks often ask how I stay so young looking. I tell them the secret is clean living."

"Yeah, I can see that," I said. "Cigarettes and whisky always make for a long, healthy life."

The old man laughed, leading to another round of chest-rattling gasps. There was something wrong with Dickson, something bad. I figured he knew that and had long since stopped caring. Of course, he caught my point, knew that I didn't believe him, but the curmudgeon didn't care. Matter of fact, he didn't look in the least concerned about my visit or my questions, which led to only one conclusion: The old man didn't see me as a serious threat. I must be ice cold.

"Where were you the afternoon of Billie's death?" I asked.

As if he couldn't be more pleased by the question, most likely because he had his answer well-planned, Dickson explained with a self-satisfied smile: "I was here at home. My accountant was with me that entire afternoon, going over my tax return, getting it ready to file an extension. He'll be happy to talk to you. You're also welcome to shoot that question past the butler, Malcolm. He brought the bean-counter and me a couple of drinks when we finished talking business."

With that, Ty Dickson grinned, giving me a parting glimpse of his not-close-to-pearly-whites.

Another dead end. As he escorted me to the door, Malcolm backed up Dickson's alibi, and on a call from the car, the accountant did the same.

I fared better at the law office of Jimmy McBride, the attorney Bobby Barker and Billie Cox had dealt with regarding their plan to purchase the Stanhope Field. I guessed that Wagner and Dickson didn't know I had McBride's name, so they hadn't ordered him to keep his trap shut. The minute McBride's secretary brought me back to his office—a small, windowless room in a nest of legal offices in a rundown building—I knew he was the third man in the photo. There was little chance of mistaking his physique. McBride was in his forties, with a fringe of dark hair around a balding dome, wearing wire-rimmed glasses. His shoulders gave him away. They sloped to the point I figured he'd have a hard time wearing suspenders.

"So, tell me about the Stanhope Field," I said, after introducing myself and explaining that I was investigating what I simply referred to as Cox's death. No reason to put him on guard by calling it a murder. "I understand that Billie Cox was interested in purchasing it for Century Oil."

"Terrible thing, her killing herself like that. Billie Cox was one smart woman," McBride said, to which I gave no argument. "Stanhope's a potentially lucrative oil field. It was developed in the thirties but abandoned in the fifties when the easy-to-reach reserves ran out. But our research suggests there's a bunch more down there."

"How can you be so sure of that?" I asked.

"We have a report that proves those wells can bring in big profits," he said. With that he flipped through the stacks on his littered desk and pulled out an inch-thick file that read: STANHOPE PROSPECTUS. He waved it at me, and then plopped it back down on his desk.

"Impressive," I said. "But my understanding is that Billie lost her enthusiasm for the deal. I've been told that she was considering backing out of the purchase just before her death. She didn't believe that oil field was as rich as your report claims."

McBride's high forehead puckered, giving him a doubtful look. "She never told me that," he said, shaking his head in disbelief. "Why, Billie told me not long before she died that she saw the purchase as one of the primary reasons she was eager to acquire Century."

"Acquire Century?" I repeated. "Billie Cox was working on a buyout of Century Oil?"

"Of course," McBride said. "Clayton Wagner and Ty Dickson were giving her a sweetheart deal. They're ready to move on, finally. I'm sure they told you that. The plans were on the Q.T., sure, but I don't know why they'd hide anything now. Since Billie's death, they've got the company publicly up for sale."

"Why are they selling?" I asked. "Some reason beyond just being old?"

"Nah. That's the main motivation. They figure time's limited, and those two old geezers want to spend their final years setting up a foundation. They're drawing up plans to build a charity hospital for kids. With no children of their own to leave their money to, they see it as their legacy, the way they'll be remembered by generations to come. The Wagner-Dickson Trust is the pride of their lives. My theory is that they see it as a way of making amends. Neither one of those two old wildcatters was particularly thrifty. They spent a bunch on big houses, cars, beautiful women. In fact, they brag about the fortunes they squandered. But with limited years ahead, they seem intent on leaving something behind that ensures they'll be remembered."

"That sure is good of them," I said. "Sounds like a great cause."

"Unlikely for the two of them, I admit. Those old scoundrels have always been better known for finagling deals than good works. For most of their lives, there wasn't a soul they wouldn't have taken advantage of for money," McBride said, with a laugh. "But in this case, looks like they've learned a new trick."

"That I don't doubt," I said with a smile.

"Since they lived large, they haven't got a bunch. Not as much as you'd think for two oil men. And to do what they want, they need more," he said. "Selling Century Oil to Billie was going to provide most of the nest egg for the trust."

Based on how freely he was talking, when I took out the photo from Cox's computer, I wasn't surprised that McBride didn't hesitate. "Sure, that's me," he said. "I didn't know anyone snapped a photo, but that's Wagner, Dickson, and me out at the field."

"When was this? Why were all of you out there?"

"It was last summer, July or so, and we went out so they could show me the property. I'd done some work for them in the past. They said they wanted me to see what I was representing so I could pass on their enthusiasm to prospective buyers," he said. "We had a lot of paperwork to pull together, so the place really didn't go up for sale until late last year, but it's been in the works for a long time."

"Now, maybe I'm getting confused, here," I admitted. "I thought you represented the owners of the field?"

"Well, yeah," McBride said. "I do represent the owners."

"You told prospective buyers that it was owned by a partnership of some kind, right?"

McBride smiled. "Well, kind of," he said, for the first time seeming reluctant to open up. Rather than offer any information, he said, "Didn't you ask Mr. Wagner and Mr. Dickson who owns Stanhope?"

"No, I'm asking you," I said. Of course, by then all the clues were tumbling into place in my brain, like those little mosaic pieces in a kaleidoscope that *click, click, click* until they form a pattern. McBride frowned, reluctant to go on, so I put my theory on the table, if for no other reason than to gauge his reaction. "What you're going to tell me is that Wagner and Dickson own that oil field. That's right, isn't it?"

McBride frowned and appeared to consider the situation.

"Remember, Mr. McBride," I cautioned. "I'm a police officer, a Texas Ranger here on official business. You need to tell me what you know."

Lawyers aren't always the best interviews. They can be reluctant to open up. But McBride paused for a minute, shrugged, and then said, "Well, I guess there's no harm. I mean, it's all really public record, if someone knew where to look and spent the time to trace all the records and the shell companies back."

"Shell companies set up to disguise the fact that Wagner and Dickson own Stanhope, right?" I asked again.

This time McBride didn't hesitate. He appeared to have convinced himself he wasn't doing his clients any harm. "Yeah, Wagner and Dickson own Stanhope. They purchased it on spec in the seventies, assuming the field wasn't played out and banking on someday being able to figure out how to get at the rest of the oil."

"Did Billie Cox know they were the sellers?"

"No," McBride said. "I'd been asked not to tell anyone, even Miss Cox, who the real owners are. It was all supposed to be done anonymously."

"Why?" I asked.

"The truth is, Lieutenant, I don't know," McBride said. "I asked both the old gentlemen, but they never said, and I was there to facilitate the deal, not figure out their motives."

"That's what you meant by most of the money for the hospital coming from the sale of Century Oil," I speculated. "The rest was coming from selling Stanhope?"

"That's right," he said. "Wagner and Dickson told me they needed enough to ensure that the trust endured well into the future. The hospital is their legacy. They didn't want to take any chances that it wouldn't survive."

It had been a cordial conversation, and, for the most part, McBride had been forthcoming. I figured he had no inkling of how important the information he'd just given me might be. It was time to give him a clue. "Mr. McBride, there's something I would suggest to you," I said.

"What's that?" he asked.

"I wouldn't tell anyone just yet that we talked, especially Clayton Wagner and Ty Dickson."

The attorney looked surprised, even startled. "Well, they're my clients. I haven't told you anything wrong, and they have a right to know."

"Billie Cox didn't commit suicide. She was murdered. If someone killed her over this oil field—I'm not saying that's what happened, but *if* someone did—your knowledge of this deal could make you a liability," I explained. "It could occur to the murderer that having you available to talk to the police isn't in his best interest. Right now, no one knows we've talked. It's best if you keep it that way."

"You're not saying that someone might murder me?" he said, suddenly alarmed.

"I'm offering you a suggestion that may keep you safe," I said. "For now, I'd forget to mention my visit. There's time enough in the future, when all this is settled, for you to bring your clients up to speed on our conversation."

That may have been the first time McBride understood the reason for my visit. A full two shades paler than when I arrived, he nodded and I left, figuring I'd shaken him up enough to buy myself at least a day before he began worrying that he may have talked too much and would hold a meeting to advise his clients.

On the drive to the ranch, I thought about what McBride had told me. It seemed that Wagner and Clayton were trying to cash in, first by getting Century Oil and Bobby's company, Barker Oil, to hand over millions more than it was worth to buy the dried-up oil field. The two old wildcatters would then be in a position to score again, by getting Billie Cox to pay an inflated price for Century, factoring in the exaggerated worth of the Stanhope holdings. If it all checked out, what McBride had given me was a motive to kill Cox. If she'd uncovered the ruse, she was in a position to expose them and not only ruin their plans, but send them to prison for conspiracy to commit fraud. Still, all I had was a theory, not one piece of real evidence.

Convinced he was somehow involved, I'd already asked Janet to subpoena financial records for Grant Roberts. Now I called her and asked her to do the same for Wagner and Dickson. To speed things up, I asked her to zero in on the past three months, the time period leading up to and continuing through Billie's murder. Next, I considered the other evidence in my possession. When and if I asked a judge to sign warrants for Wagner's and Dickson's arrests, I'd need something well beyond speculation. It would help to be able to prove they were the ones, not McBride, who lied about when the photo was taken. That meant that I needed a way to date the photo, but how? Passing time in the car on the drive back to the ranch, I used the new cell phone the captain had supplied and called Mom and Maggie.

"We're fine, Sarah," Mom said. "It's kind of nice having folks wait on us like this. We just had chocolate sundaes with whipped cream and cherries, and Maggie's already picked out pizza off the room-service menu for dinner. I'm not sure how she'll like the feta cheese and fresh basil, but Frieda and I are looking forward to it."

"Geez, and I'm still trying to work in lunch. A Big Mac would taste good right now," I said.

"Sarah, I told you, with your dad's history of heart disease you shouldn't eat like that."

"Just kidding, Mom," I said. "I knew that would get you sputtering. Put Maggie on. I miss both of you."

"Wish you could sneak away and join us," Mom said. "We'd

order you one of those sundaes. It would be worth the drive downtown."

I laughed, and then Maggie's voice came on the telephone.

"How's Warrior?" she asked, point blank.

"He was in the front pasture with Emma Lou when I left the ranch. They looked happy as clams," I said. "I'm headed back there now. Buckshot was cleaning their shed when I left, so they're probably in their little home resting up after their big outing."

"That's really good. I was worried. But Mom, this is fun," Maggie said, her voice relaxed. It sounded like the captain was right, and Mom and Maggie were enjoying their little vacation. "We've been watching movies and playing cards with the troopers. Gram told you about the sundaes?"

"Whipped cream and cherries," I said, with another chuckle. This was what I needed. Hearing their voices made the whole mess tolerable. "I'll call you before bed tonight, Maggie. Love you."

"Love you, too, Mom," she said. "Later, alligator!"

"After a while, crocodile," I replied.

I'd almost reached the house, when I had another thought, and I called back. Mom chattered about some movie they were watching about wolves, but I cut her off and told her I needed to talk to Maggie.

"Yeah, Mom," my daughter said, her voice distant, like she, too, was more interested in the wolves. "What do you need?"

"If I fax you a photo at the hotel, one with a night sky, do you think you can tell me when it was taken?" I asked.

My someday-I'll-be-an-astronomer daughter paused, and I could picture the serious look she'd have on her face, her front teeth holding down her lower lip. Then she said, "If I had my astronomy books, I might be able to say what time of the year it was when it was taken. But I probably can't tell you what year."

Thinking about the discrepancies in the two accounts, the attorney's statement that it was taken in July and Wagner's and Dickson's assertions that it was December, I said, "Time of year works. I'll send Buckshot over with the photo and your astronomy books."

"Okay, Mom," she said. "But I've got to go. Gram's got the movie paused right where the wolf cubs are chasing jackrabbits. It's really funny. The cubs keep falling down."

Once I got to the ranch, it only took a few minutes to make a copy of the photo on my workshop scanner and grab Maggie's books. Everything necessary in hand, Buckshot left in his silver pickup for the downtown Houston hotel where Maggie and Mom were watching movies. He'd make a couple of stops first, one at the feed store to buy Warrior a vitamin supplement Doc had called to say would be good for the foal and then at the drugstore, to pick up contact lens solution for Cassidy. We needed the supplies, but the stops would also help to make sure no one was following.

That done, David and I went over what the FBI had discovered in northern California. "Turns out that we had ten registered sex offenders living within fifteen miles of the trailer park during the years Cassidy and her mother lived there," David explained. "We've had some natural attrition. Two died. That leaves eight. One is confined to a state prison, has been for two years, so he's ruled out. Now we're down to seven."

"Any hunches on who's our most likely guy?" I asked.

"Our California agents faxed information on the remaining seven. I read through it and narrowed the search down to three. I'd like you to do the same. We'll see if you pick the same men," he said. "Then let's compare notes and plan our next move."

That decided, David left me with the faxed reports at the kitchen table. I grabbed a hunk of Mom's cheddar and jalapeño bread, slathered butter on top, and munched while I read. Of the ex-cons in the prospect pile, I tossed out two immediately, based on victim choice. They were all disgusting excuses for human beings, but these particular perverts weren't into young girls. Their victims of preference were adolescent boys. They might branch out to girls if presented with an easy score, but it seemed unlikely that they'd pursue Cassidy when there had to be thousands of potential young male victims who were easier to get to. Horrible folks. Those discards whittled the list down to five.

Since our guy was adept at maneuvering undetected through the cyber world, I figured Argus had to be exceptionally bright and self-taught or have a solid background in computers. Suspects number two and four both had diminished intelligence, one from a blow to the head in high school and the other mentally challenged from birth. Neither had any technical training. I drew lines through both their names on my list.

That pared the possibilities down to three.

The first, a dentist with a small private practice, was married with two kids. He lived a block from the trailer park and had an office that was only half a mile from Cassidy's old elementary school. The guy had three convictions, two for exposing himself to kids and one for the aggravated sexual assault of a twelve-year-old girl. Sure that working that close to a school was a parole violation, I figured I'd make sure California authorities heard about it one way or the other. But for the time being, I was more concerned about whether the dentist had any e-mails on his computer signed Argus.

The suspect I penciled in as choice number two, a sixty-eight-year-old ex-con, had one conviction for child molestation on his record. He lived two miles from the trailer park and worked in a nearby town, managing an office-supply store that included a computer section. He hadn't been in trouble in a couple of decades, but pedophiles often don't quit because of advancing age.

All that considered, it was number three who struck me as most likely. Forty years old, Jack Shaw not only had a first name Cassidy remembered but also a twenty-year, computer-related resume, much of it selling information technology. A decade earlier, he'd been downsized from his slot with a national cell phone company, where he worked in research and development. As recently as two years ago, he'd sold computer networking systems to small companies. Along with multiple charges of exposing himself to young girls, Shaw had child porn convictions, including selling the revolting stuff on the Internet. I found the final entry in his file upsetting: "Jack Shaw left the area approximately one year ago while under investigation for sexually assaulting an eleven-year-old girl. His location is currently unknown."

I found David in the shed brushing Emma Lou, while, to my surprise, Cassidy did the same for Warrior. The colt kept licking and nudging her, and the teenager giggled so loudly I heard her before I walked in.

"Thought we'd have a little fun with the horses," David said. "Warrior seems to have taken a real liking to Cassidy."

"What a crazy little dude," she said, with another chuckle. "Every time I run the brush down his back, he pushes me."

The kid laughed again and I didn't have the heart to tell her that the foal was probably hungry and confusing her with his mom. "Well, if you two are finished, I'd like to sit down with both of you," I said. "I'd like you to look over my list, David, see if we agree. And Cassidy, you need to look at the photos, see if any of the men look familiar."

While David paged through the files I'd selected, Cassidy stared at photos of all seven of the registered sex offenders laid out on the kitchen table, a rather bizarre lineup of possibilities. The photo of Jack Shaw was smack dab in the middle. She paused, looked at him, even picked that particular photo up and held it in her hand, but put it down and said, "Maybe this guy. I'm not sure."

"Okay," I said. "So, David, does my list match yours?"

"Yup," he agreed. "I'll call our California guys and get them to round these three up, bring them in for questioning. Since they all have priors, our guys should be able to get some kind of a warrant, at least for their computers, so we can look for files relating to Cassidy or Argus."

"Did your people indicate if they have any leads on the whereabouts of that Shaw guy?" I asked. "He looks like the most possible."

"No leads," David said. "He was my top pick in this lineup of losers, too. The California office will beat the bushes, let us know what they find out by morning, I'd guess."

After Cassidy left the room in search of a soft drink, I mentioned to David, "We only have one day left before she's scheduled to play the rodeo. Does she know she's going to have to perform even if we haven't arrested this scumbag?"

David frowned. "No," he said. "We're hoping we don't have to tell her."

"My guess is that the kid's too freaked to go along with your plan," I said. "But I hope we don't have to ask her to. I hope by then Argus is history."

"Yeah," he said. Holding up the files on our new suspects, he added, "Maybe one of these will pan out."

"Hope so," I said, but if he'd asked, I would have admitted that I had my doubts.

Half an hour later, the captain personally delivered a cooler full of hamburger meat with all the fixings. David lit the grill and cooked the burgers, and our patrol of state troopers and rangers ate in shifts at the picnic table under the corral elm tree. At dusk, the captain, David, and I took our turns, just as Maggie's lights clicked on. I thought about her and Mom and missed them.

"Rick Barron is fit to be tied about us not telling him where Collins is being kept," the captain said. Cassidy was upstairs in Maggie's room, listening to music while she ate her dinner. In addition to her burger, she covered her plate with cole slaw, potato salad, and a thick slice of Mom's egg twist bread I'd covered with melted cheddar cheese.

"You explained that no one can know, I'm sure," David said, taking a bite out of his burger.

"Yeah, but that didn't cut the mustard for him. He figures he's her head of security, and he's entitled to an answer," the captain said, dripping mayonnaise onto his plate from an overstuffed bun that held two beef patties and three slices of cheese with lettuce and tomato. It looked like one of those two-thousand-calorie burgers in the fast-food ads.

"You tell him we'll be more than happy to clue him in, but then she's going to have to come out of hiding, and he'll be responsible for protecting her," I said. "The only way she stays here is that no one, not even her own people know where to find her."

"I'm aware of that, Sarah," the captain said. "I told him to go pee on a fencepost if he needs to mark his territory, but he's not in charge of this operation. We are. The chief and the governor don't even know where Collins is, but they know we've got her in hiding for her own protection, and they're in agreement that we have no other choice. Since the girl had herself legally declared an adult in California last year, she's entitled to make her own decisions, and she's not asking to leave, so we're not telling Barron or anyone else where to find her."

"Okay," I said. "That works for me. But I wish I'd been listening in when you told him to pee on a fencepost."

"Gotta admit that the man was still angry when I hung up the telephone," the captain said with a chuckle.

I left the captain and David talking at the picnic table and settled in the living room, glad for the downtime to work on the Cox case. To get started I called Torres, the department's computer guru. He'd left a message asking me to call him about Cox's computer. The darn thing had spooked me enough that I put everything else on hold to find out what he wanted.

First thing out of Torres's mouth was, "This damn computer's jumpier than a jackrabbit eyeing a rattlesnake."

"What do you mean?" I asked.

"It keeps turning itself on," he said. "We found a short in the plug, which is odd since it's pretty new, but it's there. Fixed it, and it hasn't happened since."

"That's interesting," I said, thinking back to my experience in Cox's office. "When it happened, turned itself on, I mean, what comes up on the screen?"

"The opening screen," Torres said. Then, to my relief he added, "And about half the time, it automatically fills in that woman's password and pulls up something from memory, different every time. A couple hours ago we had her 401(k) holdings, and earlier this afternoon it flashed a photo of the victim with her sister."

"Imagine that," I said. Could it have been a coincidence that when I was in the office it pulled up a photo of the oil field? Is it possible that a simple twist of fate delivered what could be an important piece of evidence? "You're telling me that there's no rhyme or reason to what pops up?"

"Not that we can tell," he said. "We've been over and over this computer, tore it all apart, I promise. Damnedest thing I've ever seen."

"Okay," I said. From fans and TVs that turned themselves on to a computer with a mind of its own, I knew Faith would argue there were too many coincidences to be just that. For me, though, faulty wiring was at least a plausible explanation. "Thanks, Torres," I said. "Good work."

As soon as I got off the phone, I turned my attention to more concrete matters, ones that didn't make the hair on the back of my neck stand at attention. Along with dinner, the captain had brought the first batch of financial records I'd subpoenaed for Grant Roberts, Wagner, and Dickson. Janet had been busy. So far, all she'd collected on the two oilmen were credit card bills, but I'd only been at it for a couple of hours when I thought I found something interesting.

"Captain," I said, breaking into a conversation on the pros and cons of fishing with lures versus live bait. "If you can stay here to cover for us, I'd like David to come with me to talk to a possible suspect on the Cox case."

"Sure, Sarah," he said. "No problem."

Right then my new cell phone rang. "Mom, it's Maggie," my daughter said, as if I wouldn't have recognized her voice.

"Hi, Magpie. All's well here. Warrior and Emma Lou are both doing just fine," I said. "We got the colt on that new vitamin supplement Doc ordered."

"That's good. Tell Warrior I miss him, okay?" she said.

"You've got it," I said.

"Mom, I think I've got it figured out. You know that photo you sent me?"

"What did you see?"

"Well, the thing is, the sky changes depending on the time of year," she explained, very seriously. My daughter talked about someday being a teacher, and I had the distinct impression she was practicing her lecture skills on me. "Different constellations come into view while others drop away as the earth tilts on its axis."

"Okay, I understand that," I said. "So what did you see in the photo?"

"Well, it's not the best picture," she said. "It's not all that clear, but . . ."

Twenty-five

The Big Dipper, it would turn out, was the key. In the winter, this easily recognized constellation hangs low in the East Texas sky. In the photograph, Maggie had no trouble spotting the Dipper, high in the heavens. "It can't be winter," she said. "This photo was taken in the summer."

"You're sure?" I asked.

"Yeah," she said, sounding excited by the challenge. "Is that all you need? Do you want me to do more investigating?"

"That's exactly what I need, Magpie," I said. "I love you. All's well here! Tell Gram I love her, too!"

"I love you, too, Mom," she said. "Good night."

"Good night, Magpie," I said. "And thank you, again. Great work."

"Nice getup, Mr. Wagner," I said to the old man seated across from David and me. We were in his parlor where I'd been two days earlier, but this time it was after dark and he wore a flannel bathrobe over thermal pajamas and a knit cap covered his head. "Drafty in this big old place? You should consider downsizing."

"It's easier to catch a cold when you're my age," he said. "Another thing that's easier is speaking your mind. I thought we'd disposed of all this. Why are you back?"

"Agent Garrity and I are following up on the interview I had with you on Billie Cox's homicide," I said. "Some of your answers, it appears, weren't truthful. Like when that photo of you at the Stanhope Field was taken."

The old guy assessed me out of the corners of his rheumy eyes and puckered his wrinkled mouth. He would have been a natural for the part of Scrooge in *A Christmas Carol*. I wondered where the ghost of Christmas past was hiding. David and I could have passed for the ghosts of Christmas present, since we'd arrived with a large shopping bag, bulging with items wrapped in brown paper. Wagner kept staring at them. I hoped he noticed they weren't tied with ribbons and bows.

"That's not a nice thing to say to an old man, Lieutenant," he said, surveying my face and then staring yet again at the bag. "Particularly when it's not true. I happen to know that my old partner, Dickson, told you exactly the same thing I did. You got other information, it's wrong."

"Let's take a look at the photo again," I suggested. I'd put David in charge of my props. The first thing he pulled out was an envelope. He handed it to me, and I slipped out a copy of the photo in question.

"To start, I'm going to tell you how I know you lied, Mr. Wagner. First, I talked to your attorney, Jimmy McBride, the third man in this photo," I said, pointing to the younger man in the picture, the one with his back to the camera. "And what he told me is that this was taken not eight years ago in December but just this past July, last summer, when you and Mr. Dickson hired him to represent you on the sale of the oil field."

"That man's mistaken," Wagner said with a snarl. "You know lawyers. They can never keep anything straight."

Shaking my head as if perplexed, I leaned forward and tried to hand him the photo, but the old man merely sat back in his chair and shot me a look that warned I'd better be careful. "You've got my word and my partner's word against McBride's, so he's outnumbered. That ought to be enough for you."

"Only thing is, look right here," I said, taking a pen out of my pocket. Since he refused to hold the photo, I gave it to David who held it up at Wagner's eye-level, as I traced the outline of the seven stars that made up the constellation. "That's the Big Dipper. Know what's interesting about that?"

"No, but I'm bound to have the misfortune of having you explain it to me, I suppose," he said. "You know, Lieutenant, I've already lived a long life. I don't like being manipulated. It wastes my time."

"This won't be a waste of time, I give you my word," I said with a smile. Had to admit, I was enjoying every minute of this conversation, so much more than our first. "What's interesting is that in winter the Big Dipper is low over this part of Texas. The earth has shifted on its axis, and the Dipper's close to the horizon. The only time it's this high is summer, like in July, which just happens to be when Mr. McBride told us the three of you were there. Which proves, as I mentioned, that you lied to me, Mr. Wagner."

He thought about that a bit, and then smiled. "Well, maybe it was last summer. I'm an old man and I'm forgetful. Maybe I've got some of that dementia stuff my friends are all coming down with. Can't see any other explanation. Why would I lie about something like that?" he asked, with an exaggerated scowl. "Seems pretty silly."

"I wondered about that, too," I said. "Then I realized that admitting the photo was just months-old made it too easy to figure out that you were involved in the sale. And since y'all falsified that report and lied about there being oil in the field, you had a reason not to want me to learn the truth."

"Is telling a lie a jail-able offense? I don't think so," he challenged, his wispy white eyebrows knotted together, giving him a disheveled look. "Leave me alone. This is baloney. You've got no crime here."

"Ah, but I do. You know as well as I do that a lie told to bilk folks out of cash is fraud. Bet you also know that the punishment is up to ten years behind bars," I said, with a self-satisfied grin. "Still, at your age, you probably would have gotten off pretty easy, as little as a year or even probation. Mr. Wagner, you should have let it ride, come clean and settled your losses. It would have been the smarter move, even for an old wildcatter like you."

With that, Wagner dismissively shook his head. "I don't know what you're talking about," he scoffed. "I haven't heard any convincing evidence of anything, nothing to be of any concern."

"Ah, but Mr. Wagner, you should be very concerned," I said, with a wink. "There's more."

David pulled my second prop out of the bag, something rolled up in a brown paper cylinder. On the side, it read: COX MURDER: EVIDENCE NUMBER 327. BEDROOM RUG.

"What's that?" Wagner asked, looking just a speck unsettled.

"That's the Oriental rug out of Ms. Cox's bedroom, the one to the left of the bed," David explained. "I assume you'd like to know what the Lieutenant and I have discovered about this particular item?"

"Spill it," the old man said. "Then get the hell out of here. It's late. I'm old and tired, and I've had enough. So say what you will, and then leave."

"What's interesting about this particular piece of evidence is what's not on a section of it," David said. "Billie Cox's blood."

Wagner snorted dismissively, as if he saw no importance.

"You see, in a suicide, blood spatter exits the wound covering everything around the person in an uninterrupted pattern," I explained. "But on this rug, which was on the floor directly next to the body, on the side of the entrance wound, there's blood on the sides but not the center. Why? Because someone else was in the room when the shot was fired, and instead of hitting the rug, that section of blood spatter landed on the murderer."

"What does this have to do with me?" Wagner challenged.

"I'm getting to that," I said. "What's important for you to understand is that the murderer got blood on his clothes, and if we find the clothes, especially the shoes, which very few killers remember to throw out, a speck or two of blood will undoubtedly still be on them. The guys in our lab are really good at this."

"What's that?" Wagner said with a scowl. "Screwing up?"

"Not usually," I said. "Usually they don't have much trouble pulling out DNA. We already have Billie's processed and ready to compare. Once we find a match, we just have to trace the clothes to their owner and we've found her murderer."

"You think that scares me? You have my permission. Search this damn house. Search to your heart's content," the old man said with a smile. "Take every piece of clothing I own to those Neanderthals who staff that lab you're so proud of. I promise that you won't find Billie's blood. Not even a speck. I didn't kill that woman."

"Oh, but you misunderstand, Mr. Wagner. I don't think you pulled the trigger," I said. "But before we get to my theory about the role you played, I've got just a few more things to show you."

"This is starting to feel like show-and-tell in kindergarten," he said, with a tight laugh. "Have at it, Lieutenant. This isn't getting you anywhere. As far as I'm concerned, Billie committed suicide. If you can prove she didn't, you should be chasing the SOB who murdered her, not bothering an old man at bedtime."

"Ah, but we are chasing the SOB," I said. Then I whispered, "Mr. Wagner, that's why we're here."

"You said you didn't think I pulled the trigger," he said, his anger rising.

"That's right. I don't. I'm sorry if you find this confusing," I said. "It'll all make sense soon. I promise."

David pulled out our next prop, a chart I'd made with copies of receipts attached. One had Ty Dickson's name and MasterCard number on it, payment for lunch at the El Camarero Mexican restaurant, not far from Century Oil's offices. The receipt was dated the afternoon after Cox's murder, and the waiter noted that three people dined.

Wagner looked it over, then I handed him the next credit card receipt, this one for parking at the same building for the same day, the same time, on Grant Roberts's Visa.

"So who's this Roberts guy?" Wagner asked.

"You know who he is," I said. "It's Billie's brother-in-law, the one she was having an affair with. The one who was furious at her for breaking it off. He'd been counting on her money to make him rich. Too bad for him, she had second thoughts. Maybe she hated to hurt her sister. Or maybe Billie figured out that Roberts is pond scum."

"Oh, is that the man she was bedding? How embarrassing," Wagner said, with a forced laugh. "Bet her sister's not going to be delighted to hear that. But I'm confused. What in the world does any of this have to do with me?"

"Look at the final sheet of paper," I suggested.

He did. It was a computer printout I'd called the Harris County Toll Road Authority to get on a hunch, after I'd zeroed in on the two credit card receipts. The record they faxed proved that on that same afternoon, while Billie's body was in the process of being au-

topsied at the morgue, Wagner's toll tag, the one on the black
Cadillac sedan parked in his garage, left the Sam Houston Tollway
at the exit closest to the restaurant in question just five minutes before Roberts parked his car and an hour before Dickson paid for the
three Mexican lunches.

"That doesn't prove a thing," Wagner said.

"No. I only brought all of this along for fun, because I truly enjoy showing others how we piece evidence together. This is the
only item I needed," I said. Out of my purse I pulled a DVD. A
Post-it note on the top of the see-through plastic case read: COX
MURDER, SURVEILLANCE TAPE: EL CAMARERO RESTAURANT.

"Have you got a DVD player, Mr. Wagner?" I asked. "I'd like to
play this for you."

"Why?" he replied. "Is that a good movie?"

"I think you'll enjoy it. Agent Garrity and I certainly did," I
said, with a grin he must have found infuriating. "It's a video of
you, Ty Dickson, and Grant Roberts at El Camarero the day after
Billie's death. We can't hear what you're all saying, but there's a lot
to see, a lot that explains why you were all there the day after Billie died. You had a bit of business to finish up, didn't you?"

I put the DVD on the table, where he could look at it. Wagner
didn't say anything, just focused on the silver disk as if it were a bill
from the I.R.S. The old man wasn't grinning any longer.

"Now it's time for you to start talking," I suggested. "There are
three of you involved in Billie's murder, and this is the day after.
Not hard to see on this tape that what we're looking at is a payoff."

"You can't prove that!" the old man snapped. "You can't even
hear what we're saying."

"Not yet, but the jury will be able to see for themselves how delighted you all were on the day after Billie's death. Maybe we can
get someone who reads lips to interpret. You know, what's so lucky
is that the camera was pointed right at your face," I said. "I bet we'll

be able to figure out every word you said that afternoon. That is a stroke of luck."

"We were discussing the weather," he said. "You'll never be able to prove what we were talking about. I don't believe it."

"Maybe not. But the truth is that I won't need to prove it, Mr. Wagner," I said. "I'm doing you a favor here. Do you think for even a moment that your old friend Ty Dickson will go to prison to protect you? Do you have any doubt that if I'd gone to him first he wouldn't have offered you up to get on top of this thing? You know him. He's old and sick. How eager is he going to be to spend his few remaining years rotting in a cell?"

Wagner glowered at us, furious. "How dare you?" he said, spitting out the words.

"What the lieutenant is suggesting, Mr. Wagner, is pretty obvious," David said. He appeared to be enjoying our sit-down with Wagner as much as I was. Why not? It's exciting to close in on murderers. "In case you need a translation, here's one: whoever is the first, you or Dickson, to make a deal is the one who comes out of this the cleanest. Take too long and odds are that you'll die in prison."

"After all, it's not like you were the shooter," I said. "Why right now, we're getting a judge's signature on a search warrant for Grant Roberts's house. Right now our people are pulling together everything they need to collect his shoes and all of his clothes. Think we're not going to find Billie Cox's blood somewhere? That's all we need. A single drop of blood can put you in prison until the day you die. That lawyer, McBride, is a nice fella. Well, he told me that you and Dickson were trying to ensure your legacies by building a children's hospital. Imagine what a life sentence for solicitation of murder will do to your reputations."

"I don't," he blustered. "I'm going to call my—"

Before he could lawyer up, I went on, leaning toward him, my right thumb and index finger forming the smallest circle. I held it up so he could see just a speck of light through the center. "All we need is the tiniest, tiniest molecule of Billie's blood," I said. "You've seen those shows on TV. You know what our lab people can do. You have any doubt we'll find what we need?"

At that, I shut up and let the old codger consider his options.

"Like I said, I want my lawyer," he said. "Now."

"That's fine," I said, with a shrug. "As a matter of fact, Agent Garrity is going to read you your rights. We want this by the book, so there aren't any technicalities to argue later."

"You have the right to . . ." David began, reciting the warning every suspect in a criminal case is required to be told.

"That's it, Mr. Wagner. You're done. Go ahead and call your lawyer," I said, when David finished. "Meanwhile, Agent Garrity and I will be on our way across the street to Mr. Dickson's house. I'm willing to bet that he'll see this our way. He'll get the deal we were offering you."

That took Wagner back a bit. "What kind of deal?" he asked, squinting at me.

"Ten years, with a recommendation for probation in six," I said. "We've got a prosecutor lined up to sign the paperwork."

"At my age, I'd probably never live six years," he said. "Especially not in one of those hellholes."

"Maybe not," I said. "But I guarantee you won't survive a life sentence with a mandatory forty years before you're eligible for parole."

David and I sat and stared at the old geezer, silent, while I left that DVD sitting there, right where Wagner could see it. The old man extended an arthritic hand, the joints swollen and disfigured, and picked it up. He looked at what was written across the top.

"We've got it all figured out, Mr. Wagner, even your motive. You killed Billie because she threatened to tell everyone in the oil patch about your little scheme. We know because she left a note indicating she planned to fill Bobby Barker the following Monday. And that could have cost you and your partner millions and, more importantly, it could have landed you both in jail for fraud. My guess is that Billie gave you the weekend to come clean about the scam, before she went public," I said. "And that's when you two degenerates decided she had to die."

The old man looked at both our faces, his mouth twisted into a disgusted grimace. "Who would have figured they'd have cameras in a gawd-damn Mexican restaurant," he said, spitting out the words. "What's this world coming to when you can't even eat refried beans and tortillas in private?"

Two hours later, David and I finished typing Clayton Wagner's statement at my office on the 610 Loop. The old man had signed a confession that said he and Ty Dickson approached Grant Roberts with the plan and then paid him half a million dollars to murder Billie Cox. He described the money as chicken feed compared to what they planned to make selling the oil field and Century Oil. Two wrinkled old men worried about a lifetime of cashing in without giving back, they were willing to commit murder to have their names on a hospital façade, as insurance that they'd be remembered after their deaths. Unlike Dickens's Scrooge, they wouldn't be visited by the ghost of Christmas future and given the opportunity to repent to change their destinies. They'd sealed their own fates, and I doubted that either would leave prison upright.

Wagner's signed statement in hand, I dispatched two deputies to pick up Dickson at his home and to bring him downtown for booking. Then I called H.P.D. and requested two squads at the Roberts's house to back us up when David and I made the third arrest of the night. As we drove through Houston's darkened streets, I dreaded telling Faith that the murderer she'd pushed us to find was her own husband. Still, it was the truth, and although the truth could be cruel, in my experience it was pretty much always better than living a lie. Not that I was against the small white lies. Sometimes those came in handy.

"What did you have rolled up in the paper?" David asked. "We both know they wouldn't let you check Cox's bedroom rug out of the evidence room to haul around Houston to intimidate suspects."

"A horse blanket," I said. "I was kind of worried Wagner would be able to smell it, but figured he'd be too nervous to notice."

"And the surveillance DVD? That was a fake as well, I gather?"

"Blank," I said. "Clean as the day it came off the assembly line."

"What would you have done if that old man had taken your challenge and popped it in a DVD player?" David said. He was shaking his head and grinning.

"That, Agent Garrity, didn't happen," I said, smugly. "So, you'll never know."

Twenty-six

As much as I dreaded upending Faith Roberts's world more than it had been by her sister's death, I stood front and center with David and two uniformed officers at her front door. I'd posted two more at the back door, to block any escape attempt. Serving warrants in the middle of the night is a traditional police tactic; catching the bad guys at home, preferably groggy from sleep, makes the arrest easier. Most of the time, it works.

I knocked, and a few minutes passed before Faith edged the door open.

"Lieutenant?" she said, startled to see me. "Is something wrong?"

"Is your husband here?" I asked.

She nodded. "Upstairs."

"Which room?" I asked.

She looked at me questioningly, but said, "First door on the right."

The uniformed officers quickly brushed past, on their way to make the arrest.

"What's this all about?" she asked, wary. "What do you want with Grant?"

"We have a warrant for his arrest," I explained. "I'm sorry, Faith. I know this is hard, but he's been charged with Billie's murder. We have a signed statement from Clayton Wagner, the head of Century Oil, confessing that he and his partner, Ty Dickson, paid Grant five hundred thousand to murder Billie."

"Paid him? Why?" she asked.

"To cover up an oil field scam," David said.

"But why Grant? Why would he do it?"

"Because you'd inherit Billie's money, which meant he would inherit her money, and because he was furious at Billie. They had an affair," I said. "Billie dumped him."

For just a moment, Faith appeared confused, pressing her palm to her forehead as if attempting to quell the rush of thoughts and emotions that flooded through her. "I don't understand. Not Grant, he wouldn't—"

Just then, a door opened upstairs followed by sounds of a scuffle and the thud of a body slammed against a wall. On instinct, I pushed Faith out of the entryway, into a small paneled study, and motioned for her to hide behind an oversized desk, while I pulled out my .45 and hid behind one of the room's French doors. Hearing, undoubtedly, what I'd heard, David silently retreated, backing up into the living room, out of eyesight of the staircase, as heavy footsteps above us creaked floorboards beneath the worn carpeting.

My eyes on two sets of descending legs, I didn't notice Faith stand up behind me.

"Grant, stop this nonsense," Faith shouted, as she attempted to push past me toward the staircase. "This is obviously some kind of mistake."

From above us, the parade of legs grew closer, one following the other down the staircase. "Sure, Faith," Roberts said, with a short laugh. "You'll fix it, just like you've tried to fix everything in our marriage. You'll fix it like you tried to fix me, and even Billie. See how well that worked?"

"I don't understand," she cried out, as I shoved her hard toward her hiding place. "The lieutenant says you murdered Billie. Grant, you couldn't have. You wouldn't have hurt her."

"I should have known that damn ranger was here," Roberts said, seething.

Pushing harder against her, Faith at first fought me, but then I caught the first glimmer of understanding in her eyes, the first resignation that perhaps what I'd told her was true. This time, when I urged her back down, Faith hesitated, but then did as instructed.

With no good cover in the living room, David stood off to the side, his gun drawn and targeted on the stairs. On the staircase, the legs grew longer, the first two in blue uniform slacks, followed by two barefoot and wearing blue-and-white-striped pajama bottoms.

"I know you're here, Lieutenant," Roberts shouted as he pushed the young cop forward. "Come out so I can see you before I pull the trigger and kill this poor cop."

David shook his head. My impulse was to agree, until I saw the terrified kid in the cop uniform. Roberts had him by the collar, with a Glock pressed to the back of his head.

"So, what do we do now?" I said, as I stepped forward, pointing my gun at Roberts.

"You're going to put your gun down," he said. "Now. On the floor. Then stand up and back away, so I can get out that door."

I smiled. "I don't think so," I said. "In fact, I know that's not going to happen."

"If you don't, I'll kill this cop," he said. "I'll pull the trigger. I promise you, I will!"

"That's not going to happen, either," I said, being careful not to look at David, not wanting to blow his cover. "You're a smart guy, Mr. Roberts. Smart enough to realize that a dead hostage isn't any good to you."

The uniformed cop looked ready to argue the point. His stark blue eyes were bulging, and his face was drained a deathly white. I might have been sure Roberts wouldn't fire, but his hostage obviously had doubts.

Appearing not to know what to do, Roberts stopped on the stairway, on the second from the last step, and peered at me, as David came out of hiding, his pistol aimed at the back of Grant Roberts's skull.

Our suspect did a head swivel, sizing up David then back to me. "This gets more complicated all the time, doesn't it?" I said. "You really need to put that gun down."

Furious, Roberts shook his head. "Not a chance," he said. "I'm not going to prison. Won't happen. I'll kill this cop if I have to."

"That officer is all that's keeping you alive," David warned. "You kill him, and I fire. Of course, that would be poetic justice. You'll end your life the way you killed Billie Cox. The last thing you'll feel is a bullet slicing through your brain."

"Guess they didn't cover effective hostage taking in real estate school?" I said, staring him down. "Time to admit this isn't your area of expertise and move on. Better to face a murder charge than die."

For moments, Roberts stood on the steps with his gun pressed against the young officer's head, most likely playing through possible scenarios in his mind, like a chess player not yet ready to admit he's been checkmated. Finally, he must have realized he had no way out. Letting go of the kid cop, who fell forward on legs weakened by fear, Roberts turned the gun around, and held it toward me by the barrel. I grabbed it, as David pulled him down off the final step. Before he barreled up the stairs to check on his partner, the kid cop threw David a pair of handcuffs.

"There's a business card in my wallet. A lawyer, the best criminal guy in town. I've already retained his services. He's expensive, but worth the money. Call him, Faith," Roberts ordered, as David ratcheted the cuffs tight around his wrists. "You'll have Billie's money once the estate is settled. We can afford someone good."

Out from her hiding place, Faith glared at her husband. "Call that lawyer yourself, but make sure you tell him there won't be any big paycheck," she said, each word dripping in contempt. "I won't use a penny of Billie's money to defend her murderer."

"You'll do as I say. Call the damn attorney. It's all set up. I need someone good," Grant ordered yet again. "You're my wife. I expect you to stand by me."

"You expect? You have no right to expect anything," Faith said, pulling her blue terry cloth robe tight and cinching the belt around her narrow waist. "I should have known you'd target Billie. Money has always been more important to you than people. How could I not have known you were behind all this?"

"Faith, please," he said, his demands softened to pleading. "Don't believe them. Listen to me. I'm innocent. You know me. You know I couldn't kill Billie."

Without responding, she walked over to a hall table where her husband's wallet sat on a small porcelain dish. She flipped through receipts, a little folding money, a small stash of business cards, and found what I assumed was the one from the lawyer. Her hands steady, Faith stared at her husband as she tore the card up and let the pieces drift to the beige carpeted floor. Then, she grabbed four quarters out of a pile of change on the same table, and handed the coins to me. "Lieutenant, this is for my husband," she said. "So he can call a cheap lawyer."

"Why you bitch," Grant slurred.

"With the little bit we have in the bank, our meager community property, maybe you'll qualify for a public defender. Or you can use the blood money you got for killing Billie," she said.

"As soon as we find it, that'll be confiscated," I explained. "I'm afraid he'll have to find other funds."

"It's settled then," Faith said, her face a mask of calm in a room electric with tension. "Since I assure you that I won't donate a penny for your defense, a public defender it is."

"Wait until I'm free," he said. "I'll . . . You'll be . . ."

As entertaining as Grant Roberts's frustration was, we had a job to do, and I was ready to call it a night. "It'll be a long time before you'll be free," I said. "Too bad you took Wagner's and Dickson's money. Now those old men can testify against you."

"They're the ones," he snapped. "I don't know what they told you, but they're the killers. They wanted me to murder Billie, but I wouldn't do it. I'm innocent."

"You be sure to tell that to the judge and jury," David said. "Right now, you're heading downtown, for booking."

The young cop was helping his partner down the steps, an egg on his forehead the size of a quarter. While David helped them take Roberts to the squad car I lingered with Faith. She cried softly, and I put my arm around her. "I didn't want to admit it to myself, but I think I knew," she whispered. "Down deep, I suspected Grant was Billie's lover. I saw the way he looked at her, and I knew my sister better than she knew herself. I understood that as smart and beautiful as Billie was, she was still that motherless child, with an emptiness inside her that made her vulnerable to any man who said the right words. And that's something my husband excelled at, selling himself, first to me, then to my sister. What I don't understand is why he had to kill her."

"It's hard to know if Grant would have murdered Billie if Wagner and Dickson hadn't offered him the half-million," I said. "Your sister knew enough to send them to jail and cost them millions, two things those old men couldn't let happen."

Faith nodded, but her face mirrored her disgust. "My sister was worth so much more than money. How pitiful that they didn't understand that," she said. "Lieutenant, if there's anything you need from me, any way I can help with the case, please ask. Grant may technically be my husband, but only until I can get divorce papers filed, and my loyalty is to my sister."

"I understand," I said. "But now I think we'd better go. We have paperwork to complete before we call it a night. Will you be all right, or is there someone we can contact for you?"

"There's no one," Faith said, wiping her damp cheeks with the back of her hand. "Billie was everything to me, my only family."

"I'm sorry," I said. "I truly am."

"You have no reason to be. My husband and those two old men are responsible," Faith said, with certainty. "Thank you for solving my sister's murder. Thank you for believing me. Now, perhaps, Billie can rest in peace."

"Okay," I said. "But if you need someone to talk to, someone to listen and offer support, I can call the victims' assistance folks, and they'll be out here in a flash."

She shook her head. "I'll get through this, because I know it isn't forever," she said. "Thanks to Dr. Dorin, I understand that Billie and I will be together again, although not in this life, in the next."

Twenty-seven

I woke up to a ringing phone early the next morning, Monday, and, still half-asleep, I grabbed for the cell on the nightstand. I felt groggy and tired. I'd hit mom's bed at three and slept little. I wasn't sure why. It felt like something gnawed at the back of my mind. I couldn't figure out what needled me. But there was something there, just out of reach.

"Lieutenant, it's about time you picked up," Rick Barron said. "Where's Cassidy? The press is calling, and none of us know what to tell them. This thing is turning into a nightmare."

Damn, I thought. I looked at the phone in my hand. Sure enough, it was the old one, the one the captain had ordered me not to answer. Wishing I'd been awake enough to realize, I said, "Miss Collins is in a protected place. That's all I can tell you."

"Are you with her?" he asked.

"No," I lied. "I don't know where Miss Collins is, but I know that the captain has made arrangements to be sure she's being protected."

"Well, is she playing the rodeo tonight?" he asked, sounding frustrated. "We've got more than seventy-thousand fans with tickets. The captain says she is, but are you sure? Is she going to perform?"

"I'm not in touch with Miss Collins," I said, wondering if at that moment someone was tracing the signal, pinning down my location. Why hadn't I just let the damn phone ring? "All I can tell you is that the captain told me the same thing he told you, that Miss Collins will put on her show at the Houston rodeo tonight as scheduled."

"Lieutenant, does that mean you're closing in on this Argus? You'll have an arrest today?" Barron asked, sounding relieved at even the suggestion that it was possible the turmoil of the past months might finally be behind him. "Can we count on that?"

"Mr. Barron, now that we've taken over Miss Collins's security, the situation has changed. I don't know where she is, but if I did, I couldn't tell you, and details about our investigation are off limits," I said. "All you need to know is that Miss Collins is safe and she will be at the rodeo tonight, just like the captain told you. Have your crew get ready, as they would for any other performance. Good-bye."

I hung up and turned off my cell, rolled over in bed and buried my face in the pillow, when I heard someone walk in. I reluctantly squinted at the figure beside me with one eye, exhausted and just wanting to turn back over and sleep.

"No, I'm not! And you can't make me," Cassidy said, peering down at me, her hands folded across her chest in the universal stance of defiance.

"I understand how you feel," I said, pushing myself up on my side and running my fingers through my hair. It was no use. As soon as I moved my hand my frizzy mop flopped back into my eyes. "Let's talk about this, calmly. I'm sure I can explain why Agent Garrity and Captain Williams want you to perform."

"You can't force me to," she said, furious. Still, compared to the in-your-face kid who'd arrived on our doorstep, this was a new Cassidy. I could tell she was at least trying to maintain control. "Lieutenant, you can't force me to get on that stage. No one can."

"Cassidy, this isn't about your fans, it's about your future. I don't care whether or not you disappoint a bunch of teenage girls. I do care about catching Argus," I tried to explain. The kid looked ready to turn and run. I couldn't say I blamed her. "We haven't been able to get a solid lead on him. We need to draw him out."

"Sounds good. Go ahead," she said. "But you'll need another pigeon. This one's had it. When it's your life, you make the decision. Right now, this schizo wants to kill me, and he's making fools of all of you big-shot cops."

"California hasn't come up with anything to help us?" I asked, again. I'd heard it once but didn't want to believe it.

"Nothing," David said, with a shrug. "They haven't found Jack Shaw, and he remains our most likely suspect. Turns out he's the son of one of the old women who lived at the trailer park, just like Cassidy thought. The woman was Sharlene Shaw. I say 'was' because she passed away the year after Cassidy moved. The other two old ladies couldn't tell us much about him. The California office questioned the other men on our list and found no indications that they were at all involved in the stalking. In fact, they all have alibis for the periods when Argus was known to be following Cassidy. Their computers were seized as part of the search warrants on their homes and offices, and the tech guys came up dry. They arrested one man for having child porn, but nothing suggests that either one is our stalker."

"Great," I said. "It's always so good to wake up to good news. First Cassidy overhears me on the telephone with Barron. Now

California comes up dry. Everyone else is eliminated and no leads on that Shaw pervert."

"I've got to admit that it's not going particularly well," the captain said, stating the obvious. I'd called him right after the kid's blowup, and the three of us were powwowing around the kitchen table. I figured we looked like the characters in one of those old paintings, the ones with schemers around a campfire or candle, their faces etched by anxiety and glowing in the light of a flame. "Seems like we're losing instead of gaining momentum. No need to say it again, I know, but I hoped we'd be able to explain our plan to the girl with more finesse. I thought I'd talk to her this morning, since we don't have to deliver her to Reliant Stadium for the concert until about six this evening."

Whether or not he wanted to rub it in, his words hit their mark, and I squirmed a bit in the old spindle-backed chair, resulting in the complaint of wood rubbing wood as its worn joints strained. The captain rubbed his eyes and looked as fatigued as I felt. This case was wearing on all of us. I had to admit I'd felt safer having David at the ranch 24/7 since our flight out of Dallas. Having him close was comforting, even if I knew it was only temporary. But the poor guy hadn't even been able to run home to pick up his newspapers. This morning, he wore another of Bill's shirts, black with pearl-topped snaps. For a Yankee, he made a pretty fair-looking cowboy. I refocused, bringing my mind back to the job at hand.

"Obviously, I didn't realize Cassidy was walking through the hallway while I was on the phone," I said, yet again. "No excuses, but I was pretty foggy after being out most of last night. While I admit my mistake, the rodeo is tonight, Captain, so we had to tell her soon. If she won't perform, I don't see how we can help her. The only other option is to ship her back to California."

"You can't do that," Cassidy said. Mom's old house, additions tacked on over the years when she and Pop had a few extra dollars to spend, obviously had way too many nooks and crannies where folks could hide and eavesdrop on other folks. With Mom, Maggie, and me, it wasn't a problem. We didn't have many secrets. But lately, it complicated the heck out of keeping anything private.

"You can't send me to L.A.," she said. "Argus knows where I live. He'd find me. I need to stay here."

"Miss Collins, I'm not sure you've thought this through," Captain Williams said. "Sit down with us. Let's talk."

The kid ignored him and focused on me, pleading. "Lieutenant Armstrong, please don't send me back. You just can't. You need to find this creep. Please, help me."

I saw the panic in her eyes at the suggestion that we could wash our hands of the case and felt a surge of sympathy for the kid, but the truth was that we were running out of ideas.

"Cassidy," David pleaded. "If you'll just sit down with us for a few minutes as Captain Williams suggested, we'll discuss this."

"No. You have to listen," she said. She tucked her hands under opposite arms to stop them from shaking. "You have to help me. Please."

Politely asking the kid to listen didn't appear to be working, so I figured, as much as I hated to, that maybe we needed to wallop her with a heavy dose of reality. "Cassidy, the captain's right. You haven't thought this through," I said. "You're smart, but this guy has you running scared. That's putting you in even more danger. You want to help us stop this jerk? Take a breath and listen to Agent Garrity and the captain."

"Why should I?" she challenged.

"Because like you said, it's your life, and with your help, we might be able to save it," I said. "And because I don't see anyone else standing in line to help you get out of this mess."

Our eyes met, and for a long moment, she said nothing. I'd about given up hope when somehow it appeared that my words had hit their mark. "Okay," she said, her voice quaking. As frightened as she was, I had to give the kid credit for even attempting to hold it together. "I'm not agreeing to anything. But I'll listen."

The plan, as the captain explained it, was relatively simple. We wanted Argus to make his move, to act while we were fully manned and ready to pounce on him, so Cassie didn't have to worry that one day he'd attack while she was alone and vulnerable.

Unlike Dallas, at the Houston rodeo there would be no formidable show of protection around her, no visible barrier of law enforcement circling, like wagon trains in an attack. Instead, we'd employ a substantial but more discreet force, dressed to blend in with the crowd. The reason? We were tempting Argus.

"I don't like it," the kid said, as skeptical as if we claimed we had an invisible force field to throw around her, like in those sci-fi movies, the kind that mysteriously bounces off killer rays. "I'll be a sitting duck."

"No, you won't. But let's talk about alternatives," I offered. "What are your suggestions? You don't want to go home to California. You can't stay here. It's not good for my family, and it's really not helping. Eventually, you need to leave and reclaim your life. If you let this SOB scare you into obscurity, you'll have to walk away from everything you worked hard to build, your entire career, and you'll have to remain in hiding. Is that really what you want? And even if you do all that, will he leave you alone?"

"Well, I know one thing," she said. She gulped hard, and added, "I know that I don't want to die."

"Then this plan is your best bet, your only option," I said. "We need Argus to come after you where and when we're prepared to protect you. Otherwise, you'll never know when he'll strike, and it could be when you're alone, with no one to help."

"But I'll be out there on the stage, not knowing when he'll . . ."

"Cassidy, I'll be close by every minute," I promised. "Every second."

"Will you be on the stage with me?" she asked.

"No, the lieutenant won't, but we'll all be near, dressed as stage-hands, cowboys and cowgirls, spectators, sound techs, and ushers," David explained. "We'll have officers all over Reliant Stadium, all intent on keeping you safe and catching this guy."

The kid thought about that, and then frowned. "Okay, but how can you catch him when you don't even know what he looks like?"

None of us answered, because she was right. Collins was a smart kid. Without an ID, our odds of catching Argus weren't as rosy as we painted them. Still, as I saw it, she didn't have a choice. Living in fear wasn't an option.

"These types of stalkers, when they're this committed and this dangerous, well, Cassidy, they don't just go away," I explained. "This guy is fixated on you. He's not giving up."

"But I'm scared," she said. She sat down hard on the chair next to me and the spindles creaked behind her. The kitchen smelled of the breakfast tacos the captain had brought, egg, sausage, potato, and refried beans wrapped in thick flour tortillas. There were a few on a plate on the table, but the kid didn't grab one. I doubted that she had much of an appetite. The teenager closed her eyes, as if collecting her thoughts, or perhaps praying. For a few moments, no one spoke, not the captain, not David, not our celebrity charge, nor I. In the silence, I thought about what she'd said, that we didn't have a face to pin on the stalker. We had a suspect, Jack Shaw, but it was at best a long-shot guess, at worst another total misdirection. Cassidy was right. Without at the very least a description of the person we were looking for, the odds were against us. It was then that my sleep-deprived brain focused on what had kept me awake, an idea until then not fully formed.

"Cassidy," I said. "Remember when you told us that in an early e-mail Argus claimed your eyes met at a concert? That you saw him?"

She looked over at me, questioning.

"Yeah. In Atlanta," she said. "But I told you I don't remember anyone from that night. I really don't see much of anything in the crowd, from the stage. I don't see faces. That doesn't help."

"Maybe not," I admitted. "But maybe, just maybe, you did see him. And if you did, maybe there's a way to jog your memory. I'm going to make a phone call. If I can pull this together, at least we've got a shot of figuring out who we're looking for."

Twenty-eight

R elax," Dr. Dorin said, in a steady, soothing voice. "Cassidy, the most important thing is for you to let your mind rest. Concentrate on my voice and relax."

"Yeah, sure," the kid said, sounding doubtful. "Relax with that creep out there stalking me?"

"Breathe," Dorin said, drawing out the word. "One deep breath . . . two . . . three . . . breathe."

In my darkened bedroom later that morning, Cassidy lay on my bed, on top of my white eyelet comforter, while David and I watched silently from the shadows. Dorin had explained that her first task would be to lead the teenager to an imaginary place, one where she felt safe enough to set aside her anxiety. "You're in a beautiful meadow, surrounded by a rich forest and the air is thick with oxygen," Dorin said. "Flowers of every color line your path, and the air is scented with lavender. This is a place where you have nothing to fear. No one can harm you while you remain here, and you have no worries. Your only task is rest and relaxation."

Despite the doctor's assurances, on the bed, Cassidy stirred nervously. "I'm not feeling it," she said. "I'm cold."

I grabbed one of Mom's crocheted afghans off the brass quilt stand in the corner and laid it over the kid's slight frame.

"Thanks," she said, never opening her eyes.

"You're welcome," I whispered. Dr. Dorin shot me a glance, reminding me to keep quiet, but I couldn't help myself. That was the first thank you I'd heard come out of the kid. Maybe it was too much to hope for, but she did seem to be letting her guard down, at least a little. While we'd waited for Dr. Dorin to arrive, I'd watched Cassidy with Warrior, talking to the foal, brushing his coat, and almost cooing at him as she tried to reassure him that all was well. Perhaps she was attempting to convince herself as well that there was nothing to fear and all wouldn't be lost.

"Picture yourself in that meadow, my dear, surrounded by beauty," Dorin said. She still had the stripe of white roots in her dyed dark hair, and she wore what I thought was probably her uniform of sorts, a long skirt with a sensible sweater and dark brown flats. "See yourself near a small stream." At that the therapist turned on a portable CD player, and the room filled with the murmur of a babbling brook, birds high in trees, and the serenity of nature. "Feel the rhythmic motion of a hammock rocking languidly back and forth, back and forth, back and forth."

Cassidy fidgeted again on the bed. "I can't do this," she whispered. "Maybe I'm not good at getting hypnotized."

Dorin sighed. "Cassidy, I know that you've had to be strong, be on guard," she said. "Even for those who have had less stressful lives, it can be difficult to give power over to someone else and trust they have your best interests at heart. But none of the people here with you would harm you. Do you believe that we all want to help you?"

At first, Cassidy remained silent. She opened her eyes and

looked around the room, at the therapist, at David, and then at me. I smiled at her and she smiled back. Then, she closed her eyes and said in a small voice, "Yeah."

"Then release control," Dorin instructed. "Place yourself temporarily in our care. We will protect you. Listen to my voice and relax. Relax."

"Okay. I'll try," the kid said.

"Don't try," Dorin said, still in that same quiet, nurturing manner. "I can't reach you if you're working to help me. Instead, clear your mind. Breathe deeply, relax, relax, let go of your stress and wipe your mind clean. Just be. Allow yourself to blend into the bed, the mattress. Feel the slight breeze in the air as it skims your body. Imagine yourself in that meadow, a solitary place where you're protected, where you're able to lie on a blanket, close your eyes, and drift away. The sky above is blue and the clouds a pure white."

I suspected that with most subjects, Dr. Dorin didn't have to work quite this hard. It took a full fifteen minutes before the therapist nodded at me. "Cassidy," Dr. Dorin said. "Can you hear my voice?"

"Yeah," the kid said, lying on the bed, her breathing deep and steady. "I hear you."

"Listen carefully and do as I tell you," Dorin said. "But if you become frightened, if you feel unsafe, remember the meadow. You always have the meadow available to you, and you can will yourself there at any moment."

"The meadow," Cassidy said. "I have the meadow."

"That's right. No one can hurt you, because you have your safe place. You can go to the meadow at will, just by deciding you want to, instantly, and no one can follow you. No one can hurt you there," Dorin said. The girl nodded. "Now I'm going to take you back in time just a little, to this morning. I want you to tell me where you were and what you did right after waking up."

"I had to go to the bathroom. I was yawning, walking down the hallway, and I passed the lieutenant's room. I heard her on the telephone," she said. "I heard her talking to Rick, saying I was going to perform at the rodeo. I was upset. I was afraid."

Dorin looked at me for confirmation, and I nodded. "That's good, Cassidy," the therapist said. "Now let's go further back into your memory, to the night you performed in Atlanta. The show has just started. Describe what you see."

"I can't see anything," she said. "It's my opening song, and I'm wearing my costume, that gold cocoon, and I can't see through it. I can hear the crowd and the band, but I can't see anything."

"Fast-forward a little, until the cocoon is gone," Dorin said. "What do you see now?"

Cassidy paused for a few moments, and then said, "I'm looking down at the audience, flying on wires way above them. I'm singing, and the girls are reaching up at me. I see colors, lights. I see people below me."

"Look at their faces, Cassidy," Dorin said. "Isolate the men in the audience. Focus on them and describe them."

"I can't," the kid said, urgently. Agitated, she shook her head, as if looking from face to face in a crowd we couldn't see. "Everything is a blur. I can't focus. I don't see faces. All I see are arms reaching up to me, and I hear the kids screaming over the music. I'm scared."

"Slow down, Cassidy. Remember no one can hurt you. You always have the meadow. You can go there at will. So please, focus. Go into slow motion and focus. Look through the crowd and see if you can pick out a face, a man's face," Dorin said. "Any man. Tell me what he looks like."

"I see the figures of men and women, moms and dads," she said. Her expression changed from fear to one of deep sadness. "They're there with their kids. Everyone looks so excited to see me."

"You're frowning," Dorin said. "Why does that make you sad?"

"It's just," the kid said, "it's not important."

"Tell me," Dorin said. "Why does that make you sad?"

"I wonder why they're so happy."

"Why do you find that surprising, Cassidy?" Dorin asked. "Aren't they all there because of your music? To hear you sing?"

"Yes, they're there to hear me sing," she said. "It just doesn't seem right."

"Why not?"

"It just doesn't."

"Explain it to me," Dorin said. "Make me understand."

The teenager hesitated, a tear making its way down her pale cheek. "It's hard. I see the kids with their parents, and it makes me sad. I don't have a dad, and my mom hardly noticed me," she said, her voice a low whisper. "I felt like I didn't even exist."

"Why do you think that was?" Dorin asked.

"I was alone so much," Cassidy said. "Mom was drunk all the time. She never, I never felt like she loved me."

As bad as I felt for the kid, I gave Dorin a look and wound my hand in a circle, hoping she'd get the hint to speed things up. The tragedies of Cassidy's life might be interesting to explore in therapy, but this wasn't the time. We didn't have all day, and I'd explained to the doctor what we needed.

"That wasn't your fault, my dear," the therapist said, ignoring me. "Alcoholism is a disease. Your mother was sick, and you were a child. You deserved her love, but she was unable to give it. You bear no blame for her illness or her shortcomings."

"It hurts," Cassidy groaned, and each word bore deep sadness. "Why didn't she love me?"

For a moment, Dorin said nothing. I looked over at David and he shot me a glance, one that reflected the kid's pain. It was just too real, too present, too on display. I wondered if it hit the therapist as hard as it had us, or if hearing such admissions from patients made her immune to the depth of a young girl's anguish.

"I'm sure your mother loved you, Cassidy," the doctor said, softly, and from the hoarseness of her voice I knew that she too was touched. "Your mother was ill. You couldn't change or help her, no matter how hard you tried. It wasn't your fault. None of it was your fault."

"I should have done something," the girl said, and I decided perhaps it was worth not protesting to allow Dorin a few minutes to address what even I could see was an open wound. It was then that Cassidy uttered the words that must have festered deep inside her for years. "I loved my mom, but I hated her, too. Sometimes I think that I let her die."

"No, Cassidy, no," Dorin said, her voice pleading. "You were a child. You never had the power to save her."

"Yeah," she said. "Yeah, I was a kid. But I was her kid, and I watched her die."

"Cassidy, listen to me. Children aren't responsible for their parents," Dorin said, sounding like a grandmother comforting yet scolding a young child. "Your mother was the adult. Not you. You were never in control. She was there to protect you, not the other way around. Do you understand that, Cassidy?"

"She was there to protect me," the girl repeated. "I never had control. Then why do I hurt?"

I looked at my watch again, willing the session to go forward.

"You hurt because she was your mother, and you loved her," the therapist said. "Because you wanted to help her. But you couldn't. She was the only one who could help herself."

As much as I wanted to let it go on, we were losing time. I nudged Dorin's arm, and she jerked slightly, as if she'd forgotten why we were there and that David and I were waiting.

"Now Cassidy," she said, taking my cue. "Remember what we talked about. Return to that night in Atlanta, performing on the stage. Once again look out into the audience. I want you to focus on the faces, especially those of the men, and tell me about them."

"I told you that I can't see them," Cassidy said. "They're there, and I can see the outlines, but not the faces. It's a blur."

"You can't see any of them?"

"No," she said. "Not with the gold stuff all over me. When I do the cocoon, I can't wear my contact lenses. That gold stuff hurts my eyes."

"You can't see the audience at all?" Dorin asked.

"I see them," she said. "I'm looking at the audience, but without my contact lenses, I can't see faces."

I threw my head back in dismay. The kid had never mentioned not wearing her contact lenses. We had five hours before she was supposed to show up at Reliant Stadium to perform at the rodeo, and suddenly my only plan to ID Argus was hopeless. Sometimes life just doesn't play fair. It's like it leads me down a path and then, bam, it's over, my only accomplishment wasting time.

"So you can't see any of the faces of any of the men, any strangers, anyone who doesn't look as if he belongs there?" Dorin asked.

"No," the kid said. "No faces at all, just bodies and arms, and a kind of blurriness where the faces are. And I can hear the crowd shouting my name."

"Wrap it up," I whispered in Dorin's ear.

"Cassidy," the physician said. "I want you to remember what we've talked about here, about your mother and your not being at fault for her death."

"The kids are loud, screaming," she said. "I wish they'd stop."

"Cassidy, I need you to concentrate on my voice, now, it's time to end this—"

"I wonder who that sleaze is," the teenager suddenly remarked. "I haven't seen him before."

I put my hand on the doc's shoulder and squeezed.

"Who are you talking about?" she asked, pulling free of my grasp. "Tell me about him. Can you see a man's face in the audience?"

"No, I told you. I can't see any of the faces in the audience. But this guy's not in the audience. He's in the wings. Staring at me, with a really sick smile," she said, sounding puzzled. "The guys are reeling me back in, onto the stage, and they've got me stage right, ten feet from Jake. This guy's standing next to the sound mixer, so close I can see his face and that weird smile."

"Who is he?" Dorin asked.

"I don't know, but he looks familiar. He looks like someone I should know."

"Who does he look like?" Dorin asked.

"I don't know," the kid repeated. "He just looks like someone I should know or something. He just seems familiar."

"What's he doing?" I asked, and Cassidy jerked.

David put his hand on my leg and his finger to his lips, shushing me. Before the session started, Dorin had explained that David and I needed to be silent, that even the slightest interruption could disrupt, even end the session. He reached over and nudged me back in my chair. I was so drawn into what was happening, without realizing it I'd stood up and leaned over Cassidy in the bed.

"What is the man doing?" Dorin asked. "The stranger."

"He's standing next to the mixer, talking to Jake, but he keeps staring at me. He's smiling but he looks, he looks angry. Angry at me," she said, sounding puzzled. She paused, moments passed, and then she visibly relaxed. "Oh, it's nothing, I guess. Jake's talking to him."

"What's he doing now?" Dorin asked.

"He took something out of a bag. He's bending down, looking under the equipment. It looks like he's fixing the mixer. Funny they'd do that during the show, but Jake's showing him something, and the guy looks like he's brought a part. Jake's hardly paying any attention to him. Everything's okay. He looks familiar. Maybe I've seen him before?"

"Ask her to describe him," I wrote on the top sheet of my sketchpad with a charcoal pencil. Dr. Dorin and I had talked about this earlier, but I wasn't taking the chance that she'd forget. Along with sculpting clay faces on the skulls of unidentified victims, in a pinch, I sometimes use my art training to draw composites of suspects. That's what I intended to do now, with Cassidy, to draw a picture of the man she saw in Atlanta, only Dr. Dorin had to ask the questions.

"Tell me about the shape of this man's face, the stranger's," Dr. Dorin instructed, reading off my list of questions. "Describe this man, as you look at him."

"He's a big guy, not old, pretty young. His hair is a mess, thick and dark. Really stupid looking. Bushy. And his face is wide, like he has big cheeks," she said.

"Go on, Cassidy," Dorin said. "Tell me in detail what this man looks like."

"His eyes are dark and pushed back in his head kind of, or they look like it because his eyebrows are heavy."

As she talked, I drew, trying to keep up with everything she said. Beside me, David had a tape recorder running. Dorin said that depending on how the session went, we might play it for Cassidy later, to see if she remembered even more. But as the teenager described the man, the details came though remarkably clear. It sounded as if she were still in the Atlanta concert hall, as if she were at that very moment looking at his face, not resurrecting a memory.

"Is there anything remarkable about this man, a tattoo or anything that sets him apart?" Dorin asked. On my pad, the face of a young, heavyset man with dark brooding eyes took shape.

"He has a scar," Cassie said. "There's a scar on his face."

"Where?" Dorin asked.

"On the right side. It's running up and down, ending just above his lip," she said, tracing the path with her right index finger. In my mind, I saw the face of a man I'd met less than a week earlier, who had just such a scar. The man I remembered sat at a piano, composing a song.

"Do you know this man?" Dorin asked again. "Why does he look so familiar?"

Cassidy didn't answer the doctor's question.

"I know who this is," I wrote. "Wake her up."

Dorin nodded. "Cassie, I'm going to clap now, and when I do, I want you to open your eyes. You'll remember everything we've talked about, and you'll feel refreshed and happy, not at all frightened. I'm going to count now then clap on three. One. Two. Three."

Dorin clapped, but on the bed, Cassie remained silent.

"Do you hear me, Cassie?" the therapist asked. "I'm going to clap and you're going to open your eyes. The session is over."

"I feel like I know him," Cassie whispered. "Why do I feel like I know him?"

"Listen to me, Cassie," the therapist instructed. "I'm going to count to three."

"Maybe I saw him once, someplace?" Cassie mused. "Maybe I saw him before the concert sometime?"

"One, two, three," Dorin said again, then clapped her hands.

Cassidy lay still, as if waiting. "You can open your eyes now," the therapist said, and slowly the kid did. She rubbed her face with her hands, and then focused her wide green eyes on me.

"Did I do okay?" she asked. "Do you have enough?"

Twenty-nine

My sketch of the man Cassidy saw in Atlanta looked convincingly similar to Justin Peterson's driver's license photo. It was a formality, a comparison pulled together for the captain and David, who hadn't had the privilege, as I had, of meeting our prime suspect in person. We'd ruled Peterson out because he hadn't physically gone to Cassidy's concerts, believing the experts who told us he had no other way to infiltrate the sound systems. No one considered the option of bugging Cassidy's own sound equipment. I called Jake, and he confirmed that a guy in Atlanta passed himself off as a factory rep there to fix a recalled computer circuit. Whatever Peterson installed, it appeared, gave the young genius the power to hijack the mixer's output at will.

Now that we knew Peterson was our stalker, David had the FBI pulling every record they could find on the pianist, rounding up all the information they could lay their hands on.

Meanwhile, Dr. Dorin watched over Cassidy, who rested upstairs in my bed, while more troopers arrived to guard the ranch. David, the captain, and I had another job: serving a search warrant on Justin Peterson's apartment. With a little luck, we would find evidence that proved Peterson was Argus and, at the same time, take him in for questioning, hours before Cassidy walked onstage. But the clock kept ticking, and all we had left were four hours before we transported the kid to the rodeo. Meanwhile, a cobbled-together squad of two hundred officers was scheduled to descend on the stadium. No matter how this went down, we needed to be ready.

"Let's go," the captain called out. "We're rolling."

Early on a Monday afternoon, traffic was light, and we soon stood outside Justin Peterson's apartment near the Rice University campus, search warrant in hand. The captain knocked, once then again.

"Police," he shouted. "Open up, Mr. Peterson."

We'd been unable to find a manager with a key. When no one answered, the captain stepped to the side, and four officers manning a battering ram pummeled the oak door with number 35 stenciled on it. The lock gave way, and the door snapped open. I'd wanted to enter Peterson's apartment the day I'd met him on the campus. Now I found nearly every wall covered by posters of Cassidy Collins. My body felt a sudden chill, as I scanned the walls and saw what Peterson had done. In some he'd "X"ed out Cassidy's face, in others just her eyes. Over others, he'd painted red, horror-movie lips dripping blood.

"Hell of a tribute to his favorite recording artist," David said, sarcasm overflowing. "Wonder what the guy does if he doesn't like someone?"

"Lieutenant, over here," Gilberto Torres, the computer expert, called out from another room. David and I found Torres hunched over a keyboard in what was little more than a closet, a kind of hidden bedroom desk unit. The shelves held three computers, and all the screens flashed rotating images of Cassidy, many with the symbol of one Web site or TV program or another stamped in the corner. In some, she performed onstage, but most were candid shots, taken in restaurants, at parties, and clubs. Video streamed on one, rotating footage from street sightings, on a Web site called "Cassidy Collins in Real Time."

Underneath the video display, a banner read: WHERE'S CASSIDY? JOIN THE SEARCH. FIND THE SUPERSTAR AND POST YOUR VIDEO HERE.

"Does real time mean *real time?*" I asked. "Are we talking about live images of events as they happen?"

"Yeah. I think so. My guess is that these are private feeds, where viewers pay a fee to gain access," Torres said. "Looks like this particular one is a Web site where fans share cell phone video of Collins twenty-four/seven, from concerts to sightings on the street. They score a photo or video and immediately post it via PDA or cell phone." Torres clicked a few keys and images of Cassidy on the stage in Vegas popped up. Torres scouted around more and a cell phone photo showed the kid on the day of another of Argus's e-mails, this time meeting with her agent over lunch.

Perhaps the most disturbing Web site was one run by an unidentified agency that called itself "Hollywood Eye," where paparazzi photos were displayed within moments of shooting. An entire section featured photos of Collins, doing everything from shopping at Chanel to working out with her trainer on the patio of her L.A. mansion, a shot that appeared to have been taken by helicopter.

"Well, now that explains the Argus name," David said.

"What?" I asked, stunned at the extent of the cottage industry around Cassidy, the fans and paparazzi that recorded her every move. One site scanned the kid's estate with a live feed from a camera that appeared to be housed in a neighbor's window or a tree.

"Argus is the creature with a hundred eyes," David explained. "Peterson only needed two. The paparazzi and Cassie's fans supplied the other ninety-eight, and they were Argus-eyed, ever vigilant and focused on that poor kid morning to night. She didn't even have privacy in her own home. Except for his trip to Atlanta to install the chip, Peterson stalked her without ever leaving his apartment."

How sad it seemed that in the end Argus wasn't just a mythical reference by a single deluded individual but Justin Peterson bragging about being aided by a celebrity-obsessed culture.

It was then that I noticed a photo in a frame on the top shelf between two of the computers. I picked it up and held it. It was nothing special, just one of those department store portraits, this one of a young couple with two children, the oldest a dark-haired kid, maybe five or six, a boy. He sat on the father's knee, uneasy. They looked alike, thick-boned and sullen. In her arms, the woman held a small infant dressed in pink. A girl. Like the boy, the woman's body language appeared apprehensive, unsure. She was thin, blond, and pale-skinned, with delicate features.

"This is all interesting, but the important thing is that Peterson is nowhere to be found," the captain said. "Doesn't look like he's been here for at least a couple of days. His newspaper from yesterday is still outside, and the neighbors haven't seen him. The campus police tracked down his graduate advisor, and she says Peterson missed today's work session and yesterday's. He hasn't checked in at the campus clinic or the hospital where he was treated last year. No sign of him anywhere."

"So, we finally have enough to get an arrest warrant, and he's disappeared?" I said. "Anyone disagree that he's gone underground, preparing to make his move?"

Thirty

"N ow, you understand the plan?" I asked Cassidy. "You know how we want this to come down?"

In Emma Lou's shed, the kid knelt next to the tiny foal, brushing Warrior for what must have been the third time in a single day. Maggie wouldn't have anything to complain about when she and Mom got home. Expending nervous energy, Cassidy had groomed both momma and baby horses until they looked polished enough to be competing at the rodeo. In the driveway, a caravan was assembling for the drive to Reliant Stadium. It was nearly time to leave.

"Yeah, I know the drill," Cassidy said, brushing her cheek lightly against Warrior's long, thin face. "You told me everything. I'll remember. No problem. Just get that guy. Lock him up and throw away the key."

Cassidy stood up, and I frowned at the kid, wondering what to tell her. Did she need to hear it all, see it all, or could it wait? Did she deserve the truth? The captain, David, and I had been arguing about it ever since we'd figured it out. No one was sure what to do.

Damn, I thought.

"Cassie, David and I had a hunch, based what you said while under hypnosis, about why Peterson seemed familiar."

"What are you talking about?"

"We found something in Peterson's apartment, something that made me think about a possible connection between you two. So we asked the FBI to pull some records," I explained. I put both hands on her shoulders and looked into her frightened green eyes. She was so young. A tough kid, but at sixteen, how much was she capable of bearing? "Cassidy, what we learned, well, it fits into what's going on. I need to know if you want to hear it now or later, after this is all over."

"What's it about?" she asked.

"Like I said, it's about you," I repeated. "And it's about Justin Peterson."

The kid looked at me, scared. Apprehensive, she nodded.

"Okay, Lieutenant," she said. "Talk."

"Cassidy, I know this is tough, but you're going to have to just listen for a minute," I said. "First let me tell you about Peterson."

The records were easy to find. It turned out that Peterson's biological father was a housepainter and a drunk named Roy. When Justin was born they lived in a small house in Evergreen Park, outside Chicago. The local cops had an extensive file on the goings on at the house, where Peterson's mom called nine-one-one on a regular basis. The patrols arrived and found the wife with a bloody nose or bruises, once a broken arm. The local uniforms hauled Roy in on domestic violence charges, but each time they had to drop them when the wife refused to testify. The couple had a second child, a little girl, when Justin was five. Not long after, the mother disappeared with both children. The woman was never heard from again. If Roy looked for them, it wasn't for long. Even though there was never a divorce, he remarried. More battering reports came in from the new wife, she eventually left him, and then, four years ago, drunk, he drove his old work van into a tree and died."

"So that Peterson creep had a tough time. Too bad," Cassidy said, with a smirk. "So did I. Do you want me to feel sorry for him?"

"No, I don't," I said.

"I just want him out of my life," she said.

"There's more," I explained.

"What?" she asked.

I sighed. Sometimes when cases come together quickly, decisions are made on the fly, and it's tough to know what to do. I hoped we'd made the right one, telling Cassidy everything. "Okay," I said, taking the photo from Peterson's apartment out of an envelope. "Now I want you to look at something."

The kid stared at the photo doe-eyed, as if not sure what she looked at or, perhaps more important, what it meant. Finally, she put out her hands and took the framed photograph from me.

"Do you know anyone in that photo?" I asked.

The kid nodded. "Why do you have a picture of my mom?" she asked. "And who's the guy and the kids?"

"That's your father," I explained. "And the boy, he's your brother."

"I don't have a brother," she said. "I don't have any family. No one."

"Cassidy, the FBI discovered that Justin Peterson was adopted. His biological father's name was Roy Eckert, and Peterson's mother's name was Claire Eckert, just like your mother, and the baby girl Claire disappeared with was named Angie," I said. "I'm pretty sure the people in the photo are Roy and Claire Eckert and their two kids, Justin and Angie."

The kid stared at me, processing it all. "You think that Argus weirdo is my brother?"

"Yes," I said. Cassidy's eyes locked on mine. "I do."

"No," she said. "That's crap. He's not."

"The FBI has confirmed that Justin was abandoned at an orphanage in Chicago just before your mother showed up in California. A year later, he was adopted by a couple whose last name was Peterson," I said.

"Oh, my God," she said, with a look of utter disbelief. "No. This is all crap."

At that moment, the kid who'd held all of us at emotional bay turned away from me. Moments passed, but soon her shoulders heaved and she broke down, sobbing. I came up behind her and put my arms around her, and she turned and wrapped herself around me, holding tight, tears streaming. "He's my brother. My brother. My mother abandoned my brother. How could she do that? How could she?" she whispered. "Does he know who I am? Does he know I'm his sister?"

"I don't know. I can't be sure," I said. "Maybe not. Maybe your mom left him with that photo at the orphanage, and he doesn't realize the connection, that you're the baby."

"How could my mom have done that, walked away and left him?" she repeated.

"I can't answer that," I said. "But maybe she couldn't take care of both of you? Maybe she thought he'd handle it better than you would. You were just a baby."

Cassidy thought about that, and then shook her head. "Justin doesn't know I'm his sister," she said. "If he did, he wouldn't . . . If he knew, he wouldn't be threatening me. He couldn't."

That was an assumption I wasn't ready to make. "Cassie, whatever drew Justin to you, he's become obsessed," I said. "We don't know how he'll react when he's confronted with the truth. We have to assume that he's still a very, very dangerous man."

"No, you're wrong," she said, her mood changing before my eyes. She no longer appeared frightened, but something else. To my surprise, she began to look excited. "Lieutenant, he's my brother. He wouldn't hurt me. He just doesn't know."

"Cassidy, please listen to me," I cautioned. "Don't assume Justin Peterson's not dangerous. That could be a very bad mistake."

"Oh, my God. Think about it. My *brother*. I have a brother."

"Cassidy, please, slow down here," I said. "Relax and give this a little while to sink in, to think through it. We don't really know what his motives are. We don't know how he'll react."

"But he's *my brother*. My family. You can't hurt him. Promise me you won't," she insisted, holding onto me tightly. Tears still streamed down her face. "We'll explain. Once we tell him, this is over."

Thirty-one

"Y ou sure this is necessary?" I asked Germaine Dunn, while she sprayed purple and yellow stripes in my hair. "I've been meaning to get a cut and maybe some highlights, but this is a little out there for me. I usually shoot for a more traditional look. You know, something that doesn't clash with my Wranglers and holster."

Dunn stepped back, sized me up, and chuckled, then tried to camouflage her enjoyment behind a studious frown. Her own riotously colored locks hung loosely in curls around her face, and she had enough eye makeup on to play Madame Dracula onstage. "If you're going to look like one of us, yes, it's necessary," she said, diving right back in and pulling at my hair on both sides of my face to make sure she'd cut it evenly. She'd chopped it up in layers, to show off the color, which she'd repeatedly assured me would wash out. I looked at myself in the mirror and wondered what David would think, then reminded myself yet again that what he thought wasn't a concern.

At that moment, Cassie sauntered out of the trailer bedroom dressed in black leggings and a gold-sequined minidress. Since this wasn't her full stage show, there'd be no cocoon or flying about on wings. But she had on her thick stage makeup, and the kid looked five years older than an hour earlier in the horse shed.

"Wow, Lieutenant, hot look," she said, with a chuckle. "Wait until Maggie and your mom see you decked out like a Hollywood chick."

"Yeah. I can't wait. Somehow I think I'm in store for more ribbing than usual," I said. Looking at her, I considered all the teenager had and was still going through. Tough breaks. Some things didn't seem as important as they once did. "You know, we've spent a good bit of time together. I won't mind if you call me Sarah."

The girl looked surprised, but then smiled. "Okay," she said.

"Okay who?" I asked.

"Okay, Sarah," she said, looking pleased and perhaps even grateful.

The kid's mood had been lifting ever since she'd gotten the news on Peterson. All she talked about was finding him and explaining who she was. That and that alone, she insisted, would end the nightmare.

Still unsure, I'd avoided any promises that I wouldn't hurt him. The truth was that the day's revelations had made the entire situation even more complicated. All I was certain of was that Justin Peterson had to be stopped before he had time to carry out his threats. Maybe, if we were lucky, Cassidy was right, and once we had him under control, all we'd have to do was talk him through it, explain, and it would all go away. That theory, for some reason, wasn't jiving with my intuition, my subconscious voice that murmured quiet warnings. Over the years, I'd learned to pay attention when my instincts radioed all wasn't well.

"How long until the limo's here?" she said, turning to Germaine. "I'm jazzed. Ready to go."

Dunn glanced at the clock next to the mirror and said, "Forty minutes and counting."

We were in Cassie's trailer parked within a secured area, near the freight doors on the north side of Reliant Stadium, Houston's state-of-the-art football arena, part of a complex covering acres of land just inside the South 610 Loop. In the vast parking lot, cars and pick-ups sprawled as far as the eye could see, while a rambling, brightly lit carnival sold Moon Pies, chicken-on-a-stick, funnel cakes, turkey legs, popcorn shrimp, and cotton candy. I've always enjoyed carnivals. When Maggie was a little kid, we stood in line for twirls on the spinning teacups, but the Ferris wheel was my favorite. I loved soaring stories high, peering down at folks throwing rings onto bottles to win stuffed animals and catching glimpses of the banners that advertised Frog Boy and the Bearded Lady.

While we got ready in Cassidy's bus, the rodeo unfolded inside the stadium. Tons of soft brown dirt had been bulldozed over the football field, turning it into a fitting stage for muscular cowboys who wrestled steers, yanking them down by the horns or tying their legs together in a quest for speed. Bull riders cinched their hands with leather reins to hold on tight, and the crowd cheered as barrel-racing cowgirls maneuvered powerfully built horses at breakneck speeds between brightly colored barrels. A win represented fame, money, and saucer-sized, silver-belt-buckle trophies.

Just after eight, as Germaine put the finishing touches on my new look, the captain called from his position in the audience to say our forces were prepared, everyone in place. The rodeo events were over, the cowboys backstage nursing their injuries, and workers had taken over, towing a circular, white stage surrounded by a canopy of spotlights onto the floor, readying it for the evening's main event.

Opening day, the grounds pulsed with excitement, and the marquee bordering the freeway read: TONIGHT: CASSIDY COLLINS! with the notation: SOLD OUT! There was no doubt that the teenager was the year's most-sought-after ticket. Reliant held more than seventy thousand, and tonight it overflowed with a record-setting, standing-room-only audience. Every available ticket had been snapped up within fifteen minutes of sale time, a record. Scalpers sold the close-in seats for more than a grand, and the nosebleed accommodations emptied pockets by an average of two hundred bucks.

On this particular night, the crowd was young. As in Dallas, young girls filled the audience, some only eight or nine, many wearing Cassidy Collins pink T-shirts with sequined butterflies and hearts. Their faces mirrored their delight at being among the select. They were the envy of their friends, the kids the others would swarm the following morning at school, pumping for reports about all they'd seen, especially the teenage recording star, what she'd worn, what she sang, how she looked.

As the audience grew impatient, the stage was anchored into place and the crew erected three black tents behind it. That done, vans drove across the dirt-covered floor to stock the tents with equipment, props, and Cassidy's wardrobe changes. Meanwhile, digging through the dirt to find electrical outlets, the crew plugged in the stage, powering its canopy ringed with spotlights. Less than half an hour after the rodeo competition ended, the chants in the stadium built as the crowds cheered for Cassidy.

Someone pounded on the trailer door, followed by a gruff voice. "We're ready for Miss Collins, Lieutenant."

I opened the door and found Buckshot dressed in blue jeans, a plaid shirt, and his silver belly cowboy hat. "You're our driver?" I asked.

"That's my assignment," Buckshot growled. "The captain said I should drop you ladies off at the stage and pick you up at the end of the show, or sooner if that Peterson kid makes a move and we need to evacuate the girl quick."

"Great," I said, thinking the captain had made a good choice. Having Buckshot behind the wheel made me relax a bit, but just a bit. The drama Cassidy's life had been barreling toward would take place, good or bad, in the next two hours. We'd done all we could to stack the deck: two hundred cops dressed in plainclothes and carrying copies of Justin Peterson's Texas driver's license photo. Their orders: shadow anyone who looked the least bit like the kid. If they thought they had a positive ID, call for backup before confronting the suspect and moving in to make the collar.

"Cassidy, let's go," I said. The kid bustled forward, sequins chattering, with Germaine on her tail, and we headed for the black limo parked directly outside the trailer. As we scurried inside, Buckshot scanned the horizon along with a ring of cops disguised as cowboys packing their gear. Moments later, Buckshot was behind the wheel. He drove through the stadium entrance, past the pens where the bulls, horses, steers, and calves queued up for each round of competition, while inside the limo, there was silence and a fidgety, uncertain, chest-tightening anxiety that signaled the time had come.

We stopped smack dab in the middle of the stadium, and David opened the door and helped us out. He took my hand, gave me a quizzical look, and said, "Nice hair."

"Be careful," I said. "I know where you live."

He laughed. "Hey, all kidding aside," he said, suddenly serious. "Keep safe."

"You, too," I said, meaning it.

He nodded, and Cassidy turned back to yell at us before she ran onto the stage. "Sarah, remember, he's my brother. Don't hurt him. Okay?"

"We'll do our best," I shouted above the high-pitched screams of the audience, a shrill, near-ear-splitting dissonance. "And we're right here, with you."

Cassidy nodded, then turned and ran up the ramp onto the

stage. Her band was already in place, playing a pulsing, heavy beat, and she jumped in on cue. As frightened as she must have been, the kid was a trooper, fueled by the cries of her fans and the prospect of discovering a long-lost brother, even if he saw her only as his quarry.

On the stage, Cassidy joined the dancers and the backup singers, while I followed Germaine into the first black tent. Jake, the sound guy, manned the mixer. Earlier that afternoon, with his help, our computer guys had easily found the chip Peterson inserted in Atlanta. But we'd left it in place. For our plan to work, we needed Argus to believe he was the one in control.

I watched from the sidelines, hidden from the audience inside the sound tent as Cassidy performed on the stage. David stood beside me, as he had in Dallas. This time, however, we had more eyes than Argus, more than four hundred supplied by the two hundred officers, and we knew our prey's identity, a decided advantage. After the first number, Cassidy ran down the ramp and into the tent, where Germaine and the dressers waited. They went into high gear, peeling off her clothes and wiggling her into her next costume, a pair of skintight jeans that settled around her hips and a flirty sweater with holes over a white tank top.

"No sign?" she asked, as Germaine ran a brush through her hair, and picked up a tube of lipstick to repair the damage.

"No sign," I said. "We're watching. You just do your act, and we'll do the rest."

"Okay," she said, turning and quickly running back toward the stage where the dancers covered for her.

"Any reports?" David asked the captain on his walkie-talkie.

"Nothing," the captain said. "We're on full watch."

On the stage, Cassidy was on top of her game, roiling her fans into a near frenzy. Even without her golden cocoon, the kid was a sight to behold, dancing and singing, a smile as wide as her face, her long blond hair flying about her.

The concert proceeded without a glitch, as if it were any other night. There was no stopping the young superstar, as she went from song to song, carrying her fans with her. They sang along, many reciting every word. In between each set, Cassie ran back to the dressers and searched my eyes for hope that we'd made a sighting and that we had the stalker we now believed was her disturbed brother in custody. David and I shook our heads, with no assurances to give her. For more than an hour, she performed as she had many times before, putting every ounce of energy into each song. In the stands, the tens of thousands of girls sang along, waving their arms in the air as they held tiny pink flashlights and glowing pinwheels, making the stadium swim with waves of light.

"The kid's actually pretty good," David said, during the final set. "I'm kind of getting into this."

I gave him a sideways look and a smile. "Yeah, she is," I agreed. "Just don't start dancing. This isn't the time."

His eyes were focused on the audience, the stage, surveying the crowds, as we both had throughout the concert, but he laughed. "Seems to me we danced once, and I rather enjoyed it," he said.

"Seems to me we did more than that once, and I enjoyed it, too."

"Well, I do remember . . . ," he said, with a devilishly broad grin. Whatever else he planned to say was lost as his smile locked in place. His eyes focused on something in the distance, and I tracked them to the figure of a man in the front row, a heavyset guy with unruly dark hair, running toward an aisle, where a low gate led to the arena floor. The object of our attention fussed with the gate, then jumped over it, and David lifted a pair of binoculars to his eyes to get a closer look.

"Is that Peterson?" I asked.

Without answering, David bumped the captain on his walkie-talkie. "Section one-two-seven, first row, center, on the stadium floor and running," he said.

"About time," the captain said. "East center patrols move in. One-two-seven, center, on the ground and running."

Dozens of officers swarmed out of the audience toward section 127, but then, suddenly, the stadium lights flickered, blinking on, off, on again, then off. Over the loudspeaker Argus's voice came through loud and clear: "Cassidy, I'm here for you. I'm coming."

Fans screamed, and Reliant Stadium went dark. The generator kicked in and emergency aisle lights shone a bright gold, but stadium center, where Cassidy stood in disbelief staring out into the crowd, remained shrouded in shadow.

"I'll grab her," I said. "Call Buckshot and get the limo."

"He's on his way," David called out, pointing at headlights hurrying toward us.

As David rushed forward toward the suspect, I sprinted onstage, where Cassidy stood transfixed. In Dallas, the prospect of Argus claiming her had terrified her, but now she looked expectant, hopeful. I grabbed the kid by the arm, and urged her to follow, pulling her off the stage, but she resisted.

"He's here," she said. "My brother's here. He said he's coming. He won't hurt me. I just need to tell him who I am."

"No, Cassidy. You don't know how he'll react," I screamed. "We'll talk to him later, after they've got him. Now, follow me. Come on."

The limo pulled up, and I yanked the door open, stuffed the kid in, and jumped in beside her. The engine wound and the limo took off, throwing a U-turn and heading back to the north entrance.

"I need to talk to Justin. I need to find him," Cassidy cried out, reaching toward the door handle. Her hand got there before I could stop her, but the door didn't open. "Let me out. I need to find him."

I don't know what, but something didn't feel right. The glass privacy window, the one separating the rear of the limo from the driver, was up. I looked at the back of the driver's cowboy hat and thought of the last time I'd seen Buckshot, when he'd driven us into the stadium. A sense of dread flooded through me.

"This isn't right," I whispered.

"What?" Cassidy said. "What's not right? Tell him to stop and unlock the damn door. I want to go back."

"The black cowboy hat's not right. Buckshot's was regulation ranger, silver belly."

The limo tore out of the stadium through the north entrance, just as I spotted a second black limo, one with Buckshot standing beside it, tires flattened. My fellow ranger had his shotgun out, aiming at us. He looked like he wanted to shoot, maybe at the tires, like nothing would have made him happier, but there were so many folks around, workers and cowboys and their families, rushing about, trying to get a glimpse at the chaos unfolding inside the stadium, that they blocked the shot. Unlike his renowned exploit with the rustler, this time Buckshot didn't pull the trigger. Instead, he ran toward a cowboy holding the reins of a horse, pushed the man aside, threw himself up onto the stallion, and took off in pursuit.

"Isn't that our driver?" Cassidy asked, as we sped away from him, toward the gates at the edge of the parking lot. In the distance waited the freeway.

"Yeah," I said.

At the wheel, the driver tramped on the gas pedal. Behind us, Buckshot urged the horse on, into a full gallop, like the limo careening around cars and folks on foot. But the limo was too fast and the horse had too much to overcome. Before long, Buckshot and his commandeered mount faded in the distance as the limo neared the parking-lot gate.

"We're jumping. Get ready," I said. I reached down, pulled up the locking pin on the door, and, as the limo slowed to take a sharp corner, grabbed the handle. It didn't budge. I tried again, kicking at the door with the thick heels on my cowboy boots, while the limo made a wide right turn out the gate and onto the freeway access road. Again, it stayed rigid, locked. No sense in a third try. No one could hear us scream. The film over the windows was so dark, no one could see us. We were trapped.

"Sarah, is it Justin? Where's he taking us?" Cassidy asked in a small voice, a mixture of fear and excitement.

"I don't know," I whispered.

"Can he hear us?" Cassidy whispered.

"I don't know," I said. "Probably."

Immediately, Cassidy pounded with both fists on the privacy window. "Justin," she shouted. "You're my brother. We figured this out. You're my brother. That's why you're stalking me, because you don't know, but you're my brother."

The limo sped through the darkness onto the 610 Loop, with no response from the driver. Cassidy pounded again, but this time her efforts were met by a scraping noise. As we watched, black metal shields rose up from inside the window wells. Cassidy clawed at one, pushing it down, but the metal was sharp, and she pulled away her fingers, bleeding. I grabbed my Colt .45 out of my holster and fired two rounds into a side window, as a sheet of black metal slowly slid up to cover it. The tempered glass shattered into thousands of irregular pieces with bullet holes at the center, but remained intact. I lay on my back and kicked with all the force I had, but before I could break through, the metal skin closed the gap.

I turned to shoot at the driver though the privacy window, but a metal shield covered that as well.

A voice came over a speaker, one I recognized as Justin Peterson's. "Thank you for joining us, Lieutenant Armstrong," he said. "I hardly recognized you at first, but it's certainly an added bonus to have you here."

"Justin," Cassidy screamed. "Justin, you're my brother. My brother."

"There's no use in attempting to escape," he said, as if he couldn't hear her. "I've had plenty of time to outfit this limo and, as I'm sure you realize by now, I'm rather good mechanically and with technology."

"Mr. Peterson," I shouted. "Pull over and talk to us. We can explain all this. It's all a mistake."

"So I suggest you sit back and relax," he said, either not listening or choosing to ignore us. "The ride won't take long, and I think you'll both be impressed by what I have planned."

Thirty-two

Cassidy and I were entombed in the back of the limo, the doors locked and all the windows hidden behind metal shields. We drove for fifteen minutes or so, the teenager resting against me, leaning on me for support. She was terrified, and so was I. I had my gun in my right hand and my left arm over her narrow shoulders, when I felt the car make an abrupt right turn then drive down what felt like a series of steep ramps. We wove around for a few minutes, and then the car stopped, and Peterson turned the engine off. It was quiet, and we waited. Judging by the little I saw as we left the stadium and the relatively short distance he'd driven, I figured we were somewhere in downtown Houston, probably in an underground parking structure.

Most of the way, I'd told myself help was following, trailing us from the stadium. Now, looking at it logically, I figured, probably not. The kid in the front row, the one David spotted, had to be a decoy planted to draw attention. By then, Peterson had let the air out of Buckshot's tires, which gave him plenty of time, once he killed the lights, to drive into the stadium before David and the captain discovered they were chasing the wrong guy. By now, of course, they knew they'd been set up, but it was too late. We were gone. All Buckshot could tell them was that we'd pealed onto the freeway.

We were on our own.

"Lieutenant, I need your gun," Peterson said. "There's a small door on the right side, below the privacy window, that opens into a metal drawer. Put the gun in and close the door."

"Like hell," I whispered.

Again, silence, and we waited. Cassidy's body shuddered, and I held her tighter.

"I haven't heard the door open. I assume that means you've decided not to cooperate," he said.

The girl had been silent, I figured too scared to speak, but this time, hearing her brother's voice, she sat up and pounded at the metal-skinned privacy window. Tears ran down her cheeks, but her voice remained strong, determined. "Justin, it's me, Cassidy, but my real name is Angie. I'm your sister," she screamed. "Please, roll the window down. We need to talk. You're my brother."

Peterson continued on, in his calm, unconcerned tone.

"I need the gun, Lieutenant. While I'm prepared to wait for it, I don't have unlimited time until your colleagues find us. So this is the situation," he said. "Do as I instructed, please. Open the door, put the gun inside, and close the door. Or, don't. And I'll kill you both right here, right now, in the backseat of this limo, then simply walk away."

"Sarah," Cassidy pleaded. "Give him the gun, so we can talk to him. He'll understand. Once he knows who I am, he wouldn't hurt us."

I put my index finger up to my lips and shushed her.

"Give me a minute," I said. She looked uncertain, but nodded. I looked about the backseat, wondering how he planned to kill us. Then, the more I thought about it, I figured that wasn't in the cards. Considering the situation, he wanted us alive. He'd planned for too long to finish us off so unceremoniously. Why pursue Cassidy for months and then dispatch her before he had all his fun? At least, that was my best guess, one I was staking both our lives on. If Peterson wanted my gun, he'd have to come after it.

Cassidy sat so close to me, I felt her heart beating. I surveyed the headliner covering the inner roof and saw nothing. I inspected the privacy window area, acting like I was searching for the door. If Peterson wondered what I was doing, I hoped he'd think I was trying to comply. What I actually had in mind was finding the camera. There had to be a camera. He had to be watching us. He'd want to see us, to increase his enjoyment of our suffering. No fun without the visuals. I spotted a small grate in an indentation near the roof, took my jackknife out of my pocket, and used a blade to pry it open. As I suspected, I looked directly into a camera lens. I raised my right leg and kicked with my gray lizard-skin boot, smashing the lens.

"Why did you do that?" Cassidy cried out. "He'll think he has to hurt us."

I shushed her again. I could tell it was a struggle for the kid. During our time together, she'd begun trusting me. But I knew she figured I was dead wrong, that if I just did as Peterson instructed, we could talk to him and clear the whole thing up. Sounded comforting, but I still had my doubts.

"And I thought that perhaps you'd oblige me," he said. "This is disappointing."

For a moment, again only silence, as Cassidy held me and I waited, holding my gun, watching the doors. With no other ideas, I tried the door handles, again pulling up and pushing. No such luck. They were, of course, still locked. Then, I caught just the faintest hint of an unfamiliar smell, a faint but distinctly chemical odor.

"What's that?" Cassidy whispered, her entire body shaking. "It smells bad in here."

I took another whiff. I hated to say it, but I had to. "Some kind of gas I think," I said. I looked over at her, but my eyes blurred. I couldn't see her clearly, and I didn't have the strength to hold her up when she swooned, her head sinking onto my lap.

This wasn't going so well. I had to admit that maybe I needed a plan B. Quickly. Pounding on the privacy window, I screamed, "Okay. Okay," but my fists felt too heavy to lift, and my voice was little more than a mumble. The gas burned my throat, and I would remember nothing more.

"You really should have just given me the gun," Peterson said, perched on the edge of a tan metal desk. He looked miffed, but his voice didn't give away any sign of irritation. "It would have made it so much more pleasant for all of us. It wasn't easy carrying you both here. I'd only planned on the girl."

The room was floating, and everything had a yellowish hue. It felt like swimming through chicken broth. I took a look around. A metal door, gray like the walls, bolted from the inside. I could breathe but my lungs ached from the gas. As my vision cleared, I saw Cassidy across the room, on the floor. A few mops and buckets, dust rags and some spray cleaners on a shelf suggested we were in some kind of maintenance storage locker. When I looked back at Cassidy, I realized she was handcuffed and chained to a wall. I tried to move my arms and felt, instead of chains, plastic-covered electrical cord cinching my hands behind my back. I looked down and saw a length of cord anchored me to the small steel-framed chair I sat on. Only my legs were free.

Cassidy rolled over, moaning. She was waking, and Peterson, still wearing his black cowboy hat, couldn't have looked happier if he'd just finished scoring the final measure of a new symphony.

"It was nice of you to come with her, Lieutenant," he said, with a smirk. "I hadn't hoped for quite this much success. If I had, I would have made sure I had two sets of chains and handcuffs. But I believe I've adapted to the situation quite well."

"Justin, you really don't want to do this. It's all a misunderstanding," I said. "Let Cassidy tell you what we've discovered about the two of you. It'll explain why you've felt so drawn to her."

"The truth is, Lieutenant, I'm not interested," he said.

"Where are we?" I asked, again looking about the room. "We're downtown, right? Somewhere in the tunnels?"

It's one of those oddities only the locals know about. On any even vaguely inclement day, at street level Houston's main business district appears deserted, while streams of office workers mingle in air-conditioned comfort in a web of underground passageways, accessed through the city's soaring skyscrapers via a maze of stairwells, escalators, and elevators. Monday through Friday, nine to six, the tunnels are flooded with pedestrians frequenting underground shops and restaurants, dropping off dry cleaning or picking up prescriptions, all the while avoiding cold, rain, or Texas's unrelenting summer heat. After working hours, the tunnels and the skyscrapers above were mostly dark and quiet. Since it had to be ten or later, if that was where Peterson had us, we could scream, but the likelihood was that no one would hear us.

"Ah, you are good, Lieutenant," Peterson said, with a grin. "Deductive reasoning, I suppose. Length of trip, etc. Very good."

"Great, well, how about freeing us and we'll talk?" I suggested. "Cassidy has something she wants to tell you, something that'll clear all this up."

"If that's what I wanted, I would," he said with a shrug. "Too bad for the two of you, it's not."

Boy but I wanted to wipe that smirk off his face. If my hands were free I would have done just that.

"But, you don't understand," Cassidy pleaded.

All afternoon, I knew she truly believed she just had to explain their connection, to let Justin know they were sister and brother, and she'd have her happy ending. The way this guy was acting, it appeared my fears were right. Having a connection with Cassidy wasn't Peterson's only motive. There was more going on, but what?

"I'm your sister," she said. "Please listen to me. It's true. I'm your sister."

"You are?" he said, with exaggerated surprise. "How can that be?"

"Sarah can tell you. We figured it out. There are even records."

"You're sure about that?" he gasped, followed by an indulgent grin.

I gauged the delight he took in her pleas, saw how he savored having Cassidy, having both of us in his control, and I thought, *he's toying with her.*

"Listen to me, Justin," she pleaded. "I'm telling you the truth. The reason you're so interested in me, I know you don't understand, but the reason you feel drawn to me is that we're family. We're related."

"Why do I feel drawn to you, Cassidy?" he asked. "What is it about you that makes it impossible for me to think of anyone but you?"

"It's because I'm your sister, don't you see?" she said, tears coursing from her eyes, frustrated at his seeming inability to understand. "You're my brother, Justin. *My brother.*"

Then, any doubt was gone. His smug expression left no room to be mistaken. "He knows," I said. "He's known all along."

Cassidy shot me a puzzled glance, but Peterson laughed, a hard, rueful cackle that resonated off the blank walls.

"How did you figure it out?" he asked.

"I should have known from the beginning. Your e-mail, about her freckles," I said. "I thought maybe it was a good guess, based on her fair skin, but you knew. You remembered."

"There you're wrong. Actually, it was a guess. Cassie was too young for freckles when our paths diverged," he said. "But my mother had freckles as a little girl. I'd seen them in her pictures. I assumed, since they look so much alike, that my sister would, too."

"You remember?" Cassidy asked. "But Justin . . ."

"Believe me when I tell you that a five-year-old never forgets a detail of the day his mother deserts him. The day she left him at an orphanage," he said, every ounce of his being focused on his sister.

"But that wasn't me. I didn't do it," she countered, her voice small, frightened.

"True. But you were the one she picked," he said. "I was the one she left behind."

The kid looked scared but at the same time angry. "Maybe she tried, Justin. Maybe Mom wanted to be with both of us. Maybe she couldn't take care of both of us. Whatever, I don't know. But we both know she didn't have an easy life. Our mom had a lot of bad stuff, especially from our dad," the girl said. I was proud of her for standing up for her mother, at least trying to understand. "Maybe Mom thought she was doing the best she could for us, like she couldn't think of a better option."

"I don't care about her problems," he said, spitting out the words. "As for our relationship, yours and mine, well, some things are more important than sharing the same bloodline."

"Like what?" she asked. "What's more important than family?"

"To me? Revenge," he said with a surly grin. Looking at him made the acid in my stomach churn. "Cassidy, you and I have an old score to settle."

"That's not fair. I was just a baby," Cassidy said, her eyes hard on her brother. Despite her hopes, the teenager was beginning to understand that this wouldn't be the happy family reunion she'd hoped for.

Peterson gazed at the kid with utter contempt.

"How did you find me?" she asked, her voice hoarse with sadness and fear.

"That was easy. I just waited until I was old enough, and then pulled some records, looked at old files. You see, I remembered our last name. I always remembered," he said. "I went looking for Mom a few years ago, and found out she was dead. Sadly for you, the alcohol took away any opportunity to punish her. With Mom gone, you were next up. You were, I must admit, a little harder to find, but not much. You look just like her, and your face was all over the television and magazine racks."

I tugged at the cord around my wrists. Tight, too tight. It wasn't budging. And the gun, where was my gun? Maybe behind him, on the desk? Or in a drawer? Or maybe he left it in the car? Where was the damn gun? Where were the captain and David? There should have been some way to figure out where he'd taken us. Someone must have seen something.

"Instead of making up that stuff about wanting to mentor my music, why didn't you write and tell me that you were my brother?" Cassidy charged, growing ever angrier. "If you had, I would have contacted you."

"You sure?" he asked, his voice level and calm, yet contemptuous. "You're sure that's what you would have done?"

"I would have understood," she said, in a small, quiet voice. "I would have sent for you."

Peterson stood up, walked over, and peered down at Cassie, and I saw a bulge under his shirt, at the small of his back. My gun or his? It didn't matter.

"Really, you would have sent for me?" he scoffed. "And why would you have done that? Why would you have chosen me to believe? With all the crap you get every day, the fan mail, the bizarre claims. Why would you have chosen to believe me? Why wouldn't you have disregarded my letters, exactly the way you did when I wrote you offering help and friendship? Tell me that."

"I would have answered," she said, her voice aching with pain. "I would have believed you. I would have known. We have the same parents."

"Wonderful parents," he said. "Two drunks."

Peterson laughed, a derisive, searing, mocking laugh. There was no longer any question about what to do. It was obvious that Cassidy and I were part of some strange game. We wouldn't be leaving this room alive. My guess was Peterson figured he wouldn't either, but, unlike us, he didn't care.

"You're wrong about what's important. Family is family," I said to him. I didn't harbor even a glimmer of hope I could change his mind, but I needed to keep the conversation going, to buy time. "You've got a sister now, someone bound to you by the most basic human element, blood."

Peterson said nothing, only glared at Cassidy, as I went on. "Could anything be stronger? Look how much you have in common, especially music," I said. "Why not make up for lost time? Why not get to know your only living family?"

"Shut up, Lieutenant," he ordered. "The teenage superstar and I share nothing, and we're certainly not family. My father was a drunk who beat my mother. Beat me. Instead of taking me with her when she fled, my mother threw me away."

"Is that why we're here?" I asked. "So you can punish your sister for the sins of your parents?"

"Yes," he said, grinning at Cassidy. "That's precisely why we're here."

"There has to be more. There just has to. What else? You owe us an explanation," I said, but then, I knew that, too. I remembered that day at the university, as he sat at his piano, when he mentioned my name in the headlines. "You're doing this to make sure you're as famous as your sister, aren't you? It's all some kind of perverted game, a sick competition to get your name in the press. You kill her and you become famous, an instant celebrity."

"No!" Cassidy screamed. "No, Justin, please. I'm your sister."

The laugh again, that same vicious laugh.

"He's hopeless, Cassidy," I said. "Don't bother."

"But he can't mean that. He just can't," she cried.

"Yes, I can. For the first time in my life, in my entire existence, I'm in charge, with the power to make sure that the world hears my story. I planted that family photo so you'd find it," he said, turning to me. "I wanted everyone to know. Imagine what they'll assume, that I killed the superstar without knowing she's my sister. Cassidy and I will become tragic figures. They'll say things like, 'It all could have ended differently. If that poor boy had only known who she really was.'"

"And all three of us will be dead?" I said. "If you don't die here, you will of a lethal injection. You won't be around to enjoy your fame. Makes the whole exercise pointless, in my opinion."

"Too bad for you, not in mine," he said. "The way I see it, fame, at any cost, is a win. And this level of fame, that of murdering my very own superstar sister, that'll buy me a level of notoriety I could never achieve with my music."

I'd been working to free my hands, but the electrical cord wouldn't budge. If I could just get him to watch Cassidy for a while, talk to her. The final battle against Santa Anna for Texas independence only lasted eighteen minutes. I didn't need much time.

"Cassidy, tell Justin about what happened during your session with Dr. Dorin today," I said. "Tell him what you remembered about your mother. She wasn't a bad woman. Remember what the doctor said, that it was an illness."

"I don't care that she was sick," he blurted out, his eyes dark wells of anger.

"But, Sarah's right, Justin," Cassie said. "You have to listen to me. Mom didn't want our lives to be bad. Maybe she thought she was doing the best thing for us."

No matter how hard I tried, the bindings on my wrists weren't giving, so I started tugging at the knot that tied me to the chair. If I kept working, I might . . .

"Sure, and the Easter Bunny delivers colored eggs," Peterson said. "Mom was a drunk, just like Dad. That and the two of us were the only things those two had in common. When he wasn't beating one of us, he was threatening to. When Mom ran, I thought maybe we'd be all right. What does she do but give me away? At least she wanted you. At least she cared about what happened to you. Me, she threw away, like an empty booze bottle."

"Okay, maybe you're right," Cassidy shouted back. Despite everything, she wasn't sitting back taking it. "But like I said, what did I do? What did Sarah do? Why do you want to kill us?"

"The ranger's here because she ended up here. It was her fate," he said, each word laced with hate. "You? You're here because I was the one she gave away, and because killing you is the best way to make sure I don't die in obscurity."

"But your music," Cassidy argued. "Justin, you have your music. You're brilliant. Sarah told me you're some kind of a genius. You could have an amazing career."

" 'Could have' being the operative words here," he said. "Could have but probably won't have. You know how many classical musicians really make it? Hardly any. I'm not dying that way, unknown. I'm not. It won't happen."

The knot around my waist fell away and the cord went slack on my lap. I had one chance, only one. I needed him distracted. Cassidy looked at me, as if she knew, and his eyes followed hers. Peterson stared at my face, and then his eyes trailed down.

Just then, from outside the door, a voice blared on a bullhorn.

"Mr. Peterson, we have this area surrounded," David ordered. "You have thirty seconds to open up, and then we're coming in."

Startled, Peterson turned toward the door.

If I'd had more time, I might have thought of something brilliant, or at least something with a whiff of a chance of working. But I didn't, so I did the only thing that occurred to me. His back turned to me, I jumped up, dragging the chair with me, and bore down on him, knocking Peterson from behind, aiming for his kidneys. He faltered and fell, sprawled out on the floor. In the scuffle, my gun dislodged from his belt, clanking hard against the floor and skittering across the speckled beige linoleum toward Cassidy. She grabbed for it, but her chains jerked tight. Groaning, Peterson lunged for the gun.

"Justin, no," Cassidy shouted, kicking the .45 across the room. Peterson changed direction, crawling toward it, but I yanked my arms up behind me, the chair clattered to the floor, and I pulled my lizard-skin boot back and let loose a kick that caught him hard on the side. He doubled up in pain.

"Shit," he cried out, as I pushed past him. He staggered to get up, to come after me, just as I threw myself down onto the floor, aiming for the gun.

"David," I shouted. "Hurry!"

Diving nearly on top of me, Peterson strained to roll me to the side. My wrists still tied, I couldn't hold him off long. Underneath me, the gun barrel lodged against my back. I pushed up far enough to clutch the grip and held tight, then screamed, "Damn it, David. Get the hell in here. Now!"

The sounds of Cassidy's cries and the battering ram pummeling the door echoed off the cement walls. I jerked my leg up and caught a lucky break, aiming where it hurt.

With a guttural cry, Peterson rolled on his side, holding his groin. I tried to get up, but he instantly came back at me, grabbing my neck and squeezing. I dug my heels against the floor. Straining, I held my ground, my throat closing up as I struggled for air. Another booming assault on the door from the outside, as Peterson squeezed tighter. I tried to knee him again, but this time he dodged my blow, and I felt my consciousness waning. Behind me, wrists throbbing, I grasped the gun. I felt the trigger.

"Stop!" Cassidy shrieked, pleading. "Justin, stop! Don't hurt Sarah. Please, don't hurt her."

I kicked harder, and then, as the battering ram toppled the door, sending it cratering to the floor, I heard David shout my name. Peterson let go of my throat and delivered a sharp blow to my chest. Gasping for air, I rolled to the side and heard a single gunshot. A searing pain sliced through my back and left arm, and high-velocity blood spatter covered the floor beside me. David's face peered down at me, when everything went blank.

Epilogue

"Mom, wait until I show you what Cassidy did to Warrior," Maggie said, with a giggle as I sat in my favorite rocker on the porch at the ranch. "I'll get him!"

Two weeks after that night in the Houston tunnels, the bruises had faded and the stitches were gone, but the scars were still healing. In the scuffle, my gun had discharged, skimming through my back muscles but hitting my left arm full on, midway between my shoulder and elbow. In addition to the rod and screws that held together what was left of the bone, I now had a card in my wallet I'd carry into airports for the rest of my life, explaining why I set off metal detectors.

As Maggie promised, she emerged from the stable moments later with Cassidy leading the foal. Mom and I had kind of adopted the kid. She slept in Maggie's trundle bed, now that everyone was home, and they'd become fast friends. Even Strings liked her. He'd taken to bringing over his guitar to accompany the superstar while she and Maggie sang. Most of their numbers were Cassidy's compositions. I discovered I liked them without the full percussion section and a stadium full of shrieking kids.

Despite his risky beginnings, Warrior, too, was faring well, steadily gaining weight and inching taller. The sunlight glistened on his back. Solid black and growing stronger every day, he was beautiful.

"Look," Maggie said. "Doesn't he look too cute?"

Cassidy made an exaggerated bow, showing the foal off. The girls had braided Cassidy's sparkly hairpins into his sparse mane, making him look more like the filly Maggie had anticipated than a colt.

"You better not take a picture of him that way," I said, with a laugh. "When he's a full-grown stallion, he may not find this amusing."

"Oh, Mom," Maggie said. "It's just fun, that's all."

"Besides, maybe he'd like it," Cassidy added, with a laugh. "A little bling never hurt anyone, even a tough-guy horse." I chuckled along with her, but had to stop because it made my arm ache.

Surviving what threatened to be certain death made the air on the ranch smell even fresher. Or maybe it was the jasmine blooming on the porch railing, or the scent of Mom's pot roast simmering in the kitchen. In truth, I didn't care what made the sky a perfect blue or the smile on Maggie's face shine the way it did. A fluke had saved Cassidy and me. A security guard who saw the limo with the bullet holes in the window enter the garage had the good sense to call H.P.D.

I felt blessed just to be alive.

"Now, that's what I call one beautiful colt," Mom said, as she and Bobby walked out to join us, the screen door banging behind them. "You girls should rent yourselves out to the circus. You could earn a living dressing up the horses for performances."

"Heck, I'd buy a ticket," Bobby said, with a hoot. "I'd buy two, Maggie, one for your gram and one for me."

Mom gave him a playful nudge with her elbow.

Cassidy laughed, but then turned serious. "I've been thinking, it's time I get back to my real job," she said. "I called Rick and he's going to book a jet. I need to get to L.A. and figure out what to do next."

For just a moment, Maggie looked crestfallen, but I was proud of Cassidy. It was time. None of us could wall ourselves up. We all still had lives waiting to be lived.

"You're right," I said. "We'll miss you, and you're always welcome to visit, but we understand if it's time for you to go home."

"Sarah, I know you may not agree with this, I know it may not help, but I'm going to ask the prison to let me bring in someone to help Justin, like a therapist," Cassidy said. I started to protest, worried that it was better to cut all ties with Peterson, but she quickly went on. "Despite everything, he's my brother. And someday he's going to get out of jail. Maybe I'm doing it for me. I want him to get better, but I figure I'm safer if he's not so angry when he gets out."

While I figured it was probably a waste of time and money, the kid had a point. At least she could try. "That makes sense," I said. "I'll see if I can get the name of a therapist for you, someone who works with prisoners."

At that, I moved a bit in the rocker, and tried to get comfortable. If I sat too long in any one position, my arm throbbed. But that too would pass. Like Warrior, I felt better every day.

We sat there for a while, Mom and I rocking, Bobby sitting on the steps, while the meat simmered and the girls talked softly, lavishing affection on the foal. I wasn't listening, maybe just daydreaming, until Maggie walked up and stood next to me, with a strange, apprehensive look. "Mom," she said. "Cassidy and I think there's something I really need to explain to you."

"What's that?" I asked.

"Well, it's about Mr. Garrity," she started.

"Maggie," I chastised. I hated to see her ruin what was turning into a beautiful afternoon talking about a lost cause. "We've been through this. David and I are just friends, and I don't want you to worry about anything. There's no reason to be concerned."

The morning I woke up in the hospital, Mom, Maggie, Bobby, Cassidy, and David were all there. I remember thinking that anyone passing by would have thought he was part of the family. He didn't linger long. Once I was on the mend, he stopped visiting. I hadn't heard from him except for a get well card since I'd left the hospital.

Maggie looked uncertain, and Cassidy nudged her. I wondered what this could all be about when my daughter took a deep breath. "Mom," she said, again. "This isn't one of those times you should worry about me. This is one of those times when you're supposed to listen to me."

"Oh," I said. "I see."

"So, you need to listen, and then, if you're mad, you can yell at me and ground me," Maggie said. "Okay?"

"Okay," I agreed. "You have my full attention."

Ringing David's doorbell, I realized there was probably a lot I hadn't thought through. He could be with someone else, at that very moment, and I'd be interrupting. What would I do then? Mumble something about stopping in to talk about work, I guess, but since we were no longer working a case together, that would be pretty odd, or "lame" as Maggie would say. When he didn't answer immediately, I momentarily thought about turning and running back to the Tahoe. Then I thought about how I'd stopped and bought a new tube of lipstick on the way. I couldn't find my usual, and this one was called Tawny Taupe. I ran my tongue over my lips. It seemed a shame to waste it.

I rang the bell again, and waited.

"Sarah, I didn't expect to see you here," he said, when he opened the door. He had on a pair of jogging shorts and a T-shirt, looking like he was getting ready for a run. His hair was falling over his forehead, and I reached up with my good arm and pushed it behind his ears. He frowned.

"I'd been meaning to come out to the ranch and check on you, but thought maybe I shouldn't," he said.

"Are you going to invite me in?" I asked. "After all, I'd like to sit down. This arm is still pretty sore, and I'm a little weaker than usual."

A curious look, his eyes narrowed on me, he stepped back, and I walked in. I momentarily thought that life shouldn't be so complicated. People should be able to talk about the important stuff without worrying about getting hurt. Of course, that was just another of those perfect-world wishes, the kind that should be and never are. I sat down on his old corduroy couch and waited for him to join me, but he didn't.

"Maggie and I had a talk this afternoon," I said. He didn't react, and I paused. Then I said, "She mentioned a conversation the two of you had last year, about the time you stopped calling."

Looking puzzled, he sat on the couch's thick, round arm. Just being in David's place brought back memories, but I was too nervous about the troubled look on his face to relax enough to enjoy them.

"I'm not sure what she told you, Sarah," he said, cautiously. "But Maggie's been through a lot the last couple of years. I understand completely that she's not ready—"

"Well, that's the thing," I interrupted. "David, I'm not sure how you feel about me now, after all this time. But we've been through a lot. And sometimes, that brings people together. Sometimes they drift apart afterward, while other times, it forms a bond."

He was smiling. Here I was, pouring my heart out, and David was smiling at me, as if pleased by my predicament.

"I guess I'm rather amusing?"

"Not really," he said, with a soft laugh. "It's just not like you to try to explain yourself. You're more of a doer, Sarah, not much for small talk."

Why are men so aggravating, especially when a woman's trying to make herself understood? I thought.

"Okay," I said. "I admit I'm not the best at talking about feelings, it's not my thing, but in this instance, it seems necessary."

David slid down the arm of the couch, and scooted over until he sat beside me. He put one arm around my waist and wrapped the other over my shoulder. When he pulled me toward him, I winced.

"Oh, sorry," he said, loosening his grip. "The arm?"

"Still a little sore," I admitted.

That little bobble seemed to leave us hanging, so I figured, as much as I disliked it, that I'd better try to talk again. "Now, David, the reason I'm here is that Maggie told me what she said to you last year, about you and me."

"I kind of already had that figured out," he said. "And I'm glad that she did."

He was still holding me, although a bit more loosely, and he buried his face in my hair. It still had some faint purple streaks in it from Germaine's color job. She'd lied. It hadn't all washed out. But David didn't seem to mind. He took a deep breath. "I'm glad you're still using the same shampoo. I remember that scent. What is it?"

"You don't want to know," I said.

"I do," he prodded, snuggling against my neck. "What does it smell like?"

"No. You really don't want to know," I said, and he laughed. Exasperated, I said, "Now can we forget about my hair? I've prepared this entire speech."

"It's horse shampoo, isn't it?" he said.

I frowned, and then shrugged. It was hopeless. "Yeah," I admitted. "I've been using it since I was a kid. Is there a problem with that?"

"No," he said, still grinning. "In fact, I should have known."

"Now, what do you mean by that?" I asked, getting even more aggravated. "Sometimes I think you assume you know what I'm going to say before I say it."

"Sometimes I do. For instance, what you're here to tell me is that Maggie told you she asked me not to see you anymore, that she wasn't ready for you to get serious with anyone," he said. "That's it, isn't it?"

"Well, yes," I said, frowning.

"And then you were going to tell me that she's changed her mind. She's all right with it now?"

"How did you know that?"

"You wouldn't be here if she still objected," he said. I was thinking it could be maddening being involved with a profiler. Mom always said I drove her crazy, figuring out what she thought before she said it. Now David was doing it to me. Still, it was hard to get upset with him when he was kissing my neck, and when I felt his arms pulling me gently closer.

"That means, for the first time in a year, you are mine," he whispered, with what I thought was just a hint of danger.

I was glad I'd worn a shirt that buttoned down the front, so he could peel it off my arm gently before he laid me in his bed. He ran his hands over me, from my face, down my neck, cupping my breasts, trailing down to my waist. He kissed my left shoulder, the scars across my back and arm, and when he hit the tenderest spot, I winced again.

"I don't want to hurt you," he said, pulling me close. "But oh, I've missed you, Sarah."

I had only one good arm, and I pulled him closer with it. "Why didn't you tell me what Maggie said?" I asked. "Why did you let me wonder?"

"I couldn't do that to Maggie," he said. "I needed you, but she needed you, too."

The last time I kissed David was in the barn, when we were both covered with hay. So much had happened, but nothing that changed the way I felt about him. I knew in my heart that I wanted him, maybe more than he wanted me.

We made love carefully, tenderly, calmly compared to that night a year earlier when we'd first shared his bed. My arm might still be mending, but that night, in David's bed, I felt as if for the first time since Bill died that my heart had finally healed. Afterward, we lay for hours, talking and laughing, touching each other, remembering.

When morning came, we filled his old claw-foot bathtub with hot water and bubbles. David blocked out the sunlight with beach towels taped over the blinds, while I lit candles. He brought in a pillow for me to rest my sore arm on, perched on the edge of the tub, and we made love in the hot soapy water. When we were through, he sat behind me, and wrapped his arms around me, and I slept with my head on his shoulder. We woke in the water turned cold. I dried David off with a towel, then wrapped it around him and guided him back to the bed. As we made love yet again, I felt his hot, wet breath on my neck, and thought that maybe, sometimes, if we're lucky, life gives us a second chance at happiness.

"Sarah, I have one question," he whispered. I held his face and kissed him on the lips, long and hard.

"Ask away," I said finally. "Anything."

He shook his head and laughed softly, then held me close and whispered, "Where do we go from here?"

Acknowledgments

Many, many thanks to:

Retired Texas Ranger Marrie Aldridge.

Senior Crime Scene Analyst David Rossi.

My former teacher and friend Ken Hammond, for his insightful suggestions.

Mary Kay Zanoni, for helping Cassidy find her voice.

Christopher Boutros, D.V.M.

Malcolm Hackney, at Bright Star Productions.

All the wonderful folks at the Houston Livestock Show and Rodeo.

Lorrie Patel, for her tips on astronomy.

Edward Porter, for talking ideas.

T. C. and Tamara Skeete, for teaching me to two-step.

Paul Chaplo of Dallas, for his expertise with helicopters.

Liz and Ray Fitzgerald and Barbara Tavernini, for their research assistance.

Brian Weiss, M.D., for inspiring Dr. Dorin's theories on reincarnation.

Acknowledgments

Vladimir Parungao, M. D., for forensic advice.

Terry Bachman, for reading the manuscript.

David Thompson at Houston's Murder by the Book, and his entire staff, for being so kind to a local writer.

My agents, Jane Dystel and Miriam Goderich, at Dystel & Goderich, for their advice, support, and efforts on my behalf.

My St. Martin's editor, Daniela Rapp; publicists Jessica Rotondi and Hector DeSean; and copy editor NaNá V. Stoelzle.

Special thanks to Jan, Mike, Jim, Kate, John, Linda, my dad, Nick, and all the New Mexico brainstormers, especially Nicholas, Sarah, and Bethany.

Finally, thank you to all my dear friends and family, especially Brian, Kim, Emmie, Brian, Becky, Nick, Zack, and Paul. Thank you for brightening my life each and every day.